MAKE WAR

Jacquelyn Marker

Literary Wanderlust | Denver, Colorado

Published in the United States by Literary Wanderlust LLC, Denver, Colorado. www.LiteraryWanderlust.com

ISBN Print: 978-1-942856-60-3
ISBN eBook: 978-1-942856-67-2

Cover design: Pozu Mitsuma

Printed in the United States

MAKE WAR

1

Sam

I untie Jerry from the bedposts. Sometimes a woman must make do with what she can find. I found Jerry at the gym, pounding the belt on the treadmill right in front of me. It was a fabulous way to pass the time, watching his ass tighten with each stride. We both worked up a sweat, his from exercise, mine from watching, and I decided that he needed to come home with me.

Jerry is a beautiful man with chocolate brown eyes, a sharp jaw, and a thick mane of hazelnut hair. His body is sinful with sinewy muscles and smooth skin. It's almost impossible to find anything wrong. Except it isn't Jerry's face I see as I straddle him. Instead, my vision is filled with a nameless lover that I had met a couple of months ago in Barbados.

The Barbados stranger with shaggy blond hair and a beard to match has invaded every waking thought. How he smelled. How he tasted. How he felt inside me, stretching me full. The waterfall—I still get goosebumps just thinking about it. That was an experience not offered in the brochure. It's those memories that have caused me to develop a habit of masturbating. Not to say masturbation is bad, it's not. It's healthy even. However, to pleasure one's self six or seven times a day might border addiction. I was desperate for a cure and thought Jerry could be like a nicotine patch, except for sex.

I was wrong.

Jerry rubs his wrists. "That was…different."

I give him a stiff smile. I want to tell Jerry that I agree with him. That I have never slept with a man who needed so much direction. Put it here, not there. Don't stab at it; it's a vagina, not a steak. If I have to hear him call me "baby" one more time, I might have to strangle him, and not the fun way either.

He's young and dumb. Those particular qualities have never been a stopper for me. It can be a benefit to get want I want, how I want it. Unfortunately for me, and Jerry, I did not have the patience to try to teach him how to please a woman. So, I tied him up. He could do no wrong if he had no power to make the decisions. In the end, I still faked it.

I roll over, grab a cigarette out of my nightstand, and light it. "I had a great time, Jerry, but I have an early meeting in the morning. You understand, don't you?"

He huffs as he gathers the sheet around his waist and stands, searches the room for his clothes, and starts to get dressed. "Yeah, Sam. I understand. You were just using me." He jerks his pants up, stabs his arms through the sleeves of his T-shirt, and tugs it over his head. "I'm not just a dick with legs. I'm a person. I have goals and dreams for my life. Maybe you should think about that the next time you invite a man over. We have feelings too, you know." He yanks open my bedroom door then turns back to look at me.

"Okay, Jerry. I'll call you," I say, making a promise I have no intention of keeping.

He gives me a hard stare. "Jarod."

I sit my cigarette in the ashtray on my nightstand and slip on a silk nightgown. There's something sensual about silk against sexed-up skin. It's exquisite. I deserve to be pampered after my night with Jerry. Nothing fancy, just a silk nightie to make all the wrongs right.

"Hmm?" I ask, realizing that Jerry was talking to me.

"My name is Jarod. Not Jerry, or Gary, or Larry. Not any other stupid name you can come up with. Jarod." He slams the door behind him, the sound of wounded pride echoes with each footfall through the hall as he sees himself out.

I finish my cigarette, twist my long, blonde hair into a bun on top of my head, and snuggle under the covers.

The Chicago skyline winks at me as I gaze out the window. "It's okay," it says. "I'll never tell."

The sound of the ocean roars in my ears, passionate blue eyes stare back at me. I can almost feel the soft tickle of his beard as seductive kisses trail down the inside of my thigh. My hand travels beneath the covers, the ache so intense I fear I may never again be satisfied.

Reid

No matter how long I've been gone, I will never find the stench of the city charming. Some people might argue that it smells like home. I disagree. It smells like piss and exhaust. Hell, even the airport smells like piss. I grab my suitcase from the carousel and stroll toward the exit, not in any real hurry. The realization that I'm back in Chicago has made me numb, it may be the only way I'll survive with my sanity intact.

As I make my way toward a line of cabs, a tall redhead leans against a black town car, holding a sign with my name on it.

"Shit." She probably thinks she's cute. I know who she is, sign or not, and she's my ride. Of all the people to pick me up, it has to be her. I planned to hail a cab and find a cheap hotel for a few days. I'm not ready to jump back into this life. Not yet, maybe never.

"Reid," she squeals as she rushes toward me and ensnares me

in a hug.

I don't return the sentiment; instead, I remain stiff. She reeks of Chanel and shame. Judging by her outfit, I'd say she just finished a tennis lesson. Although, who was the student and who was the teacher is up for debate.

She gives a soft kiss on my cheek and takes far too long to release me. The driver takes my luggage and puts it in the trunk.

"Stella." The sting of her kiss lingers on my cheek. Her ruby red lipstick has marked me, and I wipe away the depravity with the back of my hand.

"Oh, come on now, Reid. Call me mommy."

This woman is fucked up. That is not how stepmothers talk to their stepsons. I don't answer her and instead, slide into the backseat of the car. She slips in next to me and sits so close I'm surprised she didn't try to sit on my lap.

The driver merges into traffic as I stare out the window. Visions of glossy blonde hair, beguiling blue eyes, and long silky legs wrapped around my waist haunt me. I've never regretted any decision I've made in my life, those decisions are what has made me the man I am today, albeit jaded, but it's a part of who I am. My one regret might be the vacationer I met in Barbados. I let her go, not even learning her name. If I knew anything real about her, I would have scoured the ends of the earth to find her. She insisted on anonymity, and now I'm onto the next phase of my life. Without her. Without anyone.

Stella puts her hand on my knee, and her noxious touch causes the memories to evaporate.

"You know," she says, "Frank is very excited to see you. It's been too long."

I shove her hand away and gaze out the window. "He knew where to find me." As the landscape speeds past, I consider opening the door and rolling out onto the highway.

"True," she puts her hand back on my leg, her fingers inching upward. "I've missed you too."

I haven't even started my new life, and I'm ready for it to be over.

2

Sam

The bell dings as I thrust open the door of the cafe with the best coffee in the world. It's nothing fancy. It's not Seattle-based. It's Pop's. Pop's has the best bagels, pastries, and coffees. My belly gurgles its plea for breakfast as I peruse the muffins in the glass case.

"Mornin,' Sam," the owner greets.

"Morning, Pop."

Pop wipes down the counter in front of him, and it reminds me of a soda jerk in an old black and white movie. "Your usual?"

"Wouldn't be a Monday if I had anything else."

He turns around and fires up the loud cappuccino machine. It's got to be a hundred years old, I think the rust is the secret ingredient which makes it taste so damn good.

"How's it goin,' Sam?" asks Nick as he walks out from the office behind the counter.

He's the hottest barista I've seen in my life. Tall with thick black hair, beautiful olive skin, and the kinkiest cup-bearer in the city. He loves having hot wax dripped onto his chest, is not opposed to a ball gag, and takes orders the way a man is meant to—without question. Unlike Jerry, Nick is skilled in the ways of pleasing a woman. He's never left my apartment without seeing a satisfied smile smattered across my face.

"It's good. Thanks for asking. Hey, Pop, give me one of your poppy seed muffins," I call out, licking my lips. I can almost taste it now.

"Sure thing," Pop answers.

Nick leans on the counter. "What are you up to this weekend? Haven't seen you in a few months. My plans for last Saturday fell through, and I have a brand-new set of edible paints that need to be tested. What do you say?"

"Is there banana flavored?"

"Not if you don't want there to be."

Pop hands me my drink and a bag with my muffin. I turn to Nick. "I'll think about it. Sounds fun."

A night with Nick could be the only way to right the wrong. The aftermath of Jerry had been a messy one, and I'd had to employ my trusted devices to get the job done. Unlike that lunk head, my toys function spectacularly. Four times on Saturday night, eight times on Sunday. I may need to look into a therapist at this rate.

The bell on the door dings as a customer walks in. "Large coffee. Two creamers." The deep voice licks down my spine and straight to my sex.

"Comin' right up," Pops says.

There's no need to look. The low timbre of his voice is all the confirmation I need. It's what has contributed to countless orgasms over the past two months. The waterfall guy is behind me. It requires insurmountable self-control not to toss my coffee and muffin on the ground, jump up, wrap my legs around him, and smother him with my tongue.

"Are you okay?" Nick asks. "You're blushing. I've never seen you blush. Didn't think you were capable."

"Yeah. I'm fine."

Nick shrugs. "All right. Well, give me a call and let me know."

"Okay," I answer, no longer giving my attention to Nick. My eyes are staring at him, sure, but my ears, my skin, and every other part of my body is focused on my waterfall guy.

Nick gives a rhythmic pat to the countertop and walks back to the office.

The few minutes of anticipation is getting the best of me, and I know I have to look. My stomach plummets to my toes. My memory may have undersold me on the waterfall guy's handsomeness. He's so damn tall. Despite my four-inch Milano's, he's still at least two to three inches taller than me. At five-foot-nine without my shoes, that's impressive. There is something different about him, and I can't put my finger on it. His dark blond hair has grown out and dusts his broad shoulders. And that beard. Good God, it's still as sexy as it was back when I first laid eyes on him.

Perhaps it's the clothes. In Barbados he had a penchant for board shorts and flowery shirts, but not today. Today he's dressed in a pair of well-fitted jeans and a black sweater which molds to his magnificent body. When did it get so hot in here? It's in the sixties today, but the temperature in the shop must be near boiling.

"Hi," I squeak out.

The waterfall guy hands some cash over to Pops to pay for his coffee. He turns around and his head jerks back. "Well, hi to you too. Chicago, huh?"

"I could say the same."

"You could, but I just got here a few days ago. Not quite the same thing."

"What brought you to the Windy City?" I ask as we start to walk toward the door.

He pushes the door open for me and waves me to go first. "Family business."

We head in the direction of my office. The wind bellows through the tall buildings of downtown and brings with it the fabulous city scents of pollution and urine. They should make a candle of this smell.

"You live in the city then?" he asks.

"Born and raised. Cubs fan till I die. I love the city."

"What's not to love? Homeless people on every corner, bumper to bumper traffic, corruption. It's a real gem."

"I know." I can't hold back my enthusiasm for city life.

He chuckles as he tries to take a sip from his cup. "I grew up here. Can't say I missed it much."

"How did you end up in Barbados?" I've asked this question before. His answer at the time seemed evasive. Now that he's back in the U.S., will the answer change?

I guess not because we keep walking, and he doesn't say anything. We round a corner and are only feet away from my destination. Our coincidental run-in is about to end, and I'm not sure I want it to yet.

He clears his throat. "Sometimes you have to get away and do what's right for you at the moment. Not to please anyone else or do what society thinks is the right thing. You have to do it for you."

I tip my cup to his and give a mock clink in a toast. "Cheers to that." I slow my pace as we approach the front of my office. "This is me." I point upward to the sixty-story building encased in steel and mirrored glass.

"This is where you work? Which company?"

His lips twist with suspicion, but his stare is focused on me. "A brokerage firm on the forty-second. Commercial real estate, selling businesses. Stuff like that. It's boring."

He smiles and gives a hasty laugh. Something has changed between us, but I don't know what it is. "I doubt that." Without any hint of his intention, he leans down and drops a soft kiss on my cheek.

The wind whips my hair in front of my face, and I give the loose strands an anxious tug as I tuck them behind my ears. "Maybe I'll see you around sometime."

He shoves his hands in his jean pockets and nods. "Count on it."

He turns and starts to walk back in the direction we had come.

I'm stuck in the haze of my waterfall lover. He made a promise that he would see me again. That's good, right? Maybe now I can put him to good use and break my masturbation habit. We can go to dinner, a play, the Ferris wheel—do normal coupley-type things.

"Excuse me," says a messenger as he skirts around me to enter the building.

Daydreams are entertaining, but fantasies they will stay because I still don't know his name.

As I ride the elevator to my office, I think back to my vacation in Barbados, and the first time I saw him.

3

Sam
Barbados

The view from my chair is breathtaking. Sun-kissed, toned muscles in tiny, tight swimwear, jogging on the beach—it doesn't get much better than this.

Sadly, of the fourteen men who have run past this morning, none have affected me to the point which my brain goes haywire. Until now. I sit up straight, slide my sunglasses down, and perch them on the ball of my nose, desperate for an unfettered view of the scenery. My mouth hangs open as the man makes his way in my direction. His chest is well defined and dripping with sweat from a hard, hot workout. The sunlight shimmers on his blond hair which is pulled back into a loose ponytail. Good lord, his beard is magnificent. I want to run my fingers through its coarse hair and tug as I come, riding him like the cowgirl I am.

"I'll make you break a sweat," I holler out in an attempt to blend sexy with boisterous so he can hear me over the crash of the waves. It's a tricky combination, but I think I pull it off because he lifts his chin a fraction in acknowledgment.

I slide my sunglasses back up and recline in the lounge chair and work to soak up some more sun, or at least what UV rays will penetrate my SPF five-thousand. Light skin equals burn, not bronze. I have a full itinerary of lounging for the next three days, as I have for the past seven, and a blistering sunburn would put a serious damper on those plans.

"I'll help you spike your heart rate, baby," yells a voice next to me.

I jerk my head in the opposite direction of the sexy jogger and spy a rotund man walking toward us, his feet in the surf and sinking into the sand with each step. His belly hangs over his Speedo and jiggles as he walks. I turn to look at Lizzie, but she's feigning sleep while the sun bakes her skin.

Lizzie Anderson is a giant pain in my ass, and I don't know where I would be in this world without her by my side. Except for today, where her presence may get me into something which I have no interest in at all. We've been partners in crime since we wore knee highs and pigtails.

"What the hell." I give her a shove and she laughs. I shove a little harder and tilt her off her chair. She lets out a yelp as she tumbles to the ground. "He better not think, for one second, that I'll make good on that."

Lizzie stands and dusts the sand off her bare legs and sits back down. "Oh, relax, he didn't even hear me."

"The whole beach heard you," I tell her as I rub in a liberal application of sunscreen, not wanting to burn.

I toss the lotion to Lizzie, as any good friend would do. It's eighty-five degrees, and we are basking in the sun at its closest point to the Earth. Lizzie's bikini is slinky and silver, dependent on two strings to hold up her voluptuous attributes. I cringe every time she goes in the water—one wave and that bikini is toast. Dental floss would be a sturdier option over the string she calls a bikini. The silver looks fantastic on her, and she knows it, she bought four swimsuits of the same style, all vibrant colors to reflect her Native American skin tone. Unlike my companion,

I have chosen a one-piece in black that secures the goodies and encourages the men to use their imagination.

"I don't care if you are one-sixteenth Blackfoot, your skin will turn into shoe leather with this kind of sun," I tell her.

She gives a small shrug, her long silky brunette hair falling over her shoulders as she sits forward and conservatively applies the sunscreen.

"I never would have come if I knew what pigs you guys were going to be. Men are people too. Not just objects for your hedonistic tendencies," Grayson says as he sits up and judges us from his pedestal.

Grayson Treadwell is a fine-looking man. He's a shirtless, prime piece of man-meat sitting right next to me. At least, that's how other women see him. He's a giant at six-foot-five, weighing in at two-hundred and thirty pounds. He could be a fullback for the Bears, in fact, that's precisely what he was for Notre Dame. He was heading for the big time, picked in the first round of the NFL draft. Unfortunately, pro-ball wasn't in the cards for him.

The three of us have been friends since forever, and I can't imagine my life without them.

"You're so full of shit," Lizzie says as she squirts sunscreen over Grayson's abdomen.

I join in and throw sand, not wanting to miss the fun. The mixture reminds me of glue and glitter, making abstract art on our unenthusiastic, human canvas.

"Cut it out!" he yells, hopping up from his seat.

"Hypocritical, dirty boys need sand baths." A handful of sand spills from my fingers. "And your hair is filthy."

Grayson backs up. "Don't do it, Sam. Sand is a bitch to get out."

"I guess you better start running."

Lizzie stands, and we become a united front when Grayson's attention is halted by something shiny.

A shiny, skimpy bikini that was never designed to hold up breasts of that magnitude.

Grayson flips his Ray-Bans on top of his head, to get a better look at the tone, tan, and tawdry brunette walking past. He goes in for the kill. "You're looking a little red," he tells her, dropping his voice an octave. "I'd be more than happy to rub you down."

"Not in this lifetime," the stranger tosses over her shoulder, laughing, and keeps walking.

Grayson turns his attention back to us, unable to hold back his coy smile. He is fully aware that he is no less a pig than the company he keeps. He throws his shades on the chair and runs toward the clear Caribbean waters.

Lizzie and I make chase. I'm two steps away from capturing him and launch myself at his midsection as he tries to make a dive underwater. My chest collides with the sculpted muscles of his back and Lizzie's breasts make contact with my legs, dragging us under.

I fight to grab at anything, anyone, the tug of the water makes everything slippery and misplaced. I'm not sure how it happens, but when I'm finally able to take a lungful of air, I'm pinned under one of Grayson's arms, and Lizzie under his other. He's carrying us like a frat boy with a case of beer under each arm.

Grayson lugs us up toward the beach, and Lizzie shouts, "You *pinched* my nipple. You bitch."

I look across Grayson's crotch and straight at Lizzie. "I think you have bigger problems at the moment."

Lizzie looks down to find one breast hanging out, swinging around. She begins to wiggle out of Grayson's arm. "Let me go!"

Grayson takes three more steps before giving Lizzie what she wants and sets us both down.

The warm water laps at mid-thigh, and Grayson and I form a shield from the prying eyes a hundred feet away.

Lizzie works to adjust the strap, but it's no use, it's broken, beyond repair. She covers her chest with her forearms, and Grayson and I act like her bodyguards as we walk to our towels and chairs.

Lizzie covers herself with her towel. "See, Sam, this is what happens to people who do bad things. Their karma rubs off on the innocent. That poor hot guy was only trying to get in his daily run, and you couldn't have the decency to let him be. For shame."

"For shame?" I screech. "You're the one with the bad karma. What about that old fat guy in the Speedo with the hairy ass? Right there, that's why this happened to you."

Grayson starts to clean up his beach stuff. "Cut it out, you guys. We could go round and round with this all day."

Lizzie and I shake our heads in agreement.

"You're right, Grayson. We should take a play from your goody-two-shoes playbook," Lizzie says with a smile.

Her wicked smile is my cue. I dart around Grayson and wrench his arms back to secure them. His towel and sunscreen fall to the sand. Lizzie picks up the full pitcher of frozen margarita and tugs on Grayson's swim trunks. "This oughta cool your jets," she says, dumping the contents down his shorts.

Grayson howls with surprise as the frozen drink slides down his trunks. When I release his arms, Lizzie and I don't waste a second. We scramble for our stuff and run toward the safety of the resort.

4

Sam

The evening show at the resort holds nothing back. Tonight, it's in the club attached to the hotel. With a tiki roof and sand floors, it captures the vacation vibe and is topped off with booze. The dancers parade on stage and engage the crowd. Not those kinds of dancers, these are the type who dedicated their entire childhood honing the craft. The outfits are bright and flicker under the light of the stage lamps with skirts that flume upward with each practiced twirl. I wonder if those are socks stuffed in the pants of a few dancers, and I don't resist asking Lizzie her opinion.

"No way. That one over there," she says, pointing. "One-hundred percent accurate."

"How do you know?"

"We played a game of 'I'll show you mine if you show me yours.'"

"When did you do that?" I ask, trying to remember a time when Lizzie would have been gone long enough to engage in childhood games.

"While you were in the bathroom after dinner. I went to the bar and grabbed our after-dinner drinks."

I should have known it didn't take forty-five minutes for two mojitos and a daiquiri. "Did you show him yours?"

"Of course not. I'm a lady. I pretended you sent me a text and ditched him with his pants around his ankles."

"Ah, yes. Truly lady-like."

Grayson joins us at our table after having been God only knows where. "What are we talking about?"

"We're playing the game of Boner or Bona-fide. You know, who has the junk or stuffs his treasure trunk."

"Sure. Like Jugs or Duds. The lady in the orange, her jugs are one-hundred-percent real."

I peek at the woman spinning.

"And the woman in the teal? Totally fake," he tells me.

I squint as I try to assess each set of breasts on their own merits, the difference eludes me. "How can you tell?"

"I own a strip club. It's my job to be able to see the difference."

"No, seriously. How?" I can appreciate a nice pair of ta-tas as much as the next gal, but unlike my male counterpart, I'm not as invested. In most cases, my attention is aimed a bit lower and on a different gender.

"The floppage," he says.

"Floppage?" Lizzie asks after taking a sip of her mojito.

"Yeah. Floppage. In this particular setting and how the costumes are cut, they aren't designed for the best, um, support. Miss Orange, her movements are dialed back, just enough to keep from too much floppage." He holds his hands up and uses his fingers as an imaginary camera. "She has to be at least a double D, so, it doesn't help a whole lot. Now Little Teal over there, she doesn't have that problem."

"But her tits are bigger than Orange's," I point out.

"That's true. Good eye," he compliments. "Because of the implants, her boobs are perkier and unnaturally firm. Judging by the large gap, the reconstruction was done recently and not well either."

"Definitely a shoddy job," Lizzie adds.

"And you've decided this because..."

Grayson throws his head back in exasperation. "Because the right nipple is damn near in her armpit. Do you even use your eyes?"

I take a moment and give Teal a hard once-over. He's right, her nipple is poking up toward the right armpit. "Okay, okay." I turn toward Grayson, my excitement ticking up a level. "Real or Fake? What's your preference?"

"All natural all the way. When I stick my face between a great pair of tits, I want to be engulfed in supple flesh, and motorboat until my heart's content. Not walk away with a concussion from some sort of kinky game of dodgeball."

"That has to be the most perfect answer I have ever heard," I laugh. My straw gurgles as I sip the last of my drink. It's too early in the night to run low on good-time juice. "I'm heading up to the bar for refills," I tell Lizzie and Grayson as I stand.

"Cool," Grayson says. His eyes are fixed on the dancers on stage as they begin their last set of the show. "And Sam?" he calls out before I get too far. "Beer is good and all, but—"

"Peach or strawberry?"

He smiles like a child who just got his first name-brand He-Man figure. "Peach, please."

The line at the bar is more crowded than usual tonight. Lizzie, Grayson, and I have been here for the past ten days, and there has been a sudden influx of vacationers. The resort club is typically busy, but this is above and beyond.

The club is teeming with young twenty-somethings whose naïveté is still considered endearing by society. I am many things, but naïve is not one of them. I know what I want, what it will take to get it, and the motivation to see it through to the end. Of course, it helps that I have a decade and a half worth of experience on these children posing as adults.

A gaggle of girls stands next to me, two of them are wearing tiaras. *Tiaras.* No one will take them seriously as adults or as women when they're parading around in a bar wearing tiaras. When they talk, I realize there is no hope for the future.

"O-m-g, that bartender is *so* hot," one says.

"I know, right? Like, I'd do him. Old guys are so good in bed. You know, they have, like, experience," says the other one.

I close my eyes and wish with all my heart these chickadees will take flight, tiaras and all. When I open them, I'm pleased to see that my wish has come true as the droves of girls disperse.

"A pitcher of mojitos. Oh, and a peach daiquiri, please," I shout above the music to the bartender, whose back is turned to me as he mixes a drink. Every muscle in his back flexes while he shakes the glass. That is a sight I can appreciate. I don't know what those girls were talking about. I haven't seen his face, but from the backside view alone, I'm quite sure this guy isn't that old. My age, maybe a little older. Mid-thirties if I was to guess.

The bartender turns around, and my heart skips a beat. Long, dirty blond hair rests on his shoulders in salon-perfect beach waves and gleams from the multi-colored lights above. His well-maintained beard accents his square jaw. I wonder how it would feel against my tongue.

What is it with me and beards today? First the jogger on the beach, now the bartender?

5

Sam

"Coming right up, sweetheart," the bartender says. His gaze slides from my head to my feet, and he follows it up with a wink.

Now I'm conflicted. On the one hand, him calling me "sweetheart" makes my skin crawl. The cutesie nickname is offensive and demeaning to someone who has fought her entire career to be respected as a businesswoman. A kickass businesswoman who is only months away from being number one in her profession. On the other hand, the brute act of him checking me out, the look on his face begging me to let him run his tongue over every inch of my body, makes my skin pebble with excitement.

When he turns his back to me to prepare my order, I'm delighted to watch. I already know his backside is a fine sight. The drumming bass pounds on the dance floor and every move he makes is in time with the music. The act of spirit composition by this sexy as sin bartender has become some sort of dance of seduction.

It starts with him stretching for a daiquiri glass on a shelf above. The hem of his shirt raises slightly, the bronzed skin beneath playing peek-a-boo.

Mmm. Very, very nice.

A slight twist as he turns, his shirt pulls taut, clings against him, and gives a hint to the toned abs beneath.

Good. God.

He dips his arm into the ice bin and shovels out a scoop of ice, the muscles in his forearm twitch as he removes the lid to the blender.

The better to stroke yourself with.

A line of liquor bottles sits next to the blender, and he lifts up a bottle of house rum and pours a generous amount of liquid over the ice.

Oh, the things I could pour over you. I would take my time licking up every last drop.

After a splash of peach flavoring, he places the lid back on the carafe. He presses the button once.

Yes.

Twice.

Yes.

Three, four, five, six quick pulses. The sharp blades pulverize the ice. The ingredients melt and coalesce to become one.

Yes. Oh God, *yes*.

I'm sweaty and satisfied by the time I realize there is a daiquiri and a pitcher filled to the brim with mojito in front of me.

"Bless you," he says, smiling.

"I'm sorry?" I have been in such a state of recovery from the experience of watching him make Grayson's drink, that it took a moment for it to register that he's talking to me.

"You sneezed," he clarifies.

"Oh. Oh, yeah. Well, um, thank you," I reply, flustered and embarrassed. Embarrassed because I had an orgasm as I was studiously observing his pornographic mixology show.

Sometimes, about eighty percent of the time, I sneeze when I come. My cheeks are flushed with desire, and my panties are soaked. Does he have any idea what just happened? Do I care? Not really. Good for me.

He pushes the drinks to the edge of the bar, the glassware clinking against the rail. "Normally, this would be on the house for someone as beautiful as you."

I take a deep breath and pretend to be a rational human being who does not have an orgasm in the middle of a resort bar. "It's an all-inclusive resort. Drinks are included."

He smirks. "That's usually the case." He leans over the bar, our noses almost touching. I can feel the heat of his breath on my lips when he whispers, "You owe me."

All I see is red. "Why do I 'owe' you?" With every passing millisecond, my anger rises. My post-orgasmic haze has vanished and been replaced by the ire of a woman receiving a mansplanation about waxing. Unfortunately for this guy, I am not a woman who takes crap from anyone. I *am* a woman who is feared by men. A woman with power and knows how to use it.

"I have never owed anything to a man. Men owe me." I turn around, my long, blonde hair whipping with the strength of a St. Bernard's tail.

"Whoa. Hold on," The bartender pleas as he jumps over the bar in one fluid motion. "That's not what I meant."

"Uh, huh." I take a step forward, and he grabs my arm to stop me. It doesn't hurt, but I don't like it. It takes every ounce of self-control not to deck him.

"I'm serious. It's just you promised me, uh," he stutters and rubs the back of his neck, I think he's blushing.

"I didn't promise you shit. I paid for a service, and now I'm being told I have to pay again because of some imaginary promise you were told by the voices in your head."

"No. They're not imaginary. No, no. I mean, I don't hear voices," he lets out a grunt. "I was running on the beach. Help me break a sweat?" he asks, wincing.

"Huh?"

"This morning? On the beach? I was jogging by you and your friends and—"

It comes back to me. In vivid detail. The hot jogger, the fat guy with the hairy ass, Lizzie's boobs. It's amazing how vacation naps can affect one's memory, or maybe the three mimosas with breakfast were the culprit. "And I offered to help you—"

"Uh, yeah." He turns around and walks back behind the bar. "Don't forget your drinks."

Is he giving up? Maybe I put up too much fight. Too aggressive. A strong woman can intimidate some men, perhaps he's one of them. Now, I'm not worth the trouble. No matter his opinion, it doesn't excuse my own behavior. I'm better than that. "I'm sorry. I didn't mean to be that nasty. It's just...it's a reflex."

He takes the drink order of another customer and scoops some ice into a blender. I make sure to look at anything else, I don't have it in me to hide another orgasm.

"It's okay," he says, "I don't blame you. Can't say it was an exceptionally smooth way of hitting on you. Besides, I'm sure someone like you has to be wary of her surroundings. Men are beasts."

"And you? Are you a beast?" I ask, trying to get back to the business of flirting.

"The worst kind."

"What's the worst kind?"

"The kind that never gives up—go out with me."

I pick up the cocktails from the bar. "I'll think about it."

"Do that. I get off in an hour."

"Don't count on it."

6

Sam
Chicago

"You have a lunch meeting with Silas Keogh tomorrow at noon," my assistant Ben tells me as he follows me around the office. He is a tragically beautiful man. Chestnut hair with a lean swimmer's body. Why he's chosen to be an executive assistant is beyond me. He could have been an underwear model for Calvin Klein. "Frank wants to schedule a meeting with you for some time next week," he says, referring to Frank Gallagher, President of Sterling Brokerage, a.k.a. my boss.

I stop digging through the filing cabinet. Ben has caught my attention. "Why? He doesn't need to schedule anything, he's the boss."

Ben shrugs. "I don't know, but Delores says he wants at least thirty minutes of uninterrupted time with you,"

I go back to the filing cabinet and finger through the folders until I find what I'm searching for. A dossier on Keogh's legal holdings. Not to say he has illegal holdings, but he's the kind of guy who I'm certain has off-shore accounts and shell companies. Last week Keogh contacted me and said he wanted to discuss something of a "sensitive nature." I'm not sure what he wants, but he's a whale, and any business with him would be of enormous benefit to Sterling.

I sit on the chair behind my desk. "Watch and learn," I tell Ben as I dial the phone.

"Frank Gallagher's office. This is Delores. How can I help you?" Frank's assistant answers, her nasal voice filling the air.

Ben's eyes go wide, and he sits down across from me, excited to listen to mine and Delores's conversation via speakerphone.

"Delores, how are you? How are the grandbabies? I bet they're getting big. Darius is going to break a lot of hearts."

"What do you want, Ms. Valentine?" she says, her tone clipped.

Delores hates me. She finds my lifestyle appalling and has told everyone in the office. Everyone, that is, except me. Not that I care what Delores thinks. She comes from a time where women were expected to fulfill particular roles in society. Cook, clean, raise babies. Not my kind of thing. It's not like I'm afraid of commitment, I just never found those domestic goals appealing. Business is how my mind is focused. Career and financial success are my catnip, and there is nothing wrong with that, despite Delores's views.

"Ben tells me Frank wants to schedule a meeting with me next week."

"That's correct. What day will work for you? Frank has Tuesday and Wednesday open between one and four o'clock."

I rest my finger on my chin. "Hmm. I'm looking at my calendar, and I don't know if that will work. You know, I have some free time this afternoon. If it'll work for him, that is."

"Mr. Gallagher was very clear it has to be next week. Have Ben rearrange your appointments and get back to me."

I stifle a laugh. I can hear the aggravation in her voice and the disdain for having to deal with me directly. "I'll do that. As always, it's been a pleasure, Delores."

There's an ear-splitting crack as Delores hangs up the line. I'm sure she slammed the phone down. Ben and I both wince at the noise, but can't hold back the laughter.

"That woman hates you," Ben declares as tears slide down his grinning face.

"I *know.*"

After the laughter fades, Ben fiddles on his tablet. "I can shuffle a few things around, and you can meet with Frank on Tuesday at two-thirty."

"That's fine. Send me an updated itinerary for next week, and call Delores to let her know. I don't like to push her too far. I don't want to give her any motivation to try and have me ousted," I joke. Losing my job is of no concern to me because Frank is planning to retire at the end of the year, and I am taking his place.

Ben's eyes dart around the room.

"Out with it," I tell him as I fire up my laptop.

"There's something fishy going on around here."

I slide on my reading glasses as I prepare to reply to one of my clients. I give a few taps on the keyboard. "Why do you say that?"

Ben has a pretty face, but once he opens his mouth, you don't exactly get what you paid for. He's a bit of a conspiracy nut. He's convinced there was a second gunman on the grassy knoll, insistent Oswald couldn't have orchestrated the assassination of JFK on his own. Ben also believes there is an underground race of reptilian aliens that dwell in tunnels and caves right below our feet. The JFK thing, certainly possible, but the lizards are a bit far-fetched for me.

"People are acting funny. Delores has been making rounds, talking about morale. She asked me if you had any big deals on your plate."

"Frank is fully apprised of all deals in the works on my end. Except for the Keogh thing. I'm not sure what the story will be with that."

"I know, but," Ben gives a suspicious glance around the room before getting up and closing the door. "The office across the hall. Did you notice anything different?"

I finish my email and hit send, lean back in my chair, and give Ben my full attention. I'm not sure where he's going with any of this, but I'm intrigued. "No. The door was shut, lights off, like usual."

"Last week, there were construction workers in there painting. Not to mention the movers I saw bringing in furniture. Nice furniture," he clarifies.

"Maybe Frank's switching offices."

"Not with the brand-new, high-end mahogany desk I saw. Frank loves his desk. It was his father's, and his father's father. He wouldn't give it up even if the world was ending."

I take a minute and think. "Maybe someone got a promotion." I haven't heard of any, but I could have missed an email. I'm not the best at keeping up with interoffice correspondence.

"Not according to my sources. Word on the street is, they're bringing in someone from the outside. I think there might be some underhanded dealings going on. Like, maybe we're bankrupt, or a hostile takeover."

I let out an exasperated breath as Ben spins his most ridiculous theory to date. "First, Sterling Brokerage is not bankrupt. As VP, that's something I would be privy to. I've seen the books, we're completely solid. B, even if I entertained your idea of a takeover, there is no way anyone could keep a lid on that long enough for the deal to go through unnoticed. Trust me, Ben, I'd know."

"Fine, remain ignorant." He stands and heads for the door. "When shit hits the fan, and it will, don't say I didn't warn you."

7

Sam

"Mr. Keogh, I'm excited to discuss what Sterling can do for you." If this meeting goes well, it could end up being the biggest deal ever brokered at my firm.

Sterling Brokerage is a premier commercial real estate and business broker in the Chicago Land area. We deal in small startup companies in need of their first offices, all the way to multi-billion-dollar corporations looking to sell. It's challenging work, and I'm damn good at it.

We meet in a swanky restaurant with fabulous views of Lake Michigan. Silas Keogh is a Good Fellas type of guy. His dark hair is slicked back with grease, and I wouldn't be surprised to find his suit is made from the fur of newborn lambs. The gray at his temples and prominent widow's peak reminds me of Grandpa Munster. Make no mistake, he is not as soft and huggable as the domesticated vampire. He's the kind of guy who has a lot of money, and with money comes immense power.

I pick at a slice of fresh-baked French bread and spread on a thin layer of butter, giving him a chance to speak.

"I want to sell."

"I figured as much. Tell me how I can help."

The waiter drops off our drinks, and we order our meals. Silas is having a dirty martini. I have a Macallan on the rocks. Choosing the proper drink is of the utmost importance for a woman in the business world. If I order a cosmopolitan, it could be perceived as a weakness. A high-dollar scotch is mandatory for a business meeting with a man. It makes them more comfortable and somehow elevates me to the same level as them. Which, of course, is ridiculous, but that's how the game is played.

"I want to sell Keogh Tower."

I choke on my scotch, my drink spraying across the table and onto Mr. Keogh. "Keogh Tower?"

He grabs a cloth napkin off the table and wipes the spittle off his suit. "Yes."

"I'm sorry." I wipe my chin and nose with my own napkin. "Why do you want to sell? I thought Keogh Tower was your biggest profit generator?"

"It is, but there's a need to make some cutbacks. Keogh, Inc. may have to file bankruptcy. Selling the tower will bring me out ahead and prevent inevitable downsizing."

The waiter drops off our food. My meal consists of French Onion soup and a small side salad for this lunch meeting. I've found for meals, the drink rule works in reverse. If I order a steak with all the trimmings, they think me to be greedy with no self-control.

"Okay. Any thoughts on how you want to go about this?"

"It needs to be discreet. The last thing I want is for my employees to stage a mass exodus while I'm still trying to run a business."

"Understood," I tell him as I take notes on my phone. "I have a few clients in mind. One, I know is looking to diversify. This might be right up their alley."

He cuts into a mouth-wateringly tender lamb chop—the leftovers from making his suit.

"I have a particular buyer in mind."

I take a forkful of my salad, dip it in a smidge of vinaigrette dressing in a cup on the side. As I place the fork on my tongue, Mr. Keogh drops the bomb.

"BLH."

I, once again, begin to choke. A crouton lodges in my throat, and I start to cough and pound on my chest, trying in vain to make the killer day-old bread expel itself from my airway.

"Are you choking?"

My face is turning redder by the second. I nod to Keogh, and he stands in response.

"Can someone help? She's choking," he yells, pointing at me.

I get up, stand behind my chair, and position myself so my diaphragm sits atop the back. I heave my face toward the seat of the chair in an attempt to give myself the Heimlich Maneuver.

A few people stand as if considering whether they want to save my life. Most people, however, seem to believe remaining seated and squawking about the situation is the most helpful contribution they can make.

I ram my abdomen into the chair three more times until the crouton breaks loose. The offensive food hurls out of my mouth and flies across the room, and lands with a splash into the lobster bisque of a debutante-in-training.

"And it's good," I announce, throwing my arms into the air like goal posts. Unfortunately, there is not a single diner or service worker in this restaurant with a sense of humor. Every person here is staring. I see looks of surprise, a few seem relieved, but disgust appears to be the overall consensus. My lunch companion included.

My lungs are on fire from choking, and I'm more than a little embarrassed. I pound on my chest and give a hearty grunt, hoping the act will propel me back into the Boy's Club instead of the new one I just created—Crazy Bitch Club. I throw my shoulders back, smooth out my skirt, and sit back down. I shove my salad away and opt for the soup instead, it's a safer choice.

I take a sip from the spoon and set it back down. "BLH, huh?" For the rest of this meal, I will not take a bite or a sip of anything until he's done speaking.

Bennett Luxury Hotels, or BLH, is the largest luxury hotel corporation in the United States. Second is Hotel Lux, which is suffering from internal struggles to keep it afloat. Third is Keogh, Inc. I'm surprised Mr. Keogh doesn't want to talk a deal with Hotel Lux instead. The merger of number two and number three would create a new company that would elevate both to number one.

"The Bennett's have a phenomenal reputation, and I believe they'll do right by the employees," Silas answers, seeming unfazed by my life and death plight moments ago. Perhaps he's trying to be a gentleman and nudge our meeting along to let me save face.

"They do." I don't buy into Silas's motivations. This is his company's fourth bankruptcy in the past decade. He has never had a concern for the welfare of his employees before, and I don't believe such to be the case now. However, my job isn't about finding a more profound meaning. It's about making and securing the deal.

"I asked for you specifically. I know you've dealt with Tate Bennett on numerous occasions."

"I have. In various capacities." And positions.

Silas pulls a folder out of his briefcase and passes it to me. "That's the basic info. Enough to get a conversation going."

He's right. It has everything I'll need to approach Tate with the Keogh Tower prospect.

"Besides, I'm not sure how everything will shake out after Frank's departure. This should help Sterling land on solid footing. It's a win-win."

Franks departure? I don't understand what Frank's retirement has to do with anything. There are still three months left until I take over as President. Does Keogh honestly believe Sterling will suffer under my leadership? Is it because buyers and sellers alike will lose confidence in a company ran by a woman? I don't think so. There are plenty of female CEOs in the world, and they are more than capable. Although, he may have a point; Sterling's reputation will be stronger if this deal happens.

"I see. Well, thank you," I choke out.

Mr. Keogh stands to leave. "I expect to hear back by next Thursday, Sam. If you can't make it happen, I'll find someone who can," he tells me with a tone of finality which sends shivers down my spine. The kind of shiver one gets when Tony the Tin Face threatens to slit their throat from ear to ear.

"Not a problem."

On my way back to the office, I recall the meeting with Keogh and try to strategize. My ability to focus is abysmal, and my mind becomes clouded with memories of dancing in the sand and the most extraordinary shower I have ever taken.

8

Sam
Barbados

It's late, and the bar has started to clear out. Lizzie has left with the dancer from earlier, I think she's going to show him hers. I assume the girl Grayson has been with for half the night has natural breasts because now the tiara is perched on top of his head, and somehow it looks less ridiculous on him. As Grayson and the tiara girl walk toward me, their hands clasped together, I'm quite certain I'm about to be the last person in the club.

"I think we're going to call it a night," Grayson says after he polishes off another peach daiquiri.

"Sounds good. You two sleep tight."

"There's not going to be a lot of sleeping if you know what I mean."

The girl giggles and covers her face in a sudden display of shyness. She didn't seem shy when Grayson's hand was up her skirt on the dance floor.

"I'm sure there won't," I agree. "I think I'll go for a walk on the beach."

Grayson has the good sense to be conflicted. "Do you want us to come with you? I don't want to leave you high and dry." The girl's eyes pop wide at his suggestion.

I wave at them. "No, no. Go, have a good time. I'll be heading to my room in a bit."

I don't see the bartender anywhere, and his shift should have ended over an hour ago. I wasn't hanging around for him necessarily, I still have my pride. However, I am on vacation for a few more days, so I've immersed myself in the atmosphere and am determined to make the most of it. Wild dancing and crazy drinking not excluded.

I walk from the shelter of the tiki bar and along the shoreline. The waves crash on the beach and wash the sand from my thonged feet.

I hear a shout from behind me.

"Hold up."

I turn to find the bartender jogging through the water-logged sand, trying to catch up.

"Oh, hey," I greet. "I didn't expect to see you."

He walks beside me. "Yeah, sorry. There was an emergency."

"A bartending emergency?"

He laughs. "Not quite, but I'm glad I found you."

My cheeks warm at the compliment of him wanting to see me bad enough to seek me out. "Me too."

The moon is enormous and gives the perfect amount of light to set a romantic mood. "It's a beautiful night."

He looks around but doesn't say anything.

"I'm sure the scenery becomes less impressive for someone who lives every day in paradise," I backpedal, feeling awkward.

"That's not true. Sure, you have to work, but there's still time to take in the beauty. Flip-flops and board shorts are normal workwear around here. It doesn't get much better than that."

"I suppose it doesn't. However, I am a bit partial to heels. Sand isn't known to be friendly walking grounds for four-inch pumps."

He stops in his tracks, and I can feel his gaze raking over my backside as I continue walking. "That's a damn shame," he says as he catches up to me.

I chuckle. "It is. I look fabulous in a pair of red Stilettos. Especially, when my legs are hiked up on a man's shoulders."

"Jesus," he mutters under his breath.

I'm not sure how long we have been walking, when I turn to look back toward the resort, I realize I can't see its lights anymore. "We should head back."

He agrees, and we talk, the flow of conversation is easy and natural. Not about anything significant, just ordinary things, like the weather, foods I've tried so far since I've been here and what he recommends. Maybe it's the mirage of paradise, or perhaps it's him, but I feel the calmest I've felt since...ever.

He escorts me to the empty bar. "I should get going. It's getting late."

"Wait right here." He positions me back on the beach, ten feet from the tiki hut. Moments later, strings of Christmas lights frame the straw roof and the beams holding it up. A soft tune I've never heard begins to play. He comes out and joins me and we walk a few more feet toward the beach.

He holds out his hand. "Would you do me the honor of this dance?"

I smile, and it's a genuine smile of wonderment. "I'd love to."

He tucks me close and wraps his arm around my waist. It's a fantastic feeling—he's hard and soft at the same time.

I rest my head right below his shoulder and listen to the rhythm of his heart. "What song is this?"

He begins to hum the tune and then sings about when he looks into my eyes how he loses control. "*Make Me Lose Control* by Eric Carmen," he answers.

"Never heard of him."

"It's kind of popular 'round these parts," he says with a cowboy drawl. "A big hit in the eighties."

His linen shirt is unbuttoned, and I'm wearing a thin, white tank top, sans bra, paired with a short jean skirt. I can feel his warm skin against my breasts, my nipples acknowledging that I like what we're doing and want to do more.

The song ends, and he lets go of me, taking a step back, yet still holding my hand. "I guess I shouldn't keep you any longer. I wouldn't want you to be late for…"

"Bed," I inform him, "alone."

"Jesus."

I can tell he's having at least five dirty thoughts playing like a movie reel.

I know he's thinking about these things because I am thinking these things. I have a vivid imagination, and in my mind's eye, he is tied to my bed, entirely at my mercy as I rub myself over his handsome face until his beard drips with my arousal.

"Thanks for the walk, I had a wonderful time," he tells me and places a polite peck on my cheek

As he turns to walk away, his grip on my hand begins to loosen, and the idea of a cold, lonely bed is now too much to bear. I tighten my fingers around his, and he turns to look at me.

I drag my foot through the sand. "Do you want to see my room?"

"I thought you'd never ask."

9

Sam

This fabulous resort has a unique layout that offers private cottages that are still attached to the main building. It provides privacy with immediate access to the amenities my travel agent touted.

The stranger follows me to my cottage, and I can't help but question my own sanity. My decision-making skills are killer in the boardroom but in the bedroom? I'm a single woman in a foreign country who has invited a stranger into her cottage. There are a million things that could go wrong and potentially end in murder. On the flip side, there are a million things which could go oh-so-right, culminating in a release of epic proportions. Although, it wouldn't be fair to put those kinds of expectations on one man.

"This is it." I pluck out the card to unlock my door. I stop myself mid-swipe when a realization hits me. I turn around and assess him from head to toe. A few specks of sand twinkle in his chest hair which spans from shoulder to shoulder. "I just realized, I don't know your name. But then again, maybe I don't want to."

I swipe the card through and open the door, walking in, and he follows. "There's something romantic about anonymity. Don't you think?"

He jams his hands in his pockets and looks around. "Sure. These cottages are a hot commodity. Pricey. What did you say you do for a living?"

"I didn't." I kick off my sandals, toss them in front of the TV in the living area, and make my way toward the bedroom. "I think less is more in this situation." I strip out of my clothes and don my silk robe, tying it as I walk back to the living area.

I find him in the kitchenette. He pulls out a couple of bottles of water and hands me one. "That hardly seems fair. You already know what I do."

"Good point. Okay, what if I tell you something personal about me? Then we'll be even."

He nods and clacks his bottle against mine. I saunter toward the bedroom and he follows, taking a swig of his water. We stand in my bedroom, the bed to the left, the bathroom to the right, and stare at each other. He made the first move by kissing me on the beach, I suppose sexual etiquette demands I make the second move.

I stand on my tiptoes and balance myself with my hands on his chest. "I always get my way," I whisper, and follow it up with a rough lick to the shell of his ear while I rake my nails through the coarse hair on his chest.

He clears his throat. "I think I can accommodate." He bends at the waist, and his hands travel over my ass and give a brief squeeze as they make their way to the back of my thighs. In one fell swoop, he lifts me and wraps my legs around his hips. "Tell me what you want first."

My chest heaves with excitement and anticipation. "A shower." There is sand everywhere, and I mean everywhere. Certain parts of my body require love from soap and water before inviting any form of passion tonight.

He quirks an eyebrow at my request. "As you wish."

We tumble into the bathroom, and he sets me on the sink, our mouths fused together. I slide his shirt off his shoulders and dig my fingers into the muscle. "You have amazing shoulders."

"If you take off my shorts, you'll find something better than shoulders."

I link my ankles behind him and tug him closer, kissing him hard. My hands work at the button of his board shorts until the annoying clasp finally behaves.

"No underwear," I breathe out as I shove my hands into his pants and find he's right. From the girth, weight, and length in my hand, he must be huge. More than huge. He's intimidating.

"Breathe," he whispers. "Don't let it scare you. It was born to give pleasure."

I take a deep breath as he suggested. "It doesn't scare me. I'm just wondering if it's enough to get the job done."

He scoffs and my hand falls out of his pants as he turns the water on in the shower and tests the temperature. When he returns to me, he fingers the seam of my robe at my collarbone and slides the silk down my arms and back, exposing my breasts and pooling the fabric at my waist. His eyes are nearly black with lust, and I know he likes what he sees.

The bathroom begins to fill with steam, whether it's from the shower or from us, I'm not sure. I don't have much time to consider it before he pulls at the belt of my robe, picks me up by the waist once again, and carries me toward the shower, the garment sliding off and floating to the floor. He opens the shower glass door and steps inside.

I am completely naked, and my pussy is flush against the flexing muscles of his abdomen, making me wetter than I was when we walked in the bathroom in the first place.

He sets me down and keeps his arms around me, not willing to let me go. The travertine tile is cool on my feet and has yet to heat up. The water pours over us both, and our hands and lips feverishly work to explore each other's bodies.

He pushes me against the wall, and both his hands slide

to my waist. I'm completely naked in front of this man, and I refuse to be naked alone. I shove his sodden shorts off his hips, and he steps out. He presses against me as I stand on the tips of my toes, trying to match his height. It doesn't quite work, but I'm at just the right level that I can feel his hard cock against my sex as it slides between my folds. His cock glides back and forth, and we both give a simultaneous shudder of pleasure.

I want him inside me. Need him inside me. "Do you have a condom?"

"Shit," he groans, his chest deflating.

The slightest movement and I could sheath him. My belly tightens at the thought, and he takes a step back at the exact moment I consider breaking my golden rule of STD, and of course crying baby, prevention. The decision is made for me, and I'm glad, for I would have chosen most unwisely.

Water collects in his beard as he stares down at me, and I'm eager to suck it dry. He shoves his damp, blond hair back with one hand. "I'm sorry. I didn't think to bring one. I'm not a sleep-with-a-girl-on-the-first-date kind of guy."

"That's cute. You thought this was a date?" I thought we both saw this for what it was. A one-time shot.

"I didn't say it was a date. I just wasn't getting the 'hook-up' vibe from you."

"I guess you don't subscribe to the Boy Scout's mantra to always be prepared."

His hand traces a path down my belly. "No," he answers, amused. He dips his head downward and begins to lick at the water dripping down my neck. "However, I happen to have an assortment of talents I can use to satisfy a woman." He hikes my leg onto his hip.

The air rushes out of my lungs as his fingers part my folds and slide over the bundle of nerves. "Is that so?"

"Uh-huh," he answers, as his mouth makes its way down one breast.

Strong fingers work over my most delicate area as he gently

sucks my nipple into his hot mouth. My head falls back in pure joy. His other arm falls between us, and I can feel the movements of him stroking his cock at the same time he stokes my flames.

10

Sam

There is nothing quite as erotic as a shower with a man. This bartender delivers in ways I hadn't imagined when he pushes two thick fingers inside me. Not to say this isn't anything I haven't experienced before, but it's the heat of his stare, the staccato rhythm of his breathing which elevates it from the usual to the sensual.

He captures my mouth and absorbs my cries, keeping the same rhythm on my pussy as he uses to stroke himself. The whole idea has me ready to combust.

"Touch yourself," he demands.

My fingers swirl around the spot pulsating between my legs with the perfect amount of pressure.

His body goes taut as I cry out. "Yeah, that's it. Let it go. Come all over my hand. I want to feel your pussy strangle my fingers."

Hot jets of liquid spurt onto my thigh followed by his deep roar.

"Fuck," he groans, but I can barely hear him over the blood

rushing in my ears.

No longer having the strength needed, my leg falls from his hip. He drags us both under the showerhead, and the water begins to wash away the proof of our escapade.

He grabs a washcloth and applies body wash, working up a thick, creamy lather. His touch is gentle as he cleans me, from head to toe, and it almost feels as though he's worshipping me. He bends down on one knee and washes one leg then the other, and stops when he meets the spot between my thighs. He grabs the flesh and begins to rub. "I like the way my cum looks on you. It's a damn shame I have to wash it away."

We switch positions, and I take my time exploring his body while I rub in the soap. He is beautiful, the tropical life agrees with him. His skin is golden brown, every muscle perfectly sculpted, a real-life specimen of the ideal male form. I don't think I've ever seen a man so perfect.

And his cock. Holy shit. I gently wash the muscle that was flaccid five seconds ago, and I could barely wrap my fingers around it then. Now, it's coming back to life from my touch.

He grabs my hands. "I don't have a condom," he reminds me. "And stroking it like that can only cause problems."

I laugh. "Fair enough."

We rinse the soap off our bodies and step out of the shower. I wrap a towel around myself, cinching the fabric at my breasts. He wraps his towel around his waist, and it hangs deliciously low on his hips. I try not to gape and decide we're better off if we take this into the bedroom where I can distract myself with... well, something. I flop down on top of the covers of the king-sized bed, my hair a tangled mess.

He lays down next to me. "When do you leave?"

I look over at the clock on the nightstand. It's four o'clock in the morning. "The day after tomorrow."

He sits up and offers me his hand, helping me up, and we walk out onto the lanai. Ah, yes, the lanai, a much safer distraction than the memory foam of a bed.

The night air has a slight chill compared to the blazing heat of the day. My skin tightens with gooseflesh, but I quickly adjust and drop my towel to the ground. Palm trees and large tropical plants shroud me from potential on-lookers. Distraction is overrated. I stand completely naked in front of my nameless lover. The moon and soft glow from my room mingle with the shadows of the night to conceal me in an exotic game of peek-a-boo. The stranger tugs the towel off his waist and makes himself comfortable on the wicker loveseat, patting the cushion, beckoning me.

I'm slightly confused by his contentment to stay. In my experience, men don't tend to stick around long after getting what they want, or more accurately, getting what I wanted from them. Whether it's their preference or my insistence makes no difference. Strangely enough, there is comfort in his decision to stay.

"Come on. We might not know each other's names, but after what we just did, I'd hardly consider us strangers." He pats the couch again, and this time I accept, sitting next to him, being sure to leave another body's worth of space between us.

Something about this whole situation has me off-kilter. I'm not sure what it is. Maybe it's the setting, the country, the man. The man. He's different than what I'm accustomed to, and I'm accustomed to all kinds. However, a tiki bartender is something I have never done.

He lets out a small laugh and sweeps my legs out from under me, propping them on his lap. My calf rubs against his cock as he situates me comfortably.

I lean back and relax, inhaling the salty air then twist around for something on the table next to me. I snag the object I'm rummaging for and flip open the top of the square package. "Square?" I offer as I tip out a cigarette.

"I didn't peg you for a smoker."

"Only after sex. There's nothing better than a smoke after an orgasm."

"What the hell."

I pass him a cigarette, and with a flick of my Zippo, I light his first then mine. We both take a long drag and let the nicotine, tar, and God knows what else fill our lungs. He lets out one long, slow exhale. I take my time and puff out smoke rings.

"Very cool," he says, pointing to the largest smoke ring.

"Thanks. When I was little, my dad used to smoke cigars. He made the perfect smoke rings."

He gives a slight nod and doesn't say anything for several more seconds. Then, out of nowhere, he asks, "Favorite color?"

"Purple. Yours?"

"All of them. Mountain view or ocean view?"

"Shouldn't you already know the answer to that?" I ask, waving my arm toward the beach.

His fingers rub up and down my shin, the sensation teetering between delightful and torture. "Not necessarily. Just because you're on vacation, doesn't mean you prefer ocean view. Let me clarify. If you bought a house and there was a window above the kitchen sink, what would you be staring at as you scrubbed two-day-old lasagna off a plate?"

"First of all, there are way too many carbs in lasagna, so that would never happen. B, what kind of scary, Armageddon world am I living in where I have to do the dishes?"

He takes a pull from his cigarette and blows it out. "Intriguing answer."

"What's with the third degree? I thought we were cool with the whole anonymous thing."

"I am, but just because I don't know your name, doesn't mean I don't want to get to know who you are as a person."

My idea of anonymity is not knowing any real substance about the other person, but his idea is not knowing each other's names. Interesting.

With his middle finger and thumb, he flicks his cigarette toward the beach, instead of stubbing it out in the ashtray on the table directly in front of us. He turns toward me, holding onto my legs to keep them secure across his lap. "What are you doing tomorrow morning?"

I choose to use the ashtray to stamp out my smoke. "Later today, tomorrow morning? Or tomorrow, tomorrow morning?"

"Say eleven o'clock this morning?"

Since Grayson, Lizzie and I arrived, we have made it a ritual to start the day with a late breakfast, more like brunch, and lounging in a cabana at the beach or under an umbrella at the pool. "Sipping Mai Tais by the pool. Why?"

He stands, and I notice his cock jutting out with a sway as he moves. "Meet me downstairs in the lobby at eleven. Wear your swimsuit."

For a brief second, I consider interrogating him about his plans, but as I've learned today—tonight?—is that sometimes not knowing is half the excitement.

He leans over and gives me the softest kiss on my mouth, with a flick of his tongue on my lips. "Eleven o'clock."

11

Sam
Chicago

"Today's the big day," Ben announces as he hands me a coffee.

I take a sip and set it on my desk as I resume my work, tweaking the finishing touches for the Keogh, Inc. proposal for BLH. The plan is to meet with BLH's CEO, Tate Bennett, at Grayson's club this evening. "I know. I hope I can convince BLH to bite."

"Not that. The suspicious meeting that had to be scheduled for this week. Tell me you didn't forget," Ben says as he rubs his forehead with the palm of his hand.

I raise an eyebrow in question because I don't think we're talking about the same thing.

"The meeting with Frank."

I glance at the clock at the top of my laptop screen. "Shit. What time?"

"Two-thirty," he drolls, rolling his eyes.

I lean back in my chair and relax. "Still have twenty minutes.

Just enough time to finish this. Did you confirm my meeting with Bennett for this evening?"

Ben scrolls through his tablet. "Yep. His assistant called and confirmed with me. Whiskers at seven o'clock."

I dig back into my work, trying to make the proposal perfect. What Keogh suggested the other day at lunch has been niggling in the back of my mind. I genuinely don't believe my ovaries will send clients fleeing from Sterling. Just the same, I think it would be irresponsible, and un-presidential, of me not to consider it a possibility. I need to make this work.

"*Sam,*" Ben calls out through the crack of my office door. "It's two-thirty."

I hit save on my computer and close the screen. "Calm down. It's a whole five-second walk."

Frank's office reminds me of my father's study. Wood-paneled walls full of shelves with dusty old books. It's the kind of office that makes you instantly feel at home and safe within its four walls. I give a sturdy knock, realizing I'm nervous for the first time since I was hired. I'm not sure if it's Ben's rhetoric of underhanded dealings or Silas Keogh's suggestion that the business will crumble without Frank as our captain. Whatever the reason, I'm more than grateful that Delores is not posted in front of Frank's office.

"Frank," I call out as I bulldoze through the heavy oak doors.

"Samantha," Frank greets, cheerily. "Please, please come in, my dear."

Frank Gallagher is the founder and President of Sterling Brokerage. He started this business in his basement. During the day he sought deals worth making. At night, Frank bartended in a dingy Chicago bar. He worked tirelessly for who knows how many years in an effort to support and secure a future for his wife and son.

I'm not sure what happened to Frank's son. What I do know is there were never any plans for him to run the family business. I don't know why, and it doesn't matter.

No, it does matter. The reason it matters is because of this arrangement, I'm the one primed and poised to take the reins.

Frank leans in and gives me a hug with a kiss on each cheek.

When I return the gesture, something catches my eye. A man is standing in front of the window, and he's staring out at Lake Michigan. Frank's office boasts the best view in the firm. As it should. From my position near the door, I can see the Ferris wheel of Navy Pier.

The guest seems to appreciate the scenery.

As do I.

My bottom lip begins to tingle, and I realize I'm biting into it. I shouldn't cast judgment simply from the backside of a faceless man, yet, here I am. He's lean. Tall. Taller than Frank, which isn't saying much. I'm taller than Frank without my heels. His dark blond hair is cropped short, with a little length left on top. The hairline at his neck is perfectly straight and shaped, and it's obvious this man pays close attention to his grooming. There's something so sexy about that. Well-groomed hits my hot buttons, and, so does Not-Give-A-Fuck caveman. Opposite sides of the spectrum and both can drive me wild. I guess somedays it's all about a beard and others all about the shave.

And that suit. Christ. The next time I pass by a tailor, I must make sure to walk in and shake their hands. It's a sleek gray that's measured precisely to his delectable frame.

"Samantha, please, have a seat," Frank insists, drawing me out of my ogling of the stranger who hasn't moved so much as an inch upon my entry to the office.

The jingle of coins and keys catch my attention. The guest's hands are rooted in his pockets, the light bounces off his watch, and I realize he's the cause of the jingling. Is he nervous?

I sit on one of the two club-style chairs positioned directly across from Frank's desk. Frank plops down in his chair and the springs squeak out their protests under his weight.

"How have you been?"

"Great. Fabulous, in fact." The guy at the window still hasn't introduced himself, nor has Frank made any effort in this most basic of social etiquette. I give a robust clearing of my throat, trying to rouse the rude guy. "I've got an interesting deal in the works. I think you'll be pleased."

"Wonderful, wonderful," Frank exclaims with clapping. "Of course you do, I'd expect nothing less. Always working. Always working. So? Give me details."

I look toward the guy at the window and then back to Frank in an evident gesture, except Frank doesn't notice. He's a wizard when it comes to making a deal, not so much on reading body language. Even the obvious kind.

"I'm still ironing out a few details. I'll update you by the end of the week." I pause to give one of the two men an opportunity to make some sort of introduction, however, my patience is wearing thin. "Don't you want to introduce me to your friend?" I ask Frank, pointing to the man at the window.

"Oh, yes. Of course. Where are my manners?" Frank asks rhetorically as he shakes his head. "Samantha Valentine, I'd like you to meet my son Reid. Reid Gallagher."

Well, that answers my question. Frank's son is standing in this office. Right now. Mystery solved. Why now, after how many years? I've worked for Frank for ten years, and I have never met his son. Never even knew his name.

The guest turns around, and I'm taken aback by the most intense blue eyes I have ever seen. Except I have seen them. Just last week. At the coffee shop. Also, two months ago, under a waterfall.

12

Sam

"Samantha," Reid says as he extends his hand to me. His tone is cold, and his eyes are colder. There is not a single hint of recognition in them.

I want to grab him by his tailored collar and make him feel something. Like suffocation. I want him to treat me like someone he spent an afternoon with making love, or lust. Definitions aren't important.

"Mr. Gallagher, I've heard so much about you. Welcome home. Please call me Sam," I tell him, accepting his handshake.

"No, you haven't, and thank you, Sam."

Frank points to the seat next to mine. "Have a seat, son."

Reid and I are half an arm's length away from each other. He smells different. Before, he smelled like coconut and sea salt—tasted like it too. Now, his smell isn't right. It's a high-dollar cologne that would typically drive me insane with need but somehow seems wrong for him.

Frank starts talking, but my focus is solely on the man next to me, craving his acknowledgment. I try to nonchalantly run a hand across the top button of my blouse. Oops, too much cleavage?

Reid doesn't take the bait.

I cross one knee over the other and playfully bend to rub a small cramp in my calf. A cramp which requires me to start from the top of my foot and slowly run my hand all the way to my thigh.

Reid gives a sideways glance but remains focused.

I go in for the kill and let my high-heel dangle at the end of my foot.

It works. Reid's eyes are laser-focused on my foot and leg. Foot fetish?

"What brought you back to Chicago, Mr. Gallagher?" I ask, forcing his eyes back up to my face.

"Frank," he clears his throat. "Do you want to fill her in?"

My brows narrow, and I'm sure a migraine is brewing. Denial was my friend when I entered this office, now there's no way around the truth. Nothing about this meeting can be good for me.

Frank leans back in his chair. "How long have you worked for me, Samantha?"

"Over ten years now, sir," I answer, confident.

"Yes, yes, that's right. You've worked your way up from the receptionist desk to the office," he says, pointing, "right next to mine."

"That's correct, sir."

"Now, Reid," Frank says, swiveling his seat in his son's direction. "Don't let Samantha fool you. She's a wolf in sheep's clothing. She'd been here less than a year before she marched into my office and declared that one day my desk would become hers. I admire that," he says as he turns back to me. "I knew from that moment on..."

My gaze wanders toward my stranger. I mean Reid. I mean Reid Gallagher. He's Frank's son. I don't see the resemblance. Frank is short and stodgy. Reid is...not stodgy. What happened between Frank and Reid? It didn't escape my attention that Reid called his father by his first name instead of Dad. What drives a man to call his father by his given name?

"Now that my boy, here," Frank continues, pointing toward Reid, "has decided to come home—"

Reid lets out a grunt of disgust at his father's words.

Frank gives him a side glance and continues. "I want him to become a part of our team at Sterling. Sam, I trust you above everyone else in this office. I want you to show him the ropes. He has experience in—"

"In real estate," Reid interrupts. "I worked for a large hotel company based out of New York for several years. I spent a fair amount of time acquiring land, buildings, even entire hotel chains."

The way Reid speaks is so...formal, business-like. It's sexy, yet disconcerting. I might not have spent a lot of time with him in Barbados, but this is not the man I met behind the bar. He's eloquent and well-spoken, obviously educated, probably Ivy League.

Maybe I'm being self-centered, but where does this leave me and the promotion to president when Frank retires, if his son joins the team?

"And where does this leave me, sir? Not to be uncouth, but is my position, my future position, secure?" I ask, feeling the need to address the bartender in the room.

"Oh, my goodness, yes, Samantha. Absolutely. Absolutely. I don't think Reid here has any interest in running the company. Although, I think the lawyers in HR would feel relieved if he did," Frank says with a chuckle.

Over the course of my career, I have been summoned to Human Resources on several occasions. There are some men at Sterling Brokerage who don't feel as lucky as they should when I've suggested a "meeting" in private. The lawyers in HR enjoy throwing around terms like "position of power" and "sexual harassment." I'm quite popular at the Sexual Harassment in the Workplace seminar I'm mandated to attend every year. There are a hundred and fifty guys from various Fortune 500 companies and me.

"I'm sure they would," I say, returning Frank's mirth. "But those boys need a challenge from time to time."

Frank lets out a deep laugh. "They do."

"Well, Reid, I have an appointment in a few minutes." I lie. It's as if I stepped through The Looking Glass—nothing makes sense. "I'd love to get to know you. Help you settle in," I offer.

I stand to leave. Frank and Reid both also rise in a show of old-school manners.

"I'm having some friends over for cards this weekend," I tell Reid. "We need a fourth for Euchre. Pizza, drinks, meet some new people. Pretty laid back."

"I'd love to."

I walk out the door with my shoulders thrown back, my chest pushed out, and all the confidence I can fake.

13

Reid

After Sam leaves, Frank and I sit back down. The smell of her perfume lingers, and I find myself taking a deep breath for just one more whiff of her sweet scent. She's just as beautiful as she was the first time I saw her. The day she left for the airport, and I discovered she had a boyfriend, I think my heart broke. I never thought I would be able to feel anywhere near as exposed and wanting as I did when I was with Amanda, until Sam. It was brief. It was hot. It was something I never expected.

Resigned to the fact that I would never see her again, I was shocked as hell when I ran into her at that coffee shop. When I dropped her off at the same building which houses Sterling, I convinced myself that the chances that she worked there was near impossible. Until she told me what floor she worked on and what she did for a living. That's when I knew things were about to get ugly.

"Do you think you'll ever call me 'Dad'?" Frank asks.

I prop my leg up on the opposite knee and relax in this comfortable-as-shit chair. I can say a lot of things about Frank—

some good, most bad—but I can't accuse him of being cheap.

"Is that a joke?"

Frank's frown deepens. I'm sure he's disappointed in my answer, that's nothing new. I've been a disappointment for as long as I can remember.

"I was hoping that, in light of things, you might have a change of heart."

"Hope is a dangerous thing, Frank. Be careful."

Frank let out a resigned sigh, and we sit in awkward silence. I wait patiently for him to say something, but it becomes apparent that I'm the one who will have to start the conversation.

"You didn't tell her?" I don't know why it surprises me. It shouldn't, but after everything he's been through to get me here, I find it ridiculous that he doesn't have the guts to be upfront. "And you fed her that crap that I didn't want to take over the business. You lied to her face."

"I know, I know. It's just Sam has worked so damn hard. She honestly deserves it. I don't know how I'm going to tell her. She'll be devastated." Frank says, regret tinging his words. "Have you two met before?"

"No. Never seen her in my life." Why does it matter anyway? She has a boyfriend. I was just a convenient scratch for an inconvenient itch.

"Just seems like there was something between you two," Frank theorizes.

His wife tries to molest me at dinner every night, right in front of him, and he doesn't notice. I speak two words to Sam, and he picks up on the sexual tension.

"There's not."

"I just want to make sure everything is clean as a whistle when I leave. I've worked my entire life to make Sterling what it is today. I don't want the company to take a shit the moment I walk out the door."

"Then why have me here, if you can't trust me?" I ask, bristling with anger. "I'm doing this for you. Not for me."

Frank raises his hands in surrender. "You're right. Of course, you are. I'm sorry."

This stuffy office is caging me in. I stand and button my suit jacket. "I've got a lot to catch up on if I plan to run this place within the next two weeks. You have one week to tell her, or I will."

My office is across the hall from Sam's. Frank has spared no expense to prepare it for my arrival. Which is amusing, since I will be taking his office in just a couple of weeks. I stare across the hall to Sam's office, her assistant guarding the entry. I can see Sam walking around as she digs through filing cabinets.

Fuck, she's beautiful. I'm supposed to be her new boss, not that she knows it, which means I have to keep my hands to myself. The fact that she has a boyfriend, even if she isn't the faithful type, should be enough to convince me that it could never happen.

I can't help but think back to the times we made love, the sounds she made, the smell of her arousal, the way she sneezed when she came—all of it, the whole package. She's everything I could want in a woman whom I've known for a handful of days.

Except for the boss and boyfriend thing.

Her assistant is a good-looking guy, kind of young. Maybe she likes them young. Is she sleeping with him too? I've never been a jealous man. With Amanda, I was confident in our relationship, I knew she loved me until death did us part. I rub at a spot on my chest. No matter how long ago, it is still painful, and I've spent the better part of five years mourning her loss. It's time for my life to develop some forward momentum, break out of the stagnant, predictable routine that I created. Which is part of the reason I've found myself back in Chicago.

14

Sam

Whiskers is a premier gentlemen's club where men of high society converge to be anything other than gentlemen.

Brutus guards the entrance as I walk up to the massive Greek Style pillars at the front door. I flash my onyx VIP card. In my business, I have a role to play. I need to be one of the boys, and how better to prove myself than with a membership to the most exclusive club in the Mid-West.

"Not necessary, Ms. Valentine," Brutus tells me in his deep voice. He's a large man with dark chocolate skin which makes me wonder how he would taste slathered in peanut butter.

He holds his hand out to me as I walk up to the red velvet rope. "You look divine."

I twirl in my little black dress which hugs me like a second skin. "Why, Mr. Brutus, you are too kind," I tell him, impersonating Scarlett O'Hara.

He gives me a sly smile as he unhooks the rope and allows me to pass.

"Tate Bennett will be my guest tonight," I inform him so

Tate can be let in without any trouble. Tate is a good man. A man too good to be a member of Grayson's club.

"No problem," Brutus says.

There are four bar areas on the main floor of Whiskers. I saunter up to the one in the lobby. It gives an unobstructed view of the main room and allows one to watch without being as noticeable. I slide onto a barstool and wave to the bartender.

He acknowledges me with a tilt of his chin. "He's in his office," he says, telling me where I can find Grayson as he slides a tumbler down the rail toward me. The highest shelf scotch is most delicious when in a swanky and salacious environment.

Women parade around the club in custom-made leotards. Long tails are stitched into the hind end and matching headbands with pointy ears are perched on top of their heads. They walk with grace and class as they balance trays filled with drinks while warding off unwanted attention with tact.

No matter what anyone thinks about Grayson's club, there is no denying he is a terrific boss. The girls are priority *numero uno*. Men can look, but never touch. He also supplies excellent health insurance to his employees. Better than what I get at Sterling. Grayson takes it one step further and pays each employee's premiums; single or family plan, spouse or no, Grayson pays it all.

"Hey, girl," Deanna, one of the world-class kittens, says as she passes me. Her copper hair is incorporated into her costume. I guess she'd be considered an orange domestic house cat with her orange and white striped leotard with ears and tail to match.

I wave as she walks by, balancing a tray of shots. She's serving one of the best sections in the house.

Whiskers has three stages. Two jut out toward different sides of the club, and a long platform that connects the two. The middle stage is set up for performances by the scouted talent of trained burlesque dancers. This section is referred to as "center stage" and covet the best seats in the house.

Center stage boasts three shows a night and follows up with

a grand finale with all the dancers, strippers included, in one last showdown. It's fantastic, a delicate blend of raunchy mixed with sophistication. It may seem impossible, but it's done and done well. Lizzie is the coordinator of the whole show. She's a genius when it comes to the musical art of dancing.

Upstairs are the offices. Grayson, security, Lizzie's office, and whatever else goes into managing a successful club. This floor is only accessible from the iron staircase behind the bar.

On the third level are the private showrooms with different themes. A bubble suite, an S&M room, a naughty bathroom, there are more, but I can't remember them all. Seven rooms in total, I believe.

The fourth floor houses a penthouse suite where, for a cool million or more, all of one's wildest dreams can come true, including the not-so-legal ones. They're also used to host bachelor parties, foreign diplomats, business dealings, and God knows what else.

Deanna sets down the drinks at a table in the middle section, in a semi-circular booth filled with fresh-faced men who have discovered they can take over the world. They can't, but they're still young enough to believe anything is possible.

She snubs their advances with a playful swat, and gives them an index finger, waving the no-no sign at them. They can't take the hint and continue to run their hands up her legs and jerking on her tail. Deanna warns them a second, maybe a third time, before she raises her hand in the air and brings the back of her palm to the top of her head, rubbing like a kitten grooming herself. Security has been alerted.

Brutus and another large man approach the table. I can't tell what they are saying to the young men, but if I read their lips, it looks like, "Conchee are fat lucky not torches," or whatever. I can't read lips.

Deanna walks away from the table and has a seat next to me at the bar.

I finish off the rest of my scotch. "I can't believe you cat-called them." Cat-calling is when a kitten needs the assistance of the bouncers.

"Kittens are for looking, not touching," she answers.

The bartender hands Deanna a bottle of water. She takes a slow drink of her beverage. "I have to go," she tells me as she hops off her stool. "Sit in my section. I've got center stage tonight."

"Sure thing." I toss a ten on the bar, ready to see what Grayson is up to.

I walk up the wrought iron stairs to Grayson's office and give a stern knock.

"Just a minute," he calls out, his words sounding stunted.

I decide to send him a text instead.

Me: "One minute? Or twenty?"

I ask because I'm suspicious he has a woman in there. Suspicious because of the moans seeping out from under his office door.

Grayson: "4 minutes."

I stand against the wall and fiddle with my phone. I arrived a half-hour before my meeting with Tate so I could talk to Grayson.

His door swings open and Grayson walks out, his dark hair disheveled, and a young woman on his arm. Her hair is short and spiked on top; the spikes amplify the rainbow of colors she's chosen to dye it. "You'll call me right, Gray-gray?" she asks, using the worst nickname in the entire history of nicknames.

"Of course," he croons as he guides her out the door of his office and toward the stairs.

She stops abruptly and turns to Grayson. "Oh, but I never gave you my number."

"Sure you did," he tells her as he runs his nose along her neck. "I must have banged the memory right out of your pretty little head."

I roll my eyes and Grayson catches me and gives me the finger behind his back.

He gives her a hard slap on her ass. "Now get out of here. I'll call you."

She yelps and follows it up with a giggle. It's disgusting.

"Why, Ms. Valentine, to what do I owe this pleasure?" Grayson asks, walking back into his office.

I follow him and give a few small sniffs of the air. "It smells like sex in here."

He laughs. "If it doesn't, then I've been doing it wrong for a very long time."

"Is it safe?" I ask, pointing to the couch.

He shakes his head.

"I'll just sit here." I bend to sit in the recliner.

"I wouldn't." He rifles through some papers on his desk.

"Fine. I'll sit on the desk."

He stares at me.

"You're a dirty boy, Grayson Treadwell."

He gives a huge smile. "No dirtier than you, my sweet."

I look around for a safe place to sit but figure nothing in this room is untainted. "That's gross. Come downstairs and sit with me at the bar and have a drink."

At least there the semen is anonymous.

15

Sam

We settle in at the bar, and I order an appletini and Grayson orders a scotch. When the bartender walks away to serve other patrons, we switch drinks.

"I hate the stigma that comes with a man drinking these delicious fruity drinks," Grayson says after he gulps down the entire glass. "I mean, it tastes good. Isn't that what matters? It's not like if I don't have some expensive imported beer, I'm any less of a man."

"Yeah, it's rough having testicles."

He rolls his eyes and shrugs his shoulders. He knows I'm right.

"Have you talked to Lizzie recently?" he asks.

"We meet at the gym four days a week, as usual. Why? You two aren't talking?"

"No. We are. Just making conversation. Fill me in on the wonderful life of the enigmatic Sam Valentine."

He's a liar. Neither he nor Lizzie have mentioned each other in my presence. Come to think of it, I can't remember the last time we've been together, all three of us, since Barbados. I have to summon mammoth amounts of willpower to keep from grilling him, but I know when he's ready to talk, he'll talk. Which will be on Saturday, he just doesn't know it yet.

Right now, I need to bend the ear of a good friend, and he seems willing to listen. I've been conflicted by the idea of Reid in my work life and I'm not sure how to deal with it. "Yeah, that's an interesting story. Remember the mystery guy I met in Barbados?"

"Sure."

"Turns out he's Frank's son."

"Frank Gallagher?"

"Reid Gallagher is his name. I guess he returned to the states to work at Sterling Brokerage."

"Hmm. Don't you find it...odd?"

I take a sip of my drink and consider his question. "Not really. Lots of people go to work for the family business. It's not that unusual."

"Okay. Sure. You're right. How old is this Reid guy? I mean, did he just graduate from some fancy business school, took some time off after graduation, and then was ready to work for Daddy?"

Damn. That is a good question. "I don't know. Mid-thirties maybe. It's not like I asked to see ID or anything. Hell, I didn't even know his name until today."

"Everything all right over here?"

The voice is like chocolate wrapped in silk. I still get shivers every time I hear him speak.

"Tate," I say as I stand.

Tate grabs my hand and kisses my knuckles. "Hello, Ms. Valentine. Grayson," he says, acknowledging my friend and shaking his hand.

Tate Bennett is tall and lean with coffee-colored hair and eyes so green that a girl could get lost in them. Lost I have been, several times over, in multiple positions. As much fun as we've had together, I'm not sure how compatible we are. As friends and business associates sure, but I don't think I'm quite his taste.

Grayson stands as well. "I have some work to tend to. You two have fun. Let me know if you need anything." He snaps his fingers, and the hostess appears. He gives her instructions as to where to seat us and our level of accommodation. Which, of course, is anything we want.

I give Grayson a hug. "You need to talk to Lizzie."

"Why do you say that?"

"Because it bothers you."

He nods, looks down at the ground, and shoves his hands in his pockets as he escapes to the safety of his office.

Tate and I are guided to center stage and seated in Deana's section.

"Tell me about this deal," Tate says, referring to the sale Keogh is hopeful to negotiate with BLH. His eyes are glued to a woman hanging upside down on a pole.

I've never been so glad to have a business meeting in the middle of the week in my entire career. The whole thing with Reid has thrown me for a loop, and work is the perfect distraction. This deal could make my career. Launch me into the stratosphere. I need it. I can taste it, and it smells of success.

Deanna drops off a scotch and water for Tate, and water, no scotch, for me as I explain the details of what Silas Keogh is looking to achieve.

"He's going to try and milk me for every penny he can," Tate says, still keeping his gaze on the dancer.

"Well, yeah. Isn't that the whole point? I know his reasons, whatever they are, aren't altruistic but think about the employees. If he sells to anyone else, you know jobs will be the first cutbacks made."

Tate Bennett is the new CEO of BLH, his father stepped down a few months back. Thus far, Tate has maintained his father's values. He considers the employees and how his decisions will affect them before he makes any substantial changes. The idea of laying off workers will grate against his sensibilities. Of course, I might be using this knowledge to my advantage.

"Send me the details tomorrow. I'll think about it."

"There. Business is done. See, that wasn't so bad. Now, let's have some fun."

"We agreed we can't sleep together anymore, Sam. Business and pleasure, no matter how great it is, never mix."

I laugh. "Someone has a big ego. No, I was thinking we should get lap dances."

I raise my hand in the air, and Deanna appears at our table with lightning speed. "What can I get for you, Ms. Valentine?"

I pluck out a few folded bills from my cleavage. "I want to book some time in The Kitty Cradle." The Kitty Cradle is similar to a Champagne Room in a seedy strip joint, except cleaner. It's semi-private, you pick the kitten, or kittens, who strike your fancy, and you let them rub up against you.

"Any particular kitten in mind?" Deana asks.

I point to two girls. "Yes, the short, busty kitten for him," pointing to Tate, "and the leggy Russian one for me."

I do love an exotic treat.

16

Sam
Barbados

I stand in the lobby of the hotel with my hair in pigtails, a white tank top, jean shorts, and a hot pink bikini underneath. I'm not sure what to expect for our afternoon together. I felt it best to be prepared for anything short of a formal dinner. I'm confident I can accommodate any entertainment which is sans clothing.

It took some convincing and a bit of conniving to keep Lizzie and Grayson off my back. I didn't want to tell them about last night, or who I spent it with. What would I tell them anyway? Hey, you know that stranger I called out on the beach yesterday? Turns out he took me up on the offer. By the way, I don't know his name or anything of substance, but I plan to spend the day with him, and I have no clue where he's taking me.

I'll admit, this will not rank high on my list of smart moves. A youngish, single woman in a foreign country takes up with a stranger. There are documentaries with this exact scenario. I thought long and hard about what I would tell them to keep them off my scent of deflection and defection. At breakfast this morning, I told them about a great pirate and sunken ship exhibit in town. They both groaned their disappointment and worried they would be forced to join me.

My stranger walks through the front doors, and there is a sudden change in temperature from the cool air-conditioned building to the hot and steamy quality which accompanies him. Is that what makes the tropical islands so damn warm, the hot men who occupy its land?

He looks delicious in green swim trunks that match the leaves of his tropical button-down shirt. His hair tied back in a loose ponytail, and my fingers twitch with the need to tug on it.

I can tell the exact moment he spots me because he lifts his aviator sunglasses and gives me a bright smile. I'll be damned if that isn't the most panty-melting smile I've ever seen in my life.

"Ready to go?" he asks as he approaches.

"Yup, let's do it." I secure my purse across my body.

We walk out to the parking lot, and I find myself in front of a magnificent, red Ducati Monster. "Is this a Monster?" I ask, my voice cracking in disbelief.

He leans against the motorcycle and folds his arms, smiling. "You know bikes, huh?"

"Are you kidding? I almost bought one." I walk around the bike to get a good eye-full.

"Why didn't you?"

I run my fingers along the fine Italian leather seat. "Riding wasn't conducive to my life. I wanted something that would force me to slow down and enjoy the moment. Ducati's aren't really good for that."

"What did you end up with then?" He thrusts one leg over the seat and fires up the engine, sliding his shades over his eyes.

"A Vulcan," I holler over the purr of the engine.

"An Aston Martin? They're not known for cruising the open road."

"I know. Turns out I don't want to enjoy the scenery. I want to make it blur as I pass it at two-hundred miles an hour."

The tires squeal, and I take a deep breath of burnt rubber as the force of the motorcycle tries to separate my front from the sinewy muscles of his back. My grip is so tight that physics doesn't stand a chance.

We ride on a highway littered with several different resorts and through a small town. He maneuvers the bike with practiced caution as we pass farmers' markets and other shops in the village. After the congestion of town is behind us, and there is nothing except open road, he lets loose. The scenery of the lush mountains blend with the foliage. The beauty of paradise is not lost, it's amplified.

We come to a stop in the empty parking lot of a desolate beach, and now would be a convenient time to second guess every decision I've made in my life. Riding off with a stranger in a foreign country seems like a terrible idea.

"He should be here any minute," the stranger says as he shuts off the engine.

"Who's 'he'?" I hop off the bike and start to look around, trying not to show my fear.

"You'll see."

"Is it just me, or is it weird that you have such a superlative bike in the middle of the Caribbean?"

He huffs out a small laugh. "Yeah, it's weird. When I moved here, I got rid of a lot of stuff, but," he swings a leg over to get off the bike, "I couldn't part with it. I love it too much. Unfortunately, I think this may be my last ride."

"Why is that?" I ask genuinely curious, and to keep the conversation progressing so maybe he won't slit my throat.

"Time to grow up I guess."

"That's a bummer." I glance around for signs of life anywhere I can find it. If I run, will he be able to catch me? Will I be able to find my way back to the resort?

"Here he is now," the stranger says, pointing toward a man walking with an exquisite speckled horse that has a blond mane and tail.

The man is short with creamy chocolate skin and tufts of white hair which stick out from under a baseball cap. My stranger and the new guy chat in a language I don't know. They laugh and smile at each other as the older man hands the reins to my stranger.

"I thought we could share one," my stranger says.

"That's a good idea since I've never ridden one before."

After he mounts the horse, he helps me up and positions me in front. He grabs the reins, gives a slight tap to the horse's side with his foot, and we begin to move.

The horse takes us along the shoreline and treads into the water. As we near a turn which will take us to the other side of the island, my stranger steers us toward the base of a mountain that is obscured by trees.

"Do you know where you're going?" I ask.

"Kind of, but Chester knows the way." He leans over me to rub the horse's neck.

"That makes me feel better."

"Don't worry, I'll keep you safe." He gives a slight tug on the reins and the horse comes to a stop. "Chester says we're here."

My stranger's movements are natural and smooth as he dismounts the horse. Once on the ground, he lifts his arms up to me and helps me slide off the saddle. Our bodies collide as his arms wrap tightly around my waist as he lowers me.

A gasp escapes his lips as we come face to face. The frisson of attraction is not one-sided in the least. The bright blue of his eyes captivates me, and as much as I want to stay in this moment forever, I know it's only going to last a few more hours. My fears of being kidnapped and murdered have gone by the wayside. My instincts tell me that this is where I am meant to be. They have served me well my entire life, no reason not to trust them now.

I step out of his grip and look around. Beautiful trees and tropical flowers, similar to the lanai of my resort cottage, except on a grander scale. The beauty of the island has the power to steal my breath. "What are we going to do here?"

My stranger stares at me for long moments, and I feel naked while shielded in my tank and shorts. He gives a shake of his head but doesn't answer my question. He ties Chester to a tree and talks sweet horse talk to him. It's endearing. After Chester is secured, my stranger returns his attention to me. "This way," he says, walking toward the tree line.

17

Sam

We trudge through thick vegetation, and I have a new interpretation of the adage seeing the forest for the trees. I can't see but a few feet in front of me. As a branch sticks my foot, I start to rethink my flip-flops, but it's not like I knew we were going hiking. I continue to walk, paying close attention to my feet when my stranger comes to an abrupt halt, and I slam into his back. He grunts and spreads his arms out to keep me from moving any farther.

I stand on my tiptoes and lean over his arms to get a look. We are literally standing on the precipice. Of a cliff. I'm not sure how far up we are, and no clue what awaits us below because the Earth has developed a magical ability to rise and fall right in front of my eyes. My stomach sloshes, and I tamp down the urge to throw up.

He must not notice my sudden fit of panic because my stranger toes off his shoes and peels off his shirt. Good God almighty, he is a fine specimen of a man. My sudden fear of heights vanishes at the sight of his magnificent abs.

He quirks an eyebrow and grasps for something behind me. It's a gnarly-looking, at least two-hundred-year-old, knotted rope. He gives a hard yank, and the branch cracks. "Seems sturdy."

He walks backward, taking advantage of the path we stamped down. He pulls the rope taut and sprints to the edge of the cliff and leaps off, swinging through the air. He calls out like Tarzan as he lets go of the rope, his voice echoing off the canyon walls and followed by a loud splash.

I peer down, desperate for him to rise to the top and more than worried he won't. Much to my relief, his head pokes out of the water, and his face is alight with a childish grin. At least, I think it is. He is pretty far down there.

"Hey, guy, are you okay?" I call out, not sure how he survived, also not convinced he isn't injured. The drop must be over a hundred feet, although my ability to judge distance is askew.

He shouts up to me. "Yeah, I'm fine. Come on in, the water's perfect."

Why would I want to jump from a perfectly good cliff? I bite my lip and try to decide if I will woman-up and take the plunge. Hell yeah, I will. I strip out of my shirt and shorts and fling off my flip-flops, understanding why he wanted me to wear my swimsuit. I grab the rope, yank it back as far as it can go, and make a run for it.

I swing into mid-air and let go of my only lifeline, falling. I tuck my legs in right before I collide with the water. Holy hell does that hurt. My ass and thighs feel as if they are on fire. My arms swipe and legs kick as I ascend to the surface. I break through the water and take a large gulp of air, desperate for a breath. My heart pounds in my chest, adrenaline on warp speed. I turn to look at my stranger, his eyes searching my face.

"That. Was. *Awesome*," I shout, giddy from the rush.

"I thought you might like it. Are you up for a swim? I want to show you something."

"Sure." At this point, I've got nothing to lose. Chester is a hundred feet above me secured to a tree, and I can't seem to find any way out of here that won't require extensive rock-climbing experience. Experience which I do not possess.

The perfectly warm freshwater is rejuvenating, cooling me on the outside and soothing my soul on the inside. We swim at a leisurely pace. I try the backstroke, switch to doggy paddle, and settle on the dead man's float, except facing up, so I can breathe.

A tug at my waist tips me off balance, causing me to splash like a loon. An ear-splitting squeal escapes me before I'm completely taken under. Tepid water fills my eyes as they flit open. I give a few hard blinks, and my vision begins to adjust. The water is so clear I can see the vegetation beneath my feet and the handsome man in front of me. His hair has been freed from its ponytail and is standing on end from the pull of gravity versus the water. His face is hard, serious, and assessing. He pushes his arms out to propel himself toward me until his lips make contact with mine.

My heart pounds wildly in my chest as he cups my cheek and licks into my mouth, his beard is soft against my face. We're sharing oxygen, the need to rise to the world above us seems unnecessary. Except for the tinges of white on the edges of my vision. We may be a bit heavy on the carbon dioxide side of the gas exchange. He cinches his arms around my waist, his mouth still fused to mine and kicks his feet, thrusting to the top until we meet the surface.

His hand stays on my cheek as he pulls away from my lips. I miss his taste already.

"We're here," he announces and loosens his grip.

"Wow." There is a beautiful waterfall spilling into a lagoon. Rainbows galore. The sunlight hits the fall's spray in the most perfect of ways so that there are easily a dozen multi-sized rainbows scattered around us.

"Wow is right," he whispers, his lips gliding against my ear. The swollen head of his cock nudges against my leg through his swim trunks. He turns me and wraps my legs around him. "It's hands down the best spot on the island."

"Can't argue with that."

His hand ventures to the back of my neck and his fingers loop around the knot which holds up the top of my bikini. His eyes are dark and questioning. I think he's asking me if this is okay. I give the nod, and he hikes me up, bringing my breasts to mouth level. He tugs the string to release my top, dips his head down, and draws one nipple into his mouth, giving a tug with his teeth.

A moan escapes, the roughness jerking an invisible string from my breast directly to my core. My fingers run through his long, blond hair, yanking his face closer to me still. I'm rewarded when he gives a rough tug of my nipple and then switches to the other breast, tweaking and massaging.

I could explode. I need friction. The urgency to come is consuming. I gyrate against his cock, and delight in the sensation of him against the fabric of my bathing suit. With each pivot, I can feel him growing harder, and larger.

He lets out a throaty grunt and crushes his lips into mine. His expert tongue explores my mouth. His hand travels beneath the bottom of my suit, and he slides one finger between my folds.

The feeling is sensational, lighting my skin on fire while submerged in this magnificent lagoon. Unable to resist, I take over the kiss and nip at his lip almost hard enough to draw blood.

He rears back. "You deserve better than this."

"What do you mean? This is amazing."

"You'll see." He grabs my hand and tows me through the water to step behind the waterfall.

18

Sam

My stranger and I sit in the sand with half our bodies still in the water. There is a large beach umbrella set up; underneath it lies a picnic basket and towels. It's incredibly romantic. My breath hitches as I consider how much time this must have taken. For me. A woman who called out lewd things on the beach. A woman who didn't even follow through with her promise. "You did all this?"

He rubs the back of his neck. "Yeah. Too much?"

"No. Not at all. It's stunning and thoughtful. Thank you."

"I'm glad you like it." He gets up and spreads out a beach blanket.

We lie down on our sides and stare at each other. I'm not sure what's going through my stranger's mind, but I'm wondering who is going to make the next move.

I decide it's me, and I run a finger down his chest to follow the pattern of the muscles on his abdomen. His skin pebbles beneath my touch, I take it a step further and sit up and straddle him. I grind my pelvis into his. He wraps his arms around my waist and flips us over, and I find myself on the bottom.

We kiss for a long time, our hands roaming each other's bodies, exploring, getting to know each other in the most intimate ways.

My stranger sits back on his heels, my legs spread over his thighs, my breasts exposed, and I'm panting. I need this, crave this, and worry I might go insane if I don't get it.

He slides the bottom of my suit down my legs and tosses it over my head toward the picnic basket. My knees are up and bent, and he pushes them open. His blue eyes turn sultry as he licks his lips. I could almost come from seeing the look on his face. Almost.

One finger runs over the top of my slit and then back down. My knees fall to the side out of instinct, inviting him in. The tip of his finger becomes wet with my arousal as he slowly caresses the flesh between my folds. I wiggle my hips every time he comes close to my clit, seeking pressure where I need it, but he refuses to give me what I want. This must be a new form of torture.

"Please," I beg.

He gives me an impish grin as he dips his head between my legs. *Yes.* My breathing speeds up as his tongue flicks at the bundle of nerves that pulsate with want. My hips buck, and I'm about to lose my mind. I grab him by the hair to take what I need.

"Not yet, sweetheart." His deep voice vibrates against my pussy as his tongue circles my entrance. Strong hands have a firm grip on my hips as he plunges his tongue inside me, then runs the appendage up my center to my clit.

"Oh, God," I cry.

He draws my clit into his mouth and sucks. I sit up, wild with the sensation. He looks up at me, his eyes half-closed, still sucking. He pierces my entrance with two fingers and rocks his hand back and forth.

My body goes stiff, and I fall back, unable to catch my breath. "I'm going to come," I manage to squeak out, trying in vain to hold back.

"Uh, huh," I hear him moan into me. Well, more like feel. Those two vibrations contain enough power to turn my whole world upside down. His hand pumps harder and faster, and he releases my clit from his wicked mouth to give light flicks with his thumb. There is a distinct possibility that I am speaking in tongues as the orgasm hits.

"Shit," he mutters as he watches me writhe in pleasure. He rifles around in the picnic basket just past my head, retrieves a condom, and tears the package with his teeth. He is talented. An expert multitasker because while he is in search of a condom, he continues to keep his other hand busy, his fingers moving up and down, in and out. One orgasm rolls into a second, and, oh God, a third.

I'm suddenly empty, and I raise onto my elbows to look at the amazing man who has brought me to the edge repeatedly with nothing in return. Rapt in fascination, my eyes are glued to him as he sheaths himself. Everything about him that makes him a man is bare and rubbing against my thigh. After last night, when neither one of us was prepared, I'm eternally grateful that he was thinking when he packed today because I might die if I don't feel him inside me.

He uses his forearms to position himself over me and pushes in a little bit. We both take a deep breath. He slides in a bit farther, and we both let out a sigh.

A cry of pleasure which borders on pain, exquisite pain, escapes me, and he captures each sound with his mouth, kissing me with recklessness.

His rhythm starts out slow and even, and as he hits the perfect spot, he begins to pump harder. Beads of sweat form on his chest and I lick them away, reveling the taste of a man in his purest moment of masculinity.

He tugs at my hips as he sits back on his heels, pushing and pulling as he pounds into me. His body stiffens, and he throws his head back, crying out his carnality. The thick cords of his neck strain with his release as he pushes me over the edge.

Achoo.

"Bless you," he says, looking down at me, curious.

"Thank you."

His arms quiver, and he collapses on top of me, our sweaty bodies sticking together. "Oh, man."

"You got that right."

He rolls off, removes the condom, and tosses it next to him. We lie next to each other on a dampened beach blanket behind a waterfall. I don't know if it gets much better than this.

After we lie there for a little while to catch our breath, my stranger sits up and lugs the picnic basket next to him. He removes something and takes a bite out of it like a caveman. "Fried chicken?"

"Yummy." Sex and swimming are two activities guaranteed to ratchet up the appetite. He hands me a chicken leg, and I too tear the meat off the bone, delighting in this old-fashioned picnic with a side dish of kink. "What else you got in there?"

He rifles through the basket. "Coleslaw, potato chips, brownies, and lemonade."

"I'll take some coleslaw and a lemonade."

He passes me the goodies and takes out a bag of chips for him. "What's your favorite ice cream flavor?"

I take a spoonful of slaw. It's cute that he wants to get to know me. Pointless, but cute. "Mint chocolate chip. You?"

"All—"

"And don't say all of them," I tell him, cutting him off.

"Fine, butter pecan."

"Excellent choice. Did you fry this chicken yourself?"

He takes a sip of lemonade. "Nah, got it from work."

"Amazing in bed and resourceful. Two especially important qualities. How'd you end up in Barbados?"

"Sometimes life doesn't turn out the way you planned."

"I see." His history must be a touchy subject, so I change topics. "What do you want to be when you grow up?"

"I guess I'm still trying to figure it out. What about you? What's your passion?"

"I don't want to tell you." Most men find my passion intimidating, that's why I don't typically engage in long-term relationships.

"Why not?"

"Don't want to scare you off."

He laughs. "I'm a bartender in a faraway land. What's the harm?"

"Okay, tough guy with logical reasoning, here goes—to be the best."

"The best at what?"

"Everything." I shrug my shoulders. "Life. Money. My career. Especially my career."

"What about love? I didn't hear love in your list of everything. A family?"

I take the last bite of my slaw and place the container and spoon back in the basket. "No time for love. For men who want successful careers, there's time. It's considered admirable. For a woman though, it's a weakness and an inconvenience."

"Why do you say that?" he asks as he hands me a pack of cigarettes. My brand too. "The world has evolved so much, women's rights and stuff." He lights mine first, then his.

"Not as much as you think." I take a long drag and puff out the smoke. "Despite burning our bras, standards are still different for women who aspire to reach the top."

My point must be valid because he doesn't have a response. After a few more puffs of my cigarette, I stab it out in the dirt and place the butt in a garbage bag that's packed in the basket. Next to the container of chicken, I find my swimsuit. I tug it out and slip into the damp suit. "Were you trying to hide my bikini?"

He smiles at me as he puts out his cigarette and then slides his swim trunks back on.

The sun is beginning to set, or at least from what I can see from the blips of light breaking through the plant life. "It's getting late. I should get back before my friends start to worry. Now, how do we get back up there?" I ask, pointing in the direction of the cliff we swung from.

"Same way we got down here. The rope."

I look around and spy a dirt path that wends its way up to the top. "Cute."

19

Sam

A thunderous bang on my cottage door snaps me out of a fantastic sleep filled with dreams of rainbows, waterfalls, and the hottest man I've ever met.

"Five more minutes, Mom," I call out and bury my head beneath a sea of pillows to drown out the noise.

"*Sam,*" the voice screeches, and I realize it's not my mom. It's Lizzie.

I toss the covers off, lazily stretch my limbs, and notice a fabulous soreness in my center. I can't stop smiling as the vision of my stranger hovered over me pervade my mind.

"Hurry the fuck up. We're leaving for the airport in *fifteen minutes,*" Lizzie yells.

I rub at my eyes to wipe away the sleep and take a glance at the clock next to me. "*Shit,*" I shriek, realizing I've over-slept.

Yesterday was an incredible day. One for the books. Unforgettable. Inspiring. Revitalizing. Unfortunately, it seems all that splendor has left me exhausted. Exhausted enough to forget to set my alarm to catch the plane which will whisk me away to my real life.

I don't know if I'm ready to leave. Three more years of paradise is all it would take to get my fill. Sadly, there isn't enough time for three years in paradise. I have responsibilities. An apartment. A job.

I scramble around the room, tossing my clothes into my suitcase. I throw on a tank top and a pair of capris, finger comb my hair, and toss it in a ponytail.

The pounding resumes on my cottage door, this time more persistent.

"Come on, Sam," Grayson shouts from the other side. "We need to go. Now. We're going to miss our flight."

"Okay, okay," I holler back as I slip on my flip-flops and sunglasses.

My friends are glaring at me when I open the door. I ignore their hard looks and stride past them with my suitcase rolling behind me.

"What are you guys waiting for? We're going to be late," I toss over my shoulder as I walk toward the lobby.

The refreshing climate-controlled air of the resort is sucked into the vortex of the Caribbean heat as we exit the lobby to the curb of the hotel. Christ, it's hot here. The heat of the region is almost charming, but only in small doses—like on vacation. Maybe three years is too long. Two weeks is perfect because I almost crave the unpredictable weather of home.

Lizzie and Grayson sidle up beside me as our car to the airport arrives. The cabbie pops the trunk, hops out of the driver's seat, and rounds the vehicle, collecting our luggage.

I take one last look around to commit the beauty of Barbados to memory. Lizzie is arguing with the cab driver about something. I don't know what sparked the tiff, and I don't care because I'm stricken by the sight of my stranger.

He walks up the drive with a confident stride and a bouquet of native flowers. The vibrant colors of begonias and lotuses are bested only by the brilliant smile spread across his face. It's flattering and heartwarming.

"We need to go," Grayson says as he places his hand on a small patch of exposed skin between my shirt and pants. The rear door on the passenger side is ajar, and Grayson tries to guide me into the cab.

My attention is focused on my stranger's face. Handsome, rugged edges uniquely created to attract the opposite sex, the intended complement of the soft curves of a woman. Biology's intricate design.

His smile fades, the strong line of his jaw is razor-sharp, and there is no room to misinterpret his sentiment when he tosses the beautiful bouquet into the trash. He turns and walks away, without so much as a wave goodbye.

The cab pulls out, and my heart squeezes at the knowledge that I'll never see him again, that his last memories of me will be some misunderstanding because I have no idea what just happened.

Fortunately, I don't have much time to dwell on my emotions because the experience of making it to my seat on the plane won't soon be forgotten.

The cab driver was a maniac. There were no less than three instances where I thought, "This is it. This is how I'm going to die." We made it to the airport with time to spare. Thank God we did because security in Barbados may not be as intense as the states, but it turns out, if luggage vibrates, it's some sort of international sign for bomb.

Lizzie swears up and down she did not pack a vibrator. She claimed the mysterious pulsing from her suitcase was caused by the chair massager she bought at the resort gift shop. Because a gift shop massager in a foreign country is of higher quality and more necessity than if someone was to buy it at Target. Like a normal person.

Lizzie deserved the benefit of the doubt, but because I know her as well as I do, I knew she was full of crap. That, and when security exited the room, where they graciously escorted her to privately screen her luggage, the men laughed and waved around a large purple dong. It was hilarious. I was laughing. Grayson was laughing. The fifty people behind us were laughing. Lizzie was fuming.

"It's not funny," Lizzie barked when she stomped past Grayson and me as she made her way toward our terminal.

"I totally put it in her bag," Grayson admitted, his smile wide and proud.

I doubled over with laughter.

We had been stuck on the tarmac and waiting for takeoff when Lizzie began to pelt me with questions about where I had been yesterday. The selfish part of me wanted to keep the day to myself, a delicious secret, but I decided to fill her in to help the time pass.

"And that's it? You don't even know his name?" Lizzie asks, confused and maybe offended by the way the story ends.

"That's it. It was perfect." Perfect may be the closest word I can find, but it still doesn't do the experience justice.

A flight attendant offers us champagne and hot towels when we reach our cruising altitude. I graciously accept.

"I think it's kind of romantic. One perfect day in paradise with a total stranger. Books are written from that kind of inspiration," Lizzie gushes, hearts floating from her eyes.

"Snuff films too," Grayson mutters beside me.

"They do not," I defend, giving him a playful shove to the shoulder.

"Sure they do. Think about it. A woman. On an island. No immediate means of escape. Midnight stroll on a desolate beach? No witnesses. And the jungle? Anything could have happened there. Come on Sam, horror movies are written from that kind of inspiration."

Grayson isn't wrong. I had similar thoughts myself, but I trusted my gut, and that goes to show that my instincts are on point. Grayson would never understand this, so there's no point in trying to explain. "Let's drop it." I pat Grayson on the hand and close my eyes, ready for a nap.

20

Sam
Chicago

I'd cut myself off at Whiskers after my scotch, but when the champagne was offered in The Kitty Cradle, I couldn't deny myself. When I was young, early to mid-twenties, I could drink until the sun came up, go to work, drink some more, and never suffer a hangover. The dirty secret no one talks about is that for every year after thirty, one day must be added to the hangover recovery period. This means, at thirty-three, it will require three days for me to recover from this one night. I'm on day three, and the hangover has just started to abate. The rough coating of the aspirin makes this reality just as tough a pill to swallow.

"I guess the meeting with Bennett went well on Tuesday," Ben says as he snatches a yogurt out of the fridge. "But you don't seem happy."

I wrinkle my brows at his astute power of observation. "Why do you say that?"

He points to my coffee cup. "The creamer in your coffee for the past three days tells me you're hungover. Normally, you take it black, unless you're looking for a little fat to ease the symptoms."

I stare down at my coffee and realize he's right.

"That," he continues, "and what happened to that poor girl from the mailroom on Wednesday."

"You heard about that?" On Tuesday I learned what I needed to know about my island stranger. That he's Frank's son, and he wants to learn his father's business. On its own merits, it doesn't seem like a bad thing. However, Grayson appears to be suspicious, and his suspicions only feed my own. Day one of my hangover found me in the mailroom looking to take out my anger on the innocent.

"Everybody's heard about that," Ben replies.

The argument went something like this:

Mailroom girl: "Happy Hump Day!"

Me: "What the hell are you talking about?"

Mailroom girl: "It's Wednesday. Hump Day."

My thought at the time was that if there was such a thing as "hump day," a day that can only be described as being dedicated to humping, I'm sure I would have already known about it. If by some chance this enchanting day does exist, why am I not enjoying being humped every Wednesday?

Me: "You should be careful what you say around here. The company lawyers are extremely meticulous when it comes to the slightest indication of sexual harassment. There's no such thing as Hump Day."

Mailroom girl: "Ha. You're funny."

Me: "I'm serious. Hump Day does not exist."

Mailroom girl: "Sure it does. There used to be a commercial with a camel in an office—"

Me: "Listen, I don't know what kind of joke people played on you, but there is no Hump Day. Did you even go to college?"

Mailroom girl: "Um, no. The mailroom's an entry-level position."

Me: "Well then, I suggest you go to college and learn about

the real world. A world where there's no such thing as Hump Day."

I dump the rest of my coffee down the sink. "I guess I should go and apologize."

"Don't bother, she quit. Said something about a hostile work environment."

"Shit." I give a silent prayer that this will somehow fly under the radar of HR.

"This doesn't have anything to do with Frank's son moving in across the hall does it?"

I haven't told him anything about Reid, but I'm sure he was able to figure it out on his own.

"She was right, by the way," Ben adds. "Hump Day is another term for Wednesday. You know, getting past the hump of the week?"

I don't need to acknowledge anything which will make it worse and ignore his chuckle as I walk past him and back to my office.

When I approach Reid's office at the end of the day, he's on the phone, his tone is stern and commanding. I stand in the doorway as I wait for him to finish his call and take the opportunity to drink in every fine-tuned inch that I know lies beneath that pesky three-piece suit.

I've managed to avoid him all week, bestowing him with half-hearted waves as I pass him in the hall. No real conversation, just "Good morning," or "It's nice out today." The kind of discussion you have with housekeeping while they clean the toilets, and you wash your hands.

With his office across from mine, I'd be a liar if I said he didn't catch my eye from time to time. Christ, that man is hot. No. I need to remember that I don't know his agenda. Maybe there isn't one. I asked Frank, point-blank if my position as president was secure. He gave me his word, and I have no reason to doubt him.

What I do know, is that Reid is now working for Sterling,

and I need to play nice, which is why I invited him to my place on Saturday. It seemed like a good idea at the time, and maybe it still is. However, to reunite with a vacation tryst causes a lot of questions. Did he enjoy it as much as I did? Is he still into me? Does he want to pick up where we left off? Is he as obsessed with the memories as I am?

"I don't care how inconvenient it is for you. This shit has to get done. If you can't do it in the next seventy-two hours, consider yourself fired." Reid slams the phone in the cradle and looks up, his gaze skating over me.

I delight in the power I possess as I watch him start from my red pumps, up my knees to the high waist of my pencil skirt, spend a glance past appropriate on my chest, all the way up to my high ponytail.

"Sam, I didn't see you there. Come in."

"Thank you. You seemed pretty aggravated." I point to the phone. I feel giddy and awkward. Never in my life has someone affected me this way. "Hope everything's okay?"

He waves his hand dismissively. "Oh, that? No. I mean yeah, it's fine. Just dealing with my realtor has become a pain in my ass."

"Sorry to hear. Where have you been staying for the past couple of weeks?"

"At Frank's. It's been a nightmare, but I'm hoping I'll wake up soon if this deal will ever close."

"Um." Words are lost to me, I'm a mess. What is wrong with me? "I'm not sure if you remember, but I invited some friends over tomorrow. Saturday."

"Yeah, sure. Tomorrow's Saturday. Good thing it isn't Hump Day. Saturday is three days past the hump of the week," he says, smiling.

My cheeks ignite. "You heard about that?"

He gives a hardy chuckle. It's the sexiest thing I think I've ever heard. Sadly, it's at my expense. "Sweetheart, everyone's heard about that."

"Shit," I mutter. "Um, anyway. Saturday they're coming over to play cards. You still interested in being the fourth for Euchre?"

"Yeah. That sounds great. Quick question though."

"Shoot."

"What's Euchre?"

"You've never played?"

He shakes his head.

"I thought you said you were from Chicago? Euchre is like a pre-req for pre-school."

"I was born here, but I was sent to a prep academy in Connecticut in fourth grade. Chicago never felt like home."

The idea that he was sent away from his family for his education saddens me. I can't imagine leaving my parents at such an early age. "Well, if you're going to spend any real time in the Mid-West, it's a requirement. It's fun." I grab a sticky note off his desk and a pen, and scribble down my address. "Be there around eight."

He looks down at the paper and then back up to me. "You're at the Onyx?"

"Sure. It's a great building. All the amenities you could want, a doorman, and close to everything worth doing. You've heard of it?"

"Just in passing. Okay, well, I'll see you then."

"Yeah, see you then." Even to my own ears, I sound like a love-struck teenager. I'm pathetic.

21

Sam

I spent the afternoon cleaning my apartment. It wasn't dirty but tidying up was an effective way to expel nervous energy. If it were only Grayson and Lizzie, I wouldn't bother to lift a finger. Since Reid was coming, I went above and beyond to make everything as close to perfect as possible. I typically have no desire to put forth the effort to impress a man. Impressing a man with my splendor comes naturally, but for some reason, Reid is different. We shared an extraordinary day in Barbados, but I must remember that Reid is my coworker, and there is still the tiny detail that he could be out to steal my job.

My head is deep in thought, and in the refrigerator, as I gather the ingredients for buffalo chicken dip when I hear a knock on my door.

"Yoo-hoo, is anyone home?" Lizzie calls out as she lets herself in.

"In the kitchen."

She sets a bag full of candy and a box of microwave popcorn on the counter. "What's on the agenda tonight? Action, drama, chick flick? How about *You've Got Mail?* Have you ever read *Pride and Prejudice?* They talk about that book throughout the entire movie. Turns out, it's a modern, well, modern for back then, retelling of that story. When I read the book, because of the movie, my mind. Was. Blown."

Tonight was originally scheduled as a girls' night with Lizzie. Facials, mani-pedis, movies, and junk food—the whole works. When I was at Whiskers the other night, Grayson asked if I'd talked to Lizzie recently. It struck me as odd that he hadn't, for more than one reason.

One—Lizzie is the choreographer at Whiskers. How has she avoided Grayson all this time since we've been back, or has he been avoiding her?

B—Grayson, Lizzie, and I are best friends. Why wouldn't two best friends be on talking terms, and how am I not in the loop?

"Plans changed," I inform her. "I invited the boss's son over."

"That's fine. We can watch *Die Hard* or *Predator*. I'll paint his toes. I don't discriminate." She goes quiet for a minute then says, "Frank has a son?"

"Yeah, don't sound so shocked. Frank is a good person."

"Sure. He's a fine man that one is—ugly as sin too. He's as wide as he is tall and sports the most impressive brain warmer I've ever seen. I'm surprised anyone would sleep with him, let alone procreate. When you guys are, like, walking somewhere fast together, do you ever worry he's going to gain speed and start rolling? Then, *boom,*" she says with a clap as she yells out, "*Stee-rike.*"

"Like a bowling ball?"

She nods.

I burst out laughing so hard my side aches. "No." All traces of humor gone. I can't hold back for long and begin to laugh again because Lizzie's description is spot on. I try again. "No. His wife is younger than me," I point out in an attempt to defend my boss's integrity, but at this point, it's too late. Besides, how much integrity does Frank possess? He's a cradle robber. His wife would have only escaped the womb when his son was sent off to boarding school. "Yeah, well, money makes people less ugly I guess."

She grabs some popcorn out of the bag, tosses it in the microwave, and sets if for three and a half minutes.

I mix the ingredients for the dip into the crockpot and generously sprinkle in freshly grated extra-sharp cheddar. "Remember that jogger I called out to on the beach in Barbados?" I turn the slow cooker on high.

"The one with the belly that jiggled like a bowl full of jelly?"

"No. That's Santa, and you were the caller. No, the other one. The one with the beard?"

"Oh, yeah. He was hot. Wait, wasn't he the bartender? The waterfall guy?" she asks, referring to the details I had given her on the plane ride back home. "What about him? No, no, let me guess. He's looking for a sugar momma and unwittingly finds one who can finance his get rich quick schemes. Then he knocks her up, but when he finds out about the baby, he gets spooked."

The microwave dings, and Lizzie removes the bag. Instantly my apartment stinks of burnt popcorn. She wrinkles her nose, tosses it in the trash, and grabs a new package. She puts it in the microwave, and once again, sets it for three and a half minutes.

"That's *Cocktail* with Tom Cruise, and no. Well…kind of." I remember how Reid hopped over the bar in a smooth jump. The stunt was sexy when Tom Cruise performed it, and even more so when Reid was the jumper. "Turns out," I place the wooden spoon in the sink and wipe down the counter for the sixth time, "*he's* Frank's son."

"*No,*" Lizzie says. "You're serious?"

"So serious."

"Talk about coincidence."

The microwave dings again, and like last time, it's burnt. Lizzie grabs another package, and I take it away from her. "You're grounded from making popcorn. Go open some windows," I tell her as I turn on the fan above the stove. This time I make the popcorn and set the timer for two and a half minutes. "Did you sleep with Grayson?"

A window slams and seconds later she peeks around the wall into my galley-style kitchen. Her face is pale with a slight rosiness brushed onto her cheeks, reminding me of a dead body made up for a funeral. "Why would you ask that?"

"Grayson says you two aren't talking. Are you avoiding him?" The third and final bag of popcorn is finished popping and radiated to delicious buttery perfection.

She grabs the bag out of my hand and opens it and stuffs her face. "That's ridiculous. He's my boss. It's next to impossible to avoid him," she says as popcorn and lies spill from her mouth.

"Good because I didn't want this to be awkward."

"Excuse me?"

"We needed a fourth for Euchre. I called Grayson. Is that a problem?" I know it is, and I revel in her need to cover up her discomfort.

"No way. Grayson's the best. It'll be fun. So, you're having the waterfall guy over, and that's what you're wearing?"

She's deflecting, I know her M.O., and it's working. "Yup," I answer, prepared to wow her with my analytical thought process as to the outfit I've chosen. "Because—"

I'm cut off by a knock at the door, this time it's to the tune of *Shave and a Haircut,* and I know precisely who it is. So does Lizzie. "This conversation isn't over."

22

Sam

"Two bits!" I belt out as I open the door, finishing off the song.

Grayson gives me his megawatt smile and follows with a one-armed hug, his other arm balancing two large pizzas. He crinkles his nose. "It smells like burnt popcorn in here."

I glance at Lizzie as she digs around in the candy she brought. "Some of us don't know how to cook popcorn."

Lizzie waves me off and walks into the living room, plopping down on my cream leather sofa and turning on the TV, not bothering to greet Grayson.

"What's going on between you two?" I take the pizza from Grayson's arms and set them on the counter next to the tortilla chips.

"Hell if I know."

"Bullshit. You two slept together. This better not ruin our Dynamic Trio status."

Grayson's eyes go wide. "She told you?"

"Nope. An educated guess that you, my dear friend, just

confirmed."

I don't get the reaction I was hoping for. Instead, he says, "I'm going to drain the weasel."

Reid arrives at eight o'clock on the dot with a six-pack of microbrew in hand. "I hope you don't mind. Didn't want to come empty-handed." He sets the drinks on the table.

Yesterday he looked edible in his three-piece suit, poised behind his desk, commanding the world around him. Now, he's dressed in a pair of well-worn, and I might add, well-fitted jeans with a white T-shirt. His hair is slightly mussed as if he's been running his hand through it. It's incredible how quickly he can transform back to the waterfall guy I remember.

"No, not at all. It's perfect. Welcome. Let me give you a tour," I offer. "This is the living room. The lump on the couch is Lizzie Anderson. Say hello, Lizzie."

"Hello, Lizzie," she says, staying focused on the TV. She's watching *You've Got Mail* as if our girls' night is still a plan.

I sigh. "Don't mind her. She's just PMS-ing," I tell Reid. Lizzie throws daggers at me with her eyes.

I walk him down the hall. "These two doors here," I point to the right, "are the bedrooms. This is the bathroom."

"A grand tour wouldn't be complete without getting to see the master suite," Reid says, his boyish grin making an appearance.

I laugh. "I wouldn't want to be a bad hostess."

I walk into the master bedroom, and Reid follows. He takes his time assessing my room, and I'm pretty sure he is focused on the four-poster bed. Many men have been tied to those posts, and Reid would look fabulous with all four limbs restrained. Naked. Crop marks on his chest and thighs.

Stop. It's not going to happen. It can't. Because he's the boss's son. No matter how much I want to tear off his clothes and hold that beautiful—

No. No. He's Frank's son. He's *Frank's* son. No matter how hard it is to use them, I do have moral scruples.

I do have moral scruples.

I do have moral scruples.

"It's a lovely room." He stares at me like a meal. The mention of my bedroom is just filler, as fabulous as the room may be, his attention is elsewhere.

Yoga pants, a baggy sweatshirt, and pigtails do not warrant this kind of scrutiny. I believe that clothes make the girl. An evening gown with a long slit down the leg and a deep V-cut between the breasts, makes a woman feel sexy, boosting her confidence. I like to believe the reverse holds true. Dress as if you're going through a dozen tampons a day, and you'll feel gross and self-conscious. I hope this tactic will keep me from mauling the boss's son.

"Am I interrupting anything?" Grayson asks as he walks into my bedroom.

Reid's clear blue eyes become clouded the moment he sees Grayson.

"Nope. Just giving Reid a tour," I tell Grayson.

Grayson steps up to Reid. The men are about the same height, but where Grayson has the build of a gladiator, Reid has a lean, muscled physique of a soap opera actor.

"Grayson Treadwell." Grayson introduces himself while offering his hand.

"Reid Gallagher." Reid claps his palm into Grayson's.

"Nice to meet you. That's a strong grip you have there, Reid."

"You know what they say," Reid says, still pumping Grayson's arm up and down. "Weak handshake means a weak man."

Grayson rips his hand away from Reid. "Okay. Well, this should be interesting. I'm going to set up for Euchre."

Reid turns back to me, the fire reignited but with a barely contained ire instead of the passion of the pre-Grayson introduction. "Does he know about us?" he asks, his voice low.

"About us? There is no 'us.'" This man has a lot of nerve. We've barely spoken since the office meeting with Frank, and he thinks he has some sort of claim?

"In Barbados."

"Oh, sure. Grayson knows. He doesn't care."

"What kind of man doesn't care? If you were mine..." He trails off.

We're silent for a few beats, and I'm clueless as to what is going on.

Reid takes a deep breath, his jaw hard. "I don't think I could get past a woman who cheated on me."

A thousand emotions flit through me simultaneously. Anger, disappointment, indignation, to name a few. "You think..." I leave my words hanging, stunned by the accusation and the low opinion he holds of me. "A, I didn't cheat on anyone. I'm no angel, but I'm not that kind of woman. Secondly, Grayson is a friend. An incredibly good friend, and he always will be. C, is that what you think of me? That I would invite the boss's son, a man I've slept with, to play cards and hang with me and my boyfriend?"

He shuts the door to the bedroom and now we are alone, unsupervised, in a closed room. "Shit," he mutters, and grabs me by the waist, yanking me to him. "I'm sorry. I thought..." He takes a deep breath. "I misunderstood the whole thing. God," he brushes one pigtail off my shoulder, exposing my neck, "I've missed you. I never thought I could miss someone so much."

His words melt away as his lips make their way to my neck. I've dreamt of this moment since I landed in O'Hare two months ago, and now it's happening. I let out a long sigh as he travels back up my neck and to my mouth.

I should push him away. This is wrong. It's a conflict of—

He plucks at my lips with his teeth and darts his tongue into my mouth.

A conflict of—

I don't know why it's a conflict anymore, but I need this as much as my next breath.

A knock at the bedroom door interrupts us, and we step away from each other. It's like we're teenagers, trying not to get caught being naughty.

"Yeah," I call out, my voice cracking.

"Are we going to do this or not?" Lizzie asks, her tone clipped.

"Um, yeah. We'll be out in a minute," I answer.

Reid leans his forehead on my shoulder and lets out a tempestuous breath.

"It's for the best," I tell him, and myself too.

23

Sam

Lizzie and Grayson are seated at the dining table when Reid and I join them.

"We've got a virgin here," I announce, pointing my thumb to Reid.

Reid's eyes go wide with embarrassment; Lizzie and Grayson both appear disbelieving at my announcement.

"A Euchre virgin," I clarify, rolling my eyes.

"Oh," the three say in unison.

"We need teams. How do you want to do this?" Grayson asks as he pops off a beer cap.

"Women against men," Lizzie declares.

"Of course," Grayson mutters under his breath.

I have an almost physical need to figure out what happened between these two. I'm jonesing for the story, but now is not the time or place.

We rearrange our seats so we are in a boy-girl-boy-girl arrangement. Grayson shuffles the cards and offers me the chance to cut the deck. I give a hard knock on the table, passing up the offer.

"Why didn't you cut the deck?" Reid asks.

"Euchre is considered a gentleman's game, and no real gentleman would cheat. Thus, rendering the point of cutting the deck moot," Grayson explains. As he deals out the cards, Grayson gives Reid a quick rundown on the object and rules of the game.

We play a few hands to allow Reid the opportunity to develop a strategy. For a newbie, Reid picks it up quickly. If this would have been a real game, I think he and Grayson would have legitimately won.

Lizzie takes a break and walks into the kitchen. A few minutes later she returns with a tray of Jager Bombs. She takes two shots, one right after the other. "What do you say we make this interesting?"

"How so?" I take a small glass for myself, tip my head back, and let the licorice goodness coat the back of my throat.

"Strip Euchre." Lizzie takes her seat across from me.

Animosity vibrates between Lizzie and Grayson. Strip Euchre can only lead to terrible things. "Is that a good idea?"

"I'm in," Grayson announces. "How about you Reid? You wouldn't mind seeing these two women admitting defeat while naked, would you?"

Reid takes a long swig from his beer, an eyebrow quirked and a smirk only partially hidden by the lip of the bottle. I give him a fierce stare, hoping he picks up my "No way in hell" message.

Reid turns to Grayson and taps the neck of his bottle to Grayson's. "I'm in."

One Rolex watch, two shirts, and three pairs of shoes later, and the game is not going in our favor. Lizzie and I are both topless, but the bras remain, thank God.

"No table-talking," Lizzie shrieks.

"What?" Grayson asks. "He's still new. It would be ungentlemanly of me not to assist him in some capacity."

"I don't think so. Not when my clothes are at stake," I tell

Grayson. "That's a two-book penalty, and in all fairness, you both need to remove your shirts."

Reid leans over to Grayson and whispers in his ear.

Grayson clears his throat. "My partner and I are willing to concede the shirts with one stipulation."

I cross my arms over my chest and lean back in my chair, glaring at Reid. "And what would that stipulation be?"

"The bras go," Reid says.

Lizzie and I turn around in our chairs and discuss the deal. It's not an advantage for us at this point, but if we can secure a win, it might be.

"How confident do you feel?" I whisper.

"I'll let it all hang out. I don't care."

"Not about that. How confident do you feel about winning? Do you think we can pull it off?"

"Definitely. I haven't exactly been bringing my A-game."

"I've noticed. Get your head in the game. I'm raising the stakes."

"Higher than being naked?" she squeaks.

I put my finger to my lips.

"Ladies, any day now," Grayson says.

"Trust me," I tell Lizzie. I direct my attention to the men. "Lizzie and I are prepared to make a deal. We'll take off our bras if you two strip down to your skivvies. On top of that, I would like to make another proposition. If we win this game, Grayson will have to host a Ladies Night at Whiskers."

"Deal," Grayson agrees too quickly.

No doubt Grayson thinks he has this in the bag, Whiskers hosts Ladies Night once a month already. Reid's eyes go wide at the willingness of his partner to make a deal without discussing it first.

"I'm not finished. A Ladies Night where you two are the feature. Oh, and to be clear, I'm talking the Full Monty."

Grayson appears to think it over, and if I was to guess, planning his debut.

"What's Whiskers?" Reid asks.

"Grayson owns a members-only club," Lizzie explains. "A place for high society to drink and engage in the most debauched activities known to mankind."

"You work there, what does that make you?" Grayson asks Lizzie.

"Desperate," she spits back.

I lean into Reid and whisper in his ear as the other two continue their argument. "It's a high-priced strip club."

"So, Grayson owns it, and Lizzie works it?"

"You got it."

The fighting between Lizzie and Grayson is getting to be too much and is taking the focus off our game. "You two quit it. Now," I scold. Lizzie and Grayson both lean back in their chairs and refuse to look at me or each other. "Good. Now, back to what matters. Do we have a deal?"

"And if we win?" Reid asks, picking up the negotiations. "For the Full Monty, it better be amazing."

Lizzie and Grayson are so distracted by their squabble that if I wanted, I could have gotten the deal without any concessions for losing, but not with Reid here. He must have strong negotiation skills, or Frank wouldn't have hired him, despite being his son. If Reid sold real estate in New York, I'm sure he must have been ruthless.

"If you guys win, then..." I glance around the apartment in search of something with value. The painting of the Chicago skyline which hangs above my couch is impressive, but not worth a lot. A vase from a flea market with a beautiful floral pattern, but I love it too much to put on the line. My eyes land on the TV, and I realize Lizzie must have turned off her movie because the answer to my problem is in HD. An episode of *Friends* is playing. The one where Rachel and Monica get their apartment back from Joey and Chandler. "Then Lizzie and I will make out for ten minutes on the couch after the game."

Lizzie spits out her Jager Bomb at my mad negotiation skills.

"What?" she cries.

I'm glad to see her attention is back where it belongs.

"Naked," Reid says.

"Topless."

"No bra," he counters.

"Hands above the shoulders,"

"Deal," Grayson says, jumping out of the chair to shake my hand. "Okay, to clarify, Reid and I will strip to our boxers to balance things out, and then, from this hand on, the stakes are in effect.

Reid runs his hand through his hair. "That deal isn't quite as easy for all of us."

"What do you mean?" I ask.

Reid blushes and looks down at the ground. I think back to the night we met, the shower sex, and what I discovered. "A deal's a deal, Reid. Although, I might have a solution to your problem."

24

Sam

Grayson and Lizzie argue in hushed voices as Reid and I stroll to my bedroom. I can't hear what they're saying, but I don't want to get in the middle of that mess. Not right now, anyhow. Later, though, definitely.

I open the top drawer of my dresser and start tossing panties on the bed.

"Do you have anything in cotton? Preferably without butt floss," Reid says as he scoops up my underthings to give them a close inspection.

I stand in front of the bed, assessing the selection. "Where are the pink ones?" I know I tossed the boy-short panties on the bed. I even had a brief vision of him wearing them. I was secretly hoping he would pick those.

"What pink ones? I didn't see any," Reid says.

"The pink underwear with little flowers." I root through my dresser again. "I know they were on the bed." I slam my drawer shut and turn around, still wearing only my bra.

He looks down, not into my eyes, but onto my breasts. I

shove my hands in his pockets, find the missing pair of panties, and toss them back on the bed.

I walk toward my bathroom and stop in front of the full-length mirror. Reid's gaze is fully trained on me. A raccoon could walk out of my closet singing show tunes, and I seriously doubt he would notice. "You like these, huh?" I ask as I cup my breasts.

"Yeah," he says, his voice turning to gravel.

"We're in the business of making deals." I lower my yoga pants to show off my baby blue bikini panties. I finger the edges of the lace. "I like to think I'm a strong negotiator."

"You are. Without a doubt," Reid says, tracking my fingers to the V between my legs.

I slide the panties over my thighs and step out of them. I turn around, giving him a view of my backside and bend at the waist as I pick them up off the floor, showing Reid my most intimate parts.

I stride back to him, impersonating a model on a catwalk. The underwear dangles off one finger. I lift the panties to my face and inhale deeply. "I think you'll like these better. Don't you?"

Reid nods his head with enthusiastic agreement.

"You can have these," I tell him, dragging the soft, imported lace across his cheek. "If you wear the pink ones." I pick up the pair of pink and flower boy shorts.

He nods. I'm not sure he's capable of making any decisions right now. His weakness is my advantage.

"I'll give you privacy and let you change in the bathroom. You can have these," I say, still holding the blue bikini panties, "when you've fulfilled your end of the bargain."

He snatches the pink panties from me and makes his way to the bathroom. I slide back into my yoga pants without any underwear because, why not?

When he comes out of the bathroom, I'm shocked. I never thought I would find a man in women's underwear to be sexy. It doesn't usually phase me. I've had plenty of male partners who I've insisted wear women's clothing for role play, but as I look at Reid, there is an unanticipated consequence.

He's hot.

My mouth goes dry. Reid's muscles fill out the delicate fabric, and the boy-short style shows off his...goodies. If I'm not mistaken, he's at half-mast.

He turns to the full-length mirror and looks at himself. "Am I going crazy, or do I look good?" he asks, running his hands along the seams. "And they're surprisingly comfortable."

"Come on, Narcissus." I grab him by the arm and out into the hallway.

"Is it a deal?" I holler out to Lizzie and Grayson. I don't want to parade Reid in women's underwear in front of my friends if they changed the terms.

"Yeah," Grayson calls back. "I'm in my boxers and munchin' on popcorn. Just like home."

I can hear him snicker at his own joke. "You better not have a hand shoved down your shorts. Lizzie?"

"Both hands on the table. My bra is off, so yours better be too."

I start to walk out to the kitchen, unclasping my bra and letting it fall to the ground. "Alternate arrangements had to be made for Reid. No laughing."

Grayson stares at my tits as I talk but agrees with a head nod.

They burst out laughing as soon as Reid appears. I don't know what I thought would happen. If the tables were turned, I would laugh my ass off too.

"I'd rather be in women's underwear than the only naked person at this table," Reid says, taking his seat next to me, not losing an ounce of confidence from the entire situation.

It's a close game. Lizzie and I tap into our bestie telepathy and manage to walk away the victors.

Grayson became overconfident, as I knew he would, and

called two hands as a loner, convinced he could beat us without any help from his partner. Such was not the case.

Reid was preoccupied with the breasts swaying freely around the room. What was more distracting was how he couldn't stop playing with the hem of his girly undies.

The men groan and attempt to renegotiate. It doesn't work. I, on the other hand, am super excited to see Grayson's Ladies Night Extravaganza.

Reid stays at the table, still wearing my panties, despite the fact that everyone else has gotten dressed. I think I might have found Reid's kink with women's lingerie.

"Ladies Night is next Friday," I tell Grayson as I usher him and Lizzie toward the door. "I expect you to make good on our bet."

"He will," Lizzie promises.

Grayson rolls his eyes. "Fine. See you then."

"I'll be front and center." I close the door behind him as he and Lizzie walk out.

The Reid tonight seemed more like the man I met in Barbados, laid back and funny. Not the stuffy suit, I met in Frank's office on Tuesday. Grayson and Lizzie seemed to get along with him. Who knows, we might all become friends. From what Reid has told me, he doesn't have much of a connection to the city and has spent most of his life on the East coast. He could use a few buddies. Potential competition or not, he's still human, and humans need companionship, platonic or otherwise.

I lock the deadbolt and lean against the door to find Reid stalking toward me, naked except for the panties. My breath hitches from the look he's giving me. The countdown to total exposure has begun.

25

Reid

"You can get dressed now. If you want to," Sam suggests as she leans against the door.

She's sexy as fuck. I think she was trying to ward me off with the way she was dressed. It didn't work. An oversized sweatshirt only makes me want to find out what's hidden underneath. Yoga pants. Shit, I love a woman in yoga pants. The fabric is so snug on their ass, I just want to smack it and watch it jiggle. The pigtails are enough to do me in, naughty yet virtuous at the same time.

I'm naked, except for Sam's panties, and it's been next to impossible to keep my dick in line. I've spent the entire night sitting at this table, refusing to get up. Until now.

I step toward Sam. We're so close, I can feel her tits through her shirt, rubbing up against my bare chest as her breath hitches. It's been a special kind of torture to watch her parade around the office all week. Every man she passes does a double-take. I'm not sure she knows how to open a door by herself, there is always a man there to do it. Every single one of those men eye-fucks her as she walks. Myself included.

She's pinned to the door, and she begins to gnaw on her bottom lip.

"Am I making you uncomfortable?" I run my finger along the delicate skin of her cheek.

"No," she squeaks out, but I know she's lying because she's blushing. If she isn't willing to admit it, I'm not going to back down.

I seize her lips and bite on the bottom, drawing it into my mouth to soothe it. She doesn't reciprocate at first, then she flicks her tongue and takes what she wants.

I've been dreaming about this moment since I first bumped into her at the coffee shop by the office. I want her more than I've ever wanted anything. I crave her scent, her taste, and I don't think I can wait another second before I come in these ridiculously soft panties.

I hoist her up by the back of her legs, and she wraps them around me, her pussy rubbing against my dick. I'm so hard, it hurts. I carry her down the hall toward the bedroom.

We collapse onto the bed, our hands feverishly gripping and clawing at each other.

"Fuck, I need you." I rain kisses down her neck, my hands under her shirt, playing with her perfectly pert tits.

"You're wearing too many clothes." My fingers explore beneath her yoga pants and find her soaking wet for me.

"Then take them off."

"Take them off for me, Sam. Give me a show." I dip a single finger inside her warm, wet entrance.

She moans with pleasure. "Okay."

I roll off her and scramble to the top of her bed while she slides off.

"Alexa, play my favorite song," she says.

Speakers must be hidden in her room because *Closer* by Nine Inch Nails begins to play, and I can't for the life of me figure out where the sound is emanating from.

She pulls off her sweatshirt and shakes out her hair, the pigtails messy and sexy. Her hands roam and slide down her neck to her bare breasts. She gives a small tug on her hard nipples and throws her head back.

This woman is the definition of sexy, and I can barely breathe as I watch her work her pants down. No panties. She hasn't been wearing panties the whole night because she's supposed to gift them to me.

Sam bends over, her sex glistening with slickness. When the song says "fuck" she gives a hard slap to her ass and runs a finger through her folds.

I scramble off the bed, turn her toward the mattress, and bend her over. "You're quite the tease, aren't you?" I ask, my voice thick, my throat dry.

"That's what you wanted, wasn't it?"

I fill her with two fingers and swat her ass. Her tight channel squeezes my fingers and my cock twitches.

"Fuck me, Reid," she says, gasping. "Put that big fat cock in me now, or so help me God, I will do it myself."

My fingers continue to manipulate her, despite her demand. I give a tug on one pigtail and jerk her head back. I can tell she likes it when her arousal begins to drip onto my hand. "I need a condom."

She rolls onto her back, my fingers sliding out of her. Her thighs spread wide, her essence on display.

"I'm clean," she says while her fingers rub her clit. "Are you?"

Clean? Clean how? Like drugs? No. No, she's talking about STDs. "Yeah, I'm clean."

"And I'm on the shot. I need you inside me, now."

My balls draw up from anticipation. The glint of her pussy is all the coaxing I need, and I rip off the panties she had me wear and kick them in a corner.

The fat head of my cock slips into her opening. It's warm and inviting, and I advance farther, letting her adjust to my size.

"Don't hold back, Reid."

I love the way my name sounds coming from her mouth.

"Give me what I need."

I thrust into her hard, the head of my cock rubbing against a rough patch deep inside her. "Shit," I breathe out, staving off my need to come.

Sweat beads down my chest as I pound into her. She sits up and swipes her fingers across my chest, capturing a rivulet. Bringing her fingers to her mouth, she sucks off the moisture.

"Fuck, sweetheart, if you keep doing shit like that I'm going to come."

She laughs. "Ladies first."

"Of course," I agree. I rub her clit as I continue to thrust into her.

"Oh. Oh. Oh, fuck. Yeah, just like that," she says, her pussy gripping my dick like a vice.

Her back bows and her legs spread wider as she hits her peak. The warmth and wetness of her pleasure flood around my cock, milking me.

I bend over her on the bed, needing more stability as I continue to chase after my own orgasm. "*Fuck!*" I come so hard, my arms twitch.

I roll over, and we lay side by side, both staring at the ceiling.

After several minutes of gasping for air, our breathing begins to slow, and she asks, "Was this a mistake?"

I can't blame her, I was thinking the same thing. "Unethical maybe, but not a mistake." It's true, I don't regret doing this with her. I've been thinking about her since she left the island. I haven't been this obsessed with someone since I lost Amanda. I'm not sure if that's a good thing or not. What are the chances that I would run into Sam in Chicago? Not to mention that she would be Sterling's number two. That has to mean something. Right?

"Definitely not a mistake," she says, snuggling into my chest.

"I need to tell you something." The guilt is gnawing at me. I'm going to be her boss come next Friday, and I know Frank hasn't told her yet.

She crawls to the top of the bed and pulls back the covers, patting the spot beside her, inviting me to sleep over.

"Tell me tomorrow," she says. "Whatever it is, it can wait until the sun rises."

She lays her head on my chest and falls asleep within minutes. A small puddle of drool begins to form on my pec, and I loathe myself for how much I like it.

26

Sam

Reid and I spent Sunday hanging out at my apartment. We watched bad movies with lots of explosions and ordered in, not leaving the building once until this morning. On the top of the to-do list today is to make sure I spend sufficient time sitting on an ice pack. My lady parts are sore and swollen, but I have not one regret for all the fun we had.

Reid headed back to Frank's and got ready for work early this morning. I spent what felt like a hundred hours at the gym, making up for time lost and calories gained over the course of the weekend.

As I walk up to Pop's coffee shop, Reid meets me at the door. He looks handsome in a black suit. His jaw is freshly shaven, and his hair combed back to perfection. Playing a gentleman, he opens the door for me.

"After you." He guides me inside with his hand on my lower back.

I place my order. "Morning, Nick. How'd your weekend go?"

Nick leans over the counter, his lips pressed hard. "Funny

thing about my weekend. I thought I had a date with this hot blonde I know."

I am mortified. Reid is a mere few feet from me, ordering his coffee.

"At first, I thought my phone was broken because she said she'd call me, but when Pops called, I knew it couldn't be that. What do you think happened?"

"Maybe something came up," I grate between my teeth, keeping my voice low. I don't want Reid to overhear. "Maybe she never *promised* to help you taste-test edible paints."

"Everything okay over here?" Reid asks as he approaches after having given his order with Pops.

"Yeah. Great. Everything is...great."

"Ah," Nick says, puffing out his chest. "You found someone else to paint your canvas." Nick hands me my drink and a muffin.

"Excuse me?" Reid asks Nick.

Nick hands Reid his coffee. "Nothing, man. Nothing. It's on the house." He stomps away, punching open the swinging doors to the back.

"What's that about?" Reid asks.

"That?" I ask, pointing back at the counter. "Oh, that's nothing. Nick thought we had a date this weekend. We didn't. Guess he isn't taking it well."

Our walk to work is surprisingly quiet. The tension has been rolling off Reid in waves since we stepped out of the coffee shop.

As we approach the building which houses Sterling Brokerage, Reid breaks the silence. "You dated the barista?"

"Sure. I'm not too good for a barista," I joke, hoping to dispel some of the tension.

My joke falls flat, and he just nods, not giving me any insight into what he's thinking.

The doorman at the front of the office building tips his hat to me. "Ms. Valentine." Then to Reid. "Mr. Gallagher."

"Now, remember. We didn't sleep together. We're coworkers, and that's it." I tell him as we board an empty elevator.

On Sunday we discussed the potential ramifications if word was to spread that we are sleeping together. Not to mention the headache I would have from dealing with HR. Neither one of us is sure how ethical it is. Also, there are additional concerns since I will be Reid's boss by the end of the year.

"Got it," he answers.

"Oh, yeah." I dig through the pocket of his suit jacket and snatch his phone. "We should exchange numbers. For work," I clarify. "And other things," I add, smiling. I call my phone and program myself under his Favorites. Next, on my phone, I forward a text from Grayson to Reid.

"What's this about?" he asks, reading the text.

"You have a bet to make good on. You and Grayson are meeting every night this week for rehearsal."

He gives me a tight smile. "Great."

When Reid and I step into the hallway to our offices, we make sure not to look at each other and keep walking. I find Ben standing at the doorway, glaring as Reid gives my hand a not-so-covert squeeze before turning in the opposite direction.

It's sweet.

"Good morning, boss," Ben greets, eyeing Reid.

I walk past Ben, set my stuff down on my desk and fire up my computer.

Ben sits down across from me with his tablet in hand, and we begin our ritual of scheduling for the week. "Silas Keogh called. He wants you to call him back today."

I mark it on my desk calendar. "Okay."

"Next is a meeting on Friday. Frank wants to get all the higher-ups together. Something about the direction of the company."

"Hmm."

"Weird, right?"

It is weird. "Not necessarily. He's planning to retire at the end of the year. Maybe he wants to give everyone a heads up. Inform them of my promotion."

He gives an emphatic nod. "Yeah. Maybe."

"Besides, Reid just came on, and I'm sure Frank wants to make introductions. It'll give a sense of continuity to know Frank's son is on board. Someone to keep the Sterling vision alive."

Ben looks out the door and across the hall to Reid's office. "Yeah. I'm sure that's it."

"You don't think so? I'll prove it to you." I pick up the phone and dial Delores.

"Frank Gallagher's office. This is Delores. How can I help you?"

"Delores, hearing your voice is like a ray of sunshine that brightens my entire day. How are you this morning?"

I can practically hear her eyes rolling. "What do you want, Sam?"

"I know Frank has a lot on his plate right now. I just wanted to see if he had any available time this week for lunch."

Delores doesn't answer me for a few seconds—she's probably sharpening her claws. "He's available anytime that works for you. He's requested his schedule be left open so he can help Reid adjust."

It's shocking that she would be willing to give me any details, it isn't normally her style. "I don't want to take up too much of his time. I'll just pop in later today."

"Whatever you want." When Delores hangs up the receiver, it isn't accompanied by the customary piercing of my eardrum from slamming down the phone. I think she may have hung up, like a regular person.

"That seemed...pleasant," Ben observes.

"It was." Now, I'm suspicious.

At lunchtime, I touch base with Frank. He looks pale, almost sickly. Maybe retirement can't come soon enough. We gab about office politics and nothing of real importance. Simply hanging with the boss and shooting the shit.

As much as I enjoy it just being two people lunching in a

stately office, I do have an agenda. "Ben told me there's a big meeting scheduled for Friday."

He nods.

"Anything I should be aware of?"

Frank bites off a large chunk of cheeseburger and takes an unnecessarily long time to chew. I mirror his actions and use my chopsticks to plop sushi in my mouth.

He dabs the corners of his mouth with a napkin. "Nope. Same ol,' same ol.'"

This will be the second time in the past week where I have questioned Frank's motives. Never once, in my ten years of working here, have I felt like I was being left out. Left out of something huge.

27

Sam

Reid has kept me up late and woken me up early every day since Sunday. We've been going at it like teenagers. I don't think I remember a time in my life when I've had this much fun with one man for this length of time. It's refreshing. It's new. It's exciting as hell.

Because of all the sexy times we've been having, my gym time has severely suffered. Now that Wednesday is wrapped up, I've carved out some time for an evening session of cardio.

My bag in hand, I walk down the hall toward the elevator. Reid calls out to me, and I turn around to watch him jog to catch up to me. It's like watching Harvey Spector from *Suits* doing a *Baywatch* run in the middle of Sterling.

"What's up?"

He comes to a stop in front of me. "Where are you going?" he asks, his smile suggesting other destinations.

"I'm on the path to the holistic me. The me which requires other forms of cardio besides training for the gold in the Bed Olympics.

Reid mimics boxing moves as he walks beside me. "Cool. I need to find a gym. Mind if I tag along?"

"Suit yourself, but after our workout, you have to go home. You can't keep sleeping at my place, people will notice. Besides, where does your dad think you are every night?"

We walk through the lobby doors onto the sidewalk and head toward the gym.

"Frank has his own problems right now—he doesn't have much interest in mine."

"I'm a problem now?" I tease.

"Not you. Stella. Frank's wife. She's my problem. You, sweetheart, are the solution."

Impressive. "You're good, but you still can't stay at my place."

He pouts until we get to the gym, but his mood seems to improve as I show him around the two-story facility. He fiddles with weights for a while then hops on the elliptical next to the stair master I'm climbing. His movements are long and elegant as a gazelle. I, on the other hand, am more like an elephant climbing the Statue of Liberty.

"Tell me the story about your wicked stepmother," I ask, needing to focus on something other than the burning in my calves.

"Once upon a time, a haggard old man named Frank met a beautiful, fake breasted woman who was forty years his junior."

"Wait. How old are you?"

"Thirty-five."

"And Stella?"

"Twenty-nine."

"So, you're older than your stepmom?" I ask, laughing.

"Yes. Now let me tell the story. Her name was Stella. She lived on the wrong side of the tracks, and the marks on her arms showed precisely where those tracks lead."

"She was a drug user?"

"Heroine," he confirms. "Anyway, one night, Frank was

feeling particularly lonely. He was driving down the street in his limo when he saw a woman who caught his eye. He took her back to his mansion and lavished her with the most beautiful things he could buy, and she loved it. They developed a real understanding of each other. They were talking, eating, watching reruns of *I Love Lucy* when Stella walked out onto the balcony and sat on the ledge. Now, Frank was terrified of heights—"

"Hold on," I interrupt. "Are you retelling Pretty Woman and substituting Frank and Stella's names?"

"Yeah," he admits, "but everything before the balcony part is true. Long story short, Stella liked pretty things, and Frank liked whores. So, after thirty years of marriage to my mother, Frank divorced my mom and married Stella two months later."

I ride the top step of the stair climber to the bottom, stunned by Reid's story. "Damn."

"Damn," Reid repeats. "Even though Frank is loaded, Stella has other needs he hasn't been able to meet in the past few years. Now, I have to beat her off with a stick."

Reid wrinkles his face in disgust as I double-over laughing.

"I'm sorry," I tell him through bouts of giggles. "But, beating her off with a stick?" I ask and begin to laugh again.

Reid hops off the elliptical and gives a flat-palmed whack to my ass, as I'm still bent over. "Yuck it up."

"Oh, come on, don't be such a spoilsport. You have no one to blame but yourself."

He gives me a half-smile and walks to the juice bar. "I'll buy you a drink if you'll shut up for the next ten minutes."

"Deal." I have to give somewhere.

Reid points to a couple of items on the overhead menu, and the teen behind the counter starts the blenders.

The juicer hands us our beverages, and I'm not certain letting Reid pick out my drink was a smart idea. "Mine's green," I whine. "Yours is orange."

He taps the edge of his cup to mine. "Kale. It's good for you."

I take a sip when I hear my name.

"Hey, Sam, how've you been?"

I turn to see a familiar face. "Jerry?" I'm not sure how this will go. Jerry was pretty pissed off when I kicked him out of my bed the last time I saw him. "What a surprise. Jerry, this is my good, good friend, Reid. Reid this is Jerry."

Reid extends his hand for a shake, but Jerry seems reluctant with his jaw set firm, grinding.

Finally, Jerry accepts the gesture and shakes Reid's hand. "It's Jarod. Nice to meet you. Be careful with this one. She's into some kinky shit."

"I'm sorry?" Reid tilts his head, and I worry he's ready to throw down.

Jerry, I mean Jarod, turns to me. "Have a good night, Sam."

Jarod pushes through the double doors and out to the mean streets of Chicago, leaving me here with a less than happy Reid.

"Jesus," Reid mutters, shaking his head. "On second thought, you're right, Sam. I should go home tonight."

Reid storms into the men's locker room, and I dash into the women's to grab my stuff, narrowly catching him as he makes to leave me behind.

"Wait up."

Reid stands at the edge of the street and raises his arm to hail a cab.

"Are you mad at me?"

"Did you sleep with him?" Reid asks, referring to Jerry.

"Are you serious? I won't be ashamed of my sex life. No matter how mad you get. I've had sex with lots of men. I'm thirty-three, in the prime of my life. There is nothing wrong with enjoying myself."

A cab sidles up to the curb, and Reid opens the door. "I'll see you in the morning, Sam." He steps into the back and shuts the door, leaving me alone on the sidewalk.

People continue to walk by, whereas I stand on the edge of sanity near on-coming traffic. I pluck my phone out of my purse and call Lizzie.

"Hello?" Lizzie answers.

"What are you doing for dinner tonight?" I ask, crossing my fingers that she's free. I am in desperate need of my friend right now.

"Wide open. I'm just about finished at work. What are you thinking?"

"A trashy movie, sweatpants, pizza, and my vibrator."

"Must be bad," she muses. "But you're going to have to go solo with the vibrator."

28

Reid

I'm a first-class prick. I left Sam on the sidewalk and jumped in a cab. I ditched her. For what? Because I was pissy. My entire body hums with anger. Anger at Frank because he's an ass. Anger at Stella for being a bitch. Anger at Amanda for leaving me behind. Anger at Sam because she's slept with too many men to count.

I know I shouldn't judge her for her sex life. She's a vibrant, thriving, independent woman. There is nothing wrong with what she does. If the tables were turned, and she was a man, nobody would think twice.

The run-in with Jarod at the gym confirmed my worries. Sam is a very experienced woman. The dirty talk when we're in bed, the women's panties I wore—it's the hottest sex of my life, but it has me worried that we're on the low end of Sam's kinky scale.

No matter how upset I am, justly or not, it's no excuse for what I did. What I'm going to do. I'm confident Frank hasn't filled her in yet. A part of me wants to tell her everything, confess, but

I'm selfish, and I want this to last for as long as possible. Time is almost up. By Friday afternoon, this fantasy will become my newest nightmare. I wish there was a way I could make the news of losing her promotion easier. It's going to hurt.

The answer comes to me in bright neon lights. "Drop me here," I tell the cabbie. I swipe my card and hop out, certain I've found a solution to my problem.

When I arrive back at Frank's, I try to dodge the dysfunctional family dinner and head upstairs to the room I'm temporarily using. My realtor pulled a deal off in the last minutes before I fired her, and I'll be closing on my new apartment next week. Even that's too far away.

"Reid, darling, is that you?" Stella calls up the staircase. "We just sat down for dinner. Why don't you come and join us?"

I bang my head against the door in frustration, then toss my stuff on the bed. "Yeah. I'll be right down."

Why have I done this to myself? Why in the name of God would I come back here to take over a company I don't care about for a man who doesn't care about me? Guilt. One phone call from an ICU had me hopping a plane from paradise to the dreadful city of Chicago.

"Hey, Reid. You got a phone call, man," one of the waiters yells out to me.

"Yeah, all right," I holler back and wipe my hands off with a bar towel.

I head to the office and pick up the phone, the receiver lying on the desk. Because it's an older style phone and meant for personal use, there is no "Hold" button.

"Hello?" I answer.

"Hello. I'm calling for a Mr. Reid Gallagher?" a young female voice asks.

The line crackles and must be a call from the states. "This is."

"Oh, hello, Mr. Gallagher. My name is Abby from University Hospital in Chicago," the girl begins.

I swallow the lump that has nestled in the back of my throat. "What can I do for you, Abby?"

"Your father is here in the ICU. He's had a heart attack. He asked that I call and inform you of his situation."

Of course, the old man reaches out. Five years without a single word. Not so much as a condolence card after the funeral. Now that he's had a brush with death, he expects me to...what? What is he hoping to gain by calling me now? "Fine. Inform me of his situation."

Nurse Abby begins by telling me that my father arrived at the ER with chest pain. He ended up in the Cath Lab where they diagnosed the cause and were fortunate enough to fix the problem during the same procedure. "He bought himself three stents. Including one to the Widow Maker. He's extremely fortunate."

"Sounds like it," I agree. "Thank you for letting me know, Abby. I appreciate everything you and your colleagues have done. Have a good night."

"Wait." I hear the squelch of her tiny voice as I wrench the phone away from my ear, ready to hang up. "Mr. Gallagher, he's asked to speak with you. Please give me a moment, and I'll transfer your call to his room."

Soothing music starts. A monotone voice tells me about why University Hospital is the best hospital in Chicago. In Illinois. In the country. Hell, the world.

I have no desire to speak to my father. In fact, I should hang up now, but I won't for purely selfish reasons. If he should die, I would feel like absolute shit for not at least accepting his olive branch. If there even is one.

"Son," my father says, his voice raspy and weak.

"Frank."

Frank let's out a sigh. I can tell he's annoyed that I'm not calling him dad, but he lost that privilege. He made the choice.

"I just wanted to say that I love you."

"I understand. Sorry to hear you're sick." I have barely

spoken to my father in the last eight years and not at all for the last five.

Frank gives a sickly laugh, and the line is quiet for several long seconds, until he says, "Do you think you'll ever come back home?"

"No."

"I've had some time to think."

I bet he has. His come-to-Jesus moment has shown him a lifetime of regret.

"I want to retire. I was hoping to leave my company to you."

Another long pause. The hospital is going to flip when they see the bill for an overseas call.

"I'm not a begging man, Reid. I don't expect you to forgive me."

Good. I don't think I ever will.

"But," he continues, "I'm begging."

My father is in his weakest moment, pleading to give me something. I'm a real son of a bitch because the satisfaction is immeasurable.

"Fine," I say, then hang up the phone.

Frank is at the head of the table and Stella is across from me. The maid sets out the first course, a pumpkin soup concoction that Stella has served four times a week.

"How was your day, son?" Frank asks before he slurps from his spoon.

"Fine."

"And Samantha? What do you think of her?"

"It should be Sam you promote. Not me."

Toes from under the table run up my leg and make their way to my groin. I swat it away, but Stella doesn't give up. Frank is fucking clueless.

"I know, I know, but Sterling is my legacy. I want it to stay in the family."

29

Sam

"So, what's the deal?" Lizzie asks as she throws her bag on the floor and plops down next to me on the couch.

I'm curled in a semi-fetal position in a pair of baggy sweatpants and a Columbia University T-shirt.

"It must be pretty bad for you to look like this," she says, giving me a thorough once-over.

I don't answer; instead, I queue up *Pretty Woman* on Netflix, and she orders the pizza. We don't talk much until the food arrives.

"He keeps running into my ex or kinda-ex lovers. He thinks I'm a whore. Maybe he's right." I confess.

She takes a bite of her pizza. "First of all, you aren't a whore. You never make them pay for it. You give it away for free, you heffer. Second, do you know why I hate this movie?"

"You hate *Pretty Woman?*" How can anyone hate this movie?

"Yes, because it's a movie about a prostitute who is saved by a millionaire. Why does a woman need to be saved? Why can't the woman save herself? The whole idea grates against every feminist sensibility in my body."

Lizzie begins to cry, and I'm at a complete loss. She lays her head on my lap and wipes her snot on my pants. I manage to catch the paper plate holding her pizza and set it on the coffee table before it flops onto the floor.

"Honey, what's going on?" I brush the hair out of her face.

She sits up, her eyes tired and bleary. "I'm late," she says as she leans over for a tissue and blows her nose.

"Late for what? Oh, you're late-late. How late?"

"Like last month late. I thought it was just stress, or from the altitude after flying back from Barbados, but I don't think it is."

Last month? Good Lord. I jump up and pace back and forth, biting my nails. "How? When? Who?" I ask, peppering her with questions instead of emotional support.

Lizzie looks down to the ground when I ask "who?"

"No. No. *No.* Grayson? Shit. Does he know?"

She shakes her head. I seem to be the only person talking in this conversation. Lizzie starts to cry again, and I feel like a complete jackass with the empathetic intelligence of a rock. I put my arm around her shaking shoulders. "I'm sorry. I'm not being very supportive. First things first, you need to pee on a stick."

I change into presentable clothes and walk to a drug store a few blocks from my apartment. I fumble through several different pregnancy tests. One offers a plus or minus sign, another is one or two lines, a third says pregnant or not pregnant. I pick option three and make my way to the checkout counter.

"What do you got there?" a deep voice asks as I wait in line.

I turn around to find Grayson. He's handsome in his dark suit, his tie loosened. He looks like a man on his way home after a long day of being on top of the world. The box in my hands will knock him right off his stripper pole.

"Oh, uh, nothing. Just picking up some...tampons. It's a fucking crime scene down there." I deflect by using his aversion to the natural process of womanhood.

"Gross. Have you seen Lizzie today?" he asks.

"Nope." The longer I'm in his presence, the worse this is going to get. I refuse to be the one to tell Grayson that Lizzie is carrying his spawn. Alleged spawn—we don't know if she's pregnant or not yet. I bend over and wrap my arms around my waist. "My uterus. It's like Freddy Krueger is giving me a pelvic exam," I cry, standing back up, throwing my arm up to my forehead.

Grayson turns a bit green. I believe my extraordinary vocabulary of feminine parts plays a substantial role in my success.

He steps in front of me and shoves an older lady next in line out of the way. "She's got an emergency."

Crap. Now, I have to lay the pregnancy test on the counter for the clerk to ring up. "What's that?" I ask, pointing to the back of the store.

Grayson whips around to look and the lady who was in front of me, but is now behind me, steps back in line. "What?" he asks, looking where I'm pointing.

The clerk places my purchase in a bag quick enough that when Grayson turns back, he has no clue what I bought.

"Never mind." I pick up my plastic bag. "I thought that old guy was stealing a cane. Turns out it's his," I say with a nervous laugh.

"That's my husband," the lady behind me says indignantly.

"It's flowin' like a river now. Talk to you soon." I run out of there as fast as my legs will carry me.

When I get in the front door of my apartment, I let out a deep breath. That was a close call.

"Everything okay," Lizzie asks from the couch. She changed the movie to *Pitch Perfect*. It's a good call—we could use a few laughs.

"Yeah, yeah. No worries. There was a mean-looking stray cat that followed me home. Didn't want to get rabies." There's no need to tell her about running into Grayson at the pharmacy. She'd freak out more than she already is.

I set the box on the coffee table. "One way to find out."

She stares at the box for a good two minutes before she gets off her ass to find out if she's about to become a mom.

Or Grayson a dad.

Or me an aunt.

Test in hand, she heads to the guest bathroom to do her business. I kick off my shoes, prop up my feet, and take my first bite of pizza. I'm snickering at the scene where the girl makes a vomit angel when Lizzie reappears.

"I can't look," she says, handing the stick to me.

I look down at the result. "Do you want a boy or a girl?"

I show her the test, and she looks for herself. "What am I going to do now?"

I take another bite of pizza. "I think you have to tell Grayson."

"I guess."

"You guess? Grayson needs to know. He has a right to know. Besides, even if you decide not to tell him, don't you think he'll become suspicious when you start to show? He was a business major. He can do simple math."

"No. Yeah. I mean, I know, you're right. It's just that after 'it' happened," Lizzie says, using her hands for emphasis, "he became cagey. Things haven't been the same since. Other than Euchre, I haven't talked to him."

I lie my head on her shoulder. "I don't know what to say, except that I'm here for you and Grayson. Whatever you need, I'm here."

30

Sam

Silas Keogh has become a pain in my ass. His demands are growing more ridiculous, and I still have to take those demands to Tate Bennett. Tate is beginning to lose his patience, and I can't blame him. This deal would be a major coup for me. If I could lock this down, it would prove to my future employees and clients that I have what it takes to seal the deal. Not that I was ever worried, but the impression would go a long way.

A knock on my office door jars me from my thoughts, and before I can get up from my chair, the door swings open. I expect to see Ben looking his handsome self, chomping at the bit to tell me his newest theory on the future of our company. No matter how much I try to convince him that it will be fine, he refuses to believe it.

Instead of Ben, I find a tall, lean man in a dark blue suit with regret shimmering in his eyes.

I lean back in my chair. "Hey."

"Hey," Reid parrots. "Do you have a minute?"

"Sure."

He steps into my office and closes the door behind him.

"People will talk if the door's closed," I warn him.

"I don't care what people think."

A small sarcastic laugh bubbles from my lips. Reid might not care, but I do. I already have enough problems, I don't need to battle rumors, even if those rumors are true.

"It'll only take a minute." He takes a seat on the chaise longue. "I wanted to apologize for last night at the gym. I should never have left you alone like that."

"It's fine. I've lived in this city my whole life—I don't need an escort."

He runs his hand through his hair. "No, you're right. That's not why I'm apologizing."

I dismiss him with a wave of my hand. "Don't worry about Jerry. He was a one-time pain in my ass."

"It's not Jarod that concerns me." Reid looks around the office as if we're being watched.

I mimic him and glance around. "No one's here but you and me. The door's shut. What's the problem?"

"I don't want to discuss it here. Do you think I can come over after my rehearsal with Grayson?"

"Sure." Something is off. So we had an argument, they happen all the time in relationships.

Not that this is a relationship.

It can't be.

I don't know what this is.

Reid stands and buttons his suit jacket as he takes three steps to stand in front of me. He runs his finger down my cheek. "You're the most beautiful woman I've ever seen," he says, giving me a light kiss on the cheek.

My office phone rings the moment Reid walks out the door. "Ben, it was just business."

"I didn't say anything," Ben replies dryly. "That's not why I'm calling. A hysterical model is standing in front of me."

It must be Lizzie. "Let her in."

Seconds later, Lizzie burst through my door, and she looks a wreck. She wipes her nose with a worn-out tissue, mascara running down her cheeks. "Did you tell him?" she yell-cries.

"Grayson? About?" I point to her stomach.

She nods.

"No, of course not!"

"He hunted me down today," she says, flopping onto the settee Reid had been sitting on moments earlier.

The difference between Reid occupying the seat and her is that Lizzie is partially laying down with an arm tossed above her head in distress. It's a natural and surreal sight.

"Grayson said he's tired of me avoiding him, and he ran into you last night. He told me he's tired of all these woman problems interfering in his...his...*life*," she wails, burying her face in a pillow.

Flabbergasted. That's what I am. I can't believe Grayson would be so insensitive, so ignorant. Why would he—oh.

"I wasn't ready to tell him. I don't have any idea what I'm going to do about this baby. I have options, and being a single mother isn't the only one."

"Stop." I sit on the settee. "Grayson doesn't know. He's just thoughtless. I ran into him last night. I was in line to pay for the pregnancy test when he said 'hello' and was right behind me. I gave him some story about tampons and threw in the names of a few body parts for good measure. You know how that freaks him out. He bought the whole thing. That's why he said what he did. I promise." I grab her shoulders and force a hug on her. "He doesn't know."

Lizzie relaxes into me, and we sit there for a few minutes while Lizzie's new-life hormones settle down to a reasonable level. If this is what the next nine months will look like, it's going to be rough.

§

It's well after ten o'clock at night when Reid shows up at my apartment door. He looks tired and smells sweaty. "Rough practice tonight?" Man sweat mixed with success and devilish good looks—I can barely contain myself.

He shrugs his shoulders. "A little. I'll tell you one thing though—this show is going to be awesome."

"It better be."

He slips out of his leather jacket and tosses it on the furniture. "It will."

Before I can walk away, he gently grabs me by the arms, bends at the knees, and looks me in the eye.

"What is going through that handsome head of yours?" I ask when he doesn't speak.

"Have I ever told you that your eyes are the purest shade of blue I've ever seen? I swear, I could get lost in them."

"Funny, I think the same about yours."

"We need to talk. Can we talk?" He grabs me by the hand and leads me into the dining room. Clearly, my answer is not required.

"Sit," he commands and pulls a chair up next to me so we're face to face and knee to knee. "I've been doing some thinking."

My mind starts to race like a hamster on a wheel. All the things I've done. All the things I plan to do. I don't know what's going on, but I do know it's bad news.

"Jarod said something that kind of raised my hackles."

"I told you not to worry about what Jerry said. He was a whiny mistake."

Reid covers my mouth with his hand. "Will you please let me talk? This is hard enough without you interrupting me."

I nod, now seriously curious. I don't care how bad it is, I have to know.

31

Sam

Reid sits at my dining room table and seems prepared to lay himself bare. He folds his hands in his lap and gazes at the floor. "Jarod said something that got me thinking. He mentioned that you like things a bit more varied. I don't think I'm quite as experienced as you."

"Hey." I tilt his chin up to look at me. "Experience isn't everything. However, in the name of full disclosure, how not experienced are you?" This man is so damn sexy, I can't imagine him going thirty-five years as a virgin. No way. His skills in the bedroom aren't something that can be learned from fantasizing.

He shakes his head. "It's not like I was a virgin when we met. Jesus, come on Sam."

"Well, I had to ask," I defend. "You seem so reticent about it."

"Let's be honest here. We have amazing chemistry."

"Yes, we do."

"But," he continues, "we don't know much about each other outside of that. We met like a week ago."

"That's not true. I know your favorite ice cream is butter pecan." I think back to the one question he's managed to evade each time I ask. "You know what? You're right. I still don't know how you ended up in Barbados. You went from selling large real estate in New York City to becoming a bartender. How does that happen?"

He lets out a sigh and scrubs his hand over his face. "I lost someone close to me."

"Like your dog?"

"My wife."

There it is. Reid had a wife. He's a widower. Stuff like that isn't supposed to happen to someone so young. It's for old people in nursing homes who wear diapers. Not thirty-somethings in the prime of their lives.

"I met Amanda my senior year of high school. I fell fast and hard. I didn't even know what hit me." He bites his lower lip. "She was my first."

"First what? Love?"

He raises an eyebrow at me.

I sit back in the chair. "Oh." My heart lets out a little 'awe' when I realize he married his high school sweetheart. That's adorable.

"And only. When Amanda died, the world didn't make sense anymore. So, I left everything and everyone I knew, in search of meaning in my life. I couldn't be intimate with a woman for years after Amanda. It seemed pointless. No one was ever going to be able to fill that void."

And only? "Hold on. Are you saying that I'm, what? Number two on your list of conquests?" The idea that this man would find himself in bed with a woman with my predilections is horrific.

"You say it like it's a bad thing. I found the love of my life on the first try. There's nothing wrong with that."

"There isn't, I'm just sorry that the second person you've ever had sex with was someone like me. So what changed? You lost your wife and fled to a foreign country, hiding from the world.

What made you decide to jump back into life all of a sudden?"

"You."

What? "I don't get it."

"When I saw you at the bar, it was like for the first time, in a long time, things seemed clear. I wanted you, and nothing was going to stop me. It had been five damn years since I'd had any kind of ambition. When Frank called and said he wanted me to come and run…" His words trail off. He shakes his head, getting back to the point. "It seemed like fate. When I ran into you at the coffee shop, I knew it was fate.

"I guess what I'm trying to say is that I care about you. A lot. More than I ever thought I could. I believed a part of me died when I lost Amanda, but it didn't. I just needed to find the right woman. That woman is you, Sam. I realize I'm not the most experienced man, but for you, I'm willing to try other…stuff. I don't want to leave you unfulfilled."

That has to be the sweetest thing I've ever heard. Reid has laid himself out for me, trusted me with his biggest fears. It's my responsibility to hold such delicate information near and dear to my heart.

"Okay, I can work with this." I scoot to the edge of my seat, ready to give definition to a few topics. "The whole Dom/sub thing isn't my cup of tea. Although, I do enjoy dominating a man from time to time. I also like some things a bit kinkier than other people. It certainly isn't a deal-breaker if you aren't into it. I don't want you to feel pressured into anything. We'll take it slow-ish. Just so you know, nothing about our time together has left me feeling unfulfilled.

"I don't think I'd be uncomfortable *per se*. Just more of a novice, and I'm willing to give it a try."

"Good." I grab both his hands in mine and stand. "Now, get a shower, and then we'll go play."

Reid comes out of the bathroom with a towel wrapped around his waist. I lean against the doorframe in a tight button-down shirt knotted at my belly button, a short black and white pleated skirt, white knee-high stockings, and a shiny pair of six-inch heels with a Mary Jane flare. The pigtails hanging loosely over my shoulders brings the entire naughty school girl look from fantasy to a real-life wet dream, and I happen to know he loves pigtails.

"Fuck," Reid breathes out, his gaze heavy-lidded.

I don't think there is a better compliment.

I yank the towel from his waist, the damp fabric making a whipping sound, and I toss it to the floor. Rivulets of water slide down his toned chest and I lick each drop, biting along the way.

I point to the chair next to the fireplace. "Sit."

He does as he's told.

I draw out a black silk tie. "Put your hands behind the back of the chair."

He does, and I work a complicated knot, so I know he won't be able to break loose until I want him to. "Sister Agatha taught me how to tie a slip knot. We were so slippery when we were done," I whisper in his hear.

He throws his head back and groans.

"You know what would be fun?" I ask.

He shakes his head.

I rifle around in a dresser drawer, a dedicated drawer, and present a flesh-tone, twelve-inch, silicone vibrator. Reid's eyes pop open wide.

32

Sam

Having Reid tied to a chair in my bedroom and knowing I'm the first he has ever experienced this with is beyond hot.

"There's something visceral about seeing a cock this large that makes me wet." I rub the enormous shaft of the vibrator, stroking from root to tip. I drop between his knees and prop the toy between his legs, stroking it.

Reid's cock is getting hard, and I can tell by the way his abdominal muscles are twitching that he's trying to hold back.

"Do men like to watch a woman stroke a large cock?" I ask.

"Not as much as having their own stroked."

"What about licking one?" I run my tongue from the base of the vibrator to the fake slit at the top.

"The same." His cock rises as he watches my lewd act.

"And sucking?" I cover the silicone head with my lips, and my mouth is full.

He lets out a disgruntled moan. "It doesn't change anything," he says, his voice going up an octave.

I lick and tease the vibrator with my tongue like I would the real thing. "I wonder how far down I can take it?"

"Me too."

I quirk an eyebrow and open my mouth wide, slowly sheathing the toy and working to swallow it down. I make it over halfway before I pull back. When I look up at Reid, he's still staring at the toy and the lipstick ring I left a few inches above the base. I'm pretty impressed with myself.

"So, men do like to see a woman deep throat a big. Fat. Cock. It doesn't matter if it's theirs or not," I tease, enjoying the sight of Reid's beautiful dick at full attention.

"So it would seem."

I stand up, toss the toy on the bed, and start to unbutton my shirt, exposing my red bra. Reid licks his lips as I show myself little by little. I run my fingers down the column of my neck and to the valley between my breasts. Giving my full C's a rough squeeze, letting out a long moan.

My fingers dip inside the cups simultaneously and pop my breasts out, giving them a delightful push-up effect from the underwire.

"Are those nipple clamps?" he asks.

"Yeah." I unclip one clamp and the blood rushes to the hardened bud. I straddle one of Reid's legs and shove my breast in his face, pushing him by the back of the head. "Suck it."

"Yes, ma'am." He sucks and laves at my clip-free nipple with vigor. Pressure builds low in my belly. Moisture starts to gather and slides down my leg and onto his thigh. I let out a long groan of ecstasy at the erotic moment.

I unclamp the other nipple and direct his mouth to my other breast where he gives the same attention as the one before. I grind on his leg, searching for the friction to tease myself, and the hair on his leg prickles against the flesh of my pussy.

If I continue, I'll never get to the kinky stuff which has Reid's interests so piqued. I lift my leg and dig my heel into his other thigh, earning a hiss of pain from him. My short skirt lifts upward with the pose and exposes my most intimate parts. One hand wanders to the juncture between my thighs, and I give a slow rub with one finger, parting my slit. I run a second finger through and lift it to my mouth, felating my finger. "So delicious. Would you like a taste?"

"I need a taste." He pulls at the tie.

I gather more of my flavor on my fingers and rub it across his lower lip, but before he can take a lick, I swipe the taste off his mouth with my tongue.

He struggles a bit more, fighting the restraint. "Oh, no, Mr. Gallagher. If you fight the pleasure, I will have to find a way to punish you."

"I don't care," he says, jerking his arms.

I turn back to my drawer of fun and reveal a leather crop. "You've been very bad, Mr. Gallagher." I slap the palm of my hand with the crop.

His eyes go wide. I wouldn't be surprised if he's beginning to regret his decision.

I start at his ankle, gliding the leather up to his knee. I can see the pulse in his neck pounding as the smooth leather glides upward. I give a quick snap to his inner thigh, barely missing his testicles. It was a calculated move. He jumps from the shock, maybe a little fear as well. "You liked that," I say, noticing how he exhales with relief. The cloudy euphoria in his eyes tells me I'm right. Working the crop up to his chest, I give a snap on his pec. Once again, he exhales shakily, and his cheeks turn rosy with pleasure. I continue playing with the crop, leaving marks across his body. It's a beautiful sight.

I toss the crop to the floor and straddle him, staring into his eyes. I reach between us, wrap my fingers around his cock, and give a hard squeeze. "You're hard as stone." I tug at his bottom lip with my teeth.

I lick away the hurt and press my mouth against his, compelling his mouth open, and sweeping my tongue in, robbing him of any dominance he may have left.

"Do you want to come?" I ask.

"Fuck yes."

I turn around and sit on his cock, slowly sheathing him with my dripping entrance. We both moan in delight at the same time. The anticipation has only amplified my need to have him inside me, and now that he's here, I don't ever want him to leave. I lift slowly and sit back down. I stand again until he's almost entirely out of me, and slam down. The head of his cock hits the furthest part inside me, giving a pang of pleasure followed by a delightful cramp of things to come. I lift and slam down again, and we both cry out. The tempo increases and the force lessens, sending me spiraling over the edge. I can feel him growing inside me. "I'm going to come all over your cock, and you don't get to come until I say so."

"I don't know—"

I cut him off with a loud cry of rapture. My pussy is quivering when I hop off him, and his face is filled with distress from the need to come. Squirting lube into my hand, I jerk him from root to tip. "Come on my tongue," I command, sticking my tongue out to catch his seed. "Watch."

Reid looks down at me, and jets of warm, tangy liquid hit my pallet as he roars through his orgasm. His head falls back on the chair, exhausted from our fun time. I untie him, and he turns to look at me, a satisfied smile lighting up his face.

33

Sam

Thank God Delores is away from her desk when I stop into Frank's office on Friday. I don't have it in me to fuck with her this morning. I give a gentle knock on his door and peek my head inside. "You busy?"

"Samantha. Come in. Come in. What can I do for you?"

I sit in a chair across from him. "Remember that deal I was telling you about a couple of weeks ago?" I ask, referring to the meeting where I first met Reid.

"Sure."

"Well, I thought I should fill you in." This is a strategic move. This afternoon is the meeting Frank scheduled with the team, and I assume it's for a formal introduction of Reid and what his role will be at Sterling. With Frank's retirement coming up in the next few months, now would be an ideal time to announce that I'll be taking over his position.

"I got a call a couple of weeks ago," I begin, "from Silas Keogh. He's looking to sell Keogh Tower."

Frank stiffens. "Keogh. Interesting. He called you?"

"Yes. He sought me out. He wants to sell to BLH."

"Hmm. Why's he selling?"

"Keogh's looking to scale back and wants to unload the tower."

"This would be a major win for you, Samantha. Huge for Sterling. So, what's the problem?"

That's part of the reason I wanted to talk this morning. I thought it would help improve morale after Frank announces his retirement if the staff knew how hard I work and precisely how capable I am to take the helm of the S.S. Sterling. "Why would you assume there's a problem?"

"Why else would you be here telling me about it, if you didn't need to talk it out? You tend to keep your deals, especially the big ones, close to the vest."

He's right. Keogh has become a real princess over the last week. Every time I think I have it locked down, and am ready to start the paperwork, Silas raises the price. It's been constant negotiations. I'm worried that Silas is playing me, or playing BLH. Although, I haven't a clue as to his motive.

"As you know, Sterling also reps BLH. I've been doing fairly well managing the negotiations, but, to be honest, I'm feeling a bit pulled apart, trying to secure the best deal for both parties."

"I imagine Silas is the root of your problem?"

I don't bother to confirm his suspicion, it was more of a rhetorical question anyway.

"And your solution?"

"I want to invite Reid into this." I'm not sure if Reid has his licensing exams and applications completed yet, but I think it would be valuable to bring him in on the negotiations. I imagine that once Frank steps down, and I step up, Reid will become the next VP. This kind of deal needs to be handled by someone at the top. "I was thinking that since Keogh asked for me specifically, maybe Reid could represent BLH's interests."

"Hmm."

The tick-tock of the clock hanging on the wall is the only

sound in the office. Frank chews on the inside of his cheek like he's conflicted. Why is he so hesitant? Something like this should be celebrated, shouted from the rooftops.

"Good thinking. I'll talk to him," is all Frank has to say.

A half-hour before the big afternoon meeting Reid knocks on my office door. Ben is taking a long lunch, and the break was hard-earned. This Keogh thing has put us both through the wringer.

"Afternoon, sweetheart," Reid says, a bright smile lighting up his face. He closes the door.

"Hello to you too. Did Frank talk to you?"

"No. Why?"

"Just curious. So, what's up?"

Reid holds out a plastic bag of the nondescript variety. Its lack of description tells me everything I need to know. I round my desk and rub my breasts against his vested chest. "Ooh, what you got there, sailor?"

"A gift."

"That's not the kind of package I expect for," I grab a fistful of his crotch, "a pearl necklace."

He lets out a harsh breath, and his cock grows hard in my hand. He cups the back of my head and crashes his mouth to mine, securing my body to his by wrapping an arm around my waist. As much as I hate what the impression of us being behind a closed door at work suggests, I can't seem to stop myself. I crave him. Papers slide off my desk as Reid lies me down, the bag tossed next to me. He searches under my skirt and gives a rough snag to my panties. I groan into his mouth turned on by his animalistic act.

Oh, tit for tat. I could get used to this.

Two fingers penetrate me, and I gasp.

"You're already wet." He removes his fingers and brings them up to my mouth, spreading my slickness on my lips.

I dart out my tongue for a taste. "Delicious."

Then I feel something hard and rubbery penetrating me

while simultaneously covering my clit.

Reid steps away and stands back. "Do you have any idea how sexy you look right now?" he asks as he fiddles with his phone.

At first, I thought he was going to snap a picture. Kinky, but always a bad idea. I'm mortified when he slides his thumb across the screen. "Are you checking your email? Seriously?"

He looks up at me and smiles, and it's a wicked grin.

Vibration. Vibration here, there, everywhere. Simultaneous pulsations wring through my body. I fall back on my desk, staring at the ceiling tile, a sweat breaking out from the delicious sensation.

"I thought I'd provide the kink today. Technology is a marvelous thing. It turns out there are sex toys that can be controlled by your phone. From anywhere in the world. One click away from an orgasm at all times."

My head snaps up, and I look at the clock on my desk. We have a meeting in ten minutes. A meeting filled with people. Not a 'show me the money' meeting with five or six people. No, a big, State of the Business assembly.

The pulse below begins to duel. Clit. Pussy. Clit, clit, clit. Pussy, pussy. Clit.

"Oh, fuck," I rasp, my head falling back onto my desk.

"Eminem. Turns out you can use the beat from songs too. Are you a fan of rap?"

"I am now."

He grabs my hand and hauls me up from the desk. "Good. We have a meeting to attend."

34

Sam

The room is filled wall to wall with people. I greet and shake hands with several coworkers, making chit-chat, trying to give the impression of unflappable stoicism. The long walnut table seats over twenty people, and each spot has a paper tent assigning our seats.

Frank is at the head. I'm to his right, where the VP should be. The tension in the room is palpable. Lenora from accounting is chittering apprehensively to Jim from commercial. A worry-wrinkle mars Jim's brow as they talk. Everyone in here looks like they're about to shit their pants with nervousness.

Except for Reid. He trails in the door and does the greeting ritual, twiddling with his phone the entire time.

Why does he seem so relaxed? The thought doesn't last long, as a pulsation begins to phase in and out beneath my skirt. I bite my lower lip and close my eyes, trying to suppress a moan.

When Frank enters the room, he too engages in the ritual of hellos. He walks up to Reid and the pair talk, smiling at each other, and embrace in a one-armed man hug. Reid sidles up to the opposite side of the table from me and sits to the left of Frank.

"Welcome. Welcome," Frank announces, as he takes his place at the head of the table. "Please, everyone have a seat."

The table is crammed full, people standing and lined up along the windows and walls.

"I want to start off by thanking everyone for making time in their day to be here," Frank begins.

The vibrations down below change tempo and I have to adjust in my seat to compensate. I peer across the table to Reid. A smug look of satisfaction illuminates his face.

Bastard.

"First order of business. We have another big deal in the works. Samantha," Frank says, "Why don't you fill us in."

The Keogh deal is still a mess, and I'm surprised at Frank's willingness to announce it so soon. I haven't yet had the opportunity to discuss with Reid what his role will be, or more like, that he has a role.

"Thanks, Frank." The little device shifts ever so slightly as I stand, and my heart rate ticks up a notch. I clear my throat. "Hello, everyone. I, like Frank, am excited to see so many people here today. Yes, we have a big deal on the table. I have been working tirelessly with Silas Keogh and Tate Bennett for the sale of Keogh Tower."

Several people gasp in surprise.

"It's very exciting stuff. As many of you know, we here at Sterling Brokerage have been the sole brokers for BLH for quite some time. Our reputation must precede us because Mr. Keogh sought out our firm. Things have been going very smoothly and amicably, but I would not be a good leader," I toss in, trying to build my audience's faith in me, "if I didn't recognize that a deal of this magnitude, potentially the largest sale on record for our company, can't be done by one person alone.

"For those of you who have been living under a rock for the past week, or who haven't had the chance to meet him, I would like to introduce—" The pulsing slows down, more of a long hum, alternating from inside to on top. Jesus. "I would like to introduce," I repeat, my voice a little higher this time around, "Reid Gallagher."

The room fills with applause. Reid stands for a moment and takes a bow, sits back down and grabs his phone. This little idea of Reid's is deliciously naughty. Awkward, but fun none the less.

"Thank you, Reid. As I was saying," I continue, "that with a deal of this size, I think it would be beneficial to bring on another person to help advocate for our clients. I can't think of anyone better than Reid Gallagher."

Again, another round of applause.

Reid's head snaps up from his phone, his face ashen. I'm not sure what the problem is, nor is this the place to ask. Maybe it's shock. This is an important deal, and I wonder if Reid feels up to the challenge, especially since he hasn't been here for long. Perhaps he's overwhelmed.

"Wonderful. Wonderful. Thank you, Samantha," Frank boasts.

I resume my seat and Frank continues to clap with the crowd.

After the cheering dies down, Frank begins again. "Now, I know you're wondering why I've summoned us all here today. Yes, the BLH/ Keogh deal was part of that," he lies. "There have been some rumors going around lately, about my retirement and the future of Sterling."

The pulse under my skirt smooths to a continuous vibration, inside and out. I can feel sweat forming at my hairline, my cheeks beginning to flush. I'm close.

"It's true. In light of recent health issues, I've decided to bump up my retirement. Instead of waiting until the end of the year, as originally planned, I'll be retiring next week."

The room goes completely silent. Within seconds, the room fills with murmurs of discontent.

"Calm down. Calm down. I know, this wasn't what any of us

were expecting," Frank says.

My stomach tightens along with every muscle in my body. Shit. I'm going to—

"Bless you," Frank says, handing me a tissue.

I just came in a room full of forty-plus people. Not like at the resort bar, where I was anonymous. This time it's in a crowded room with people who know and respect me, and it's surprisingly sexy.

"Bless you again."

Another one. The vibrations pitch up, and another sneeze follows. This time my hearing plugs up from the pressure in my head. There's a dull roar in the room, the fluid in my ears must have shifted from sneezing so hard.

"Goodness, Samantha. I hope you're not catching a cold," Frank says leaning toward me, clapping.

Once again, the whole room is clapping. Standing. People talking amongst themselves, some smiling, some look scared, angry even.

Frank steps to the side, edging toward me as Reid stands and buttons his suit jacket. "Thank you. You're too kind," Reid says, stepping to the head of the table. Where Frank reigns king.

I think I've missed something.

"I know many of you have never heard of me and my arrival has come as a bit of a surprise. Bless you," Reid says, looking to me, giving a wink.

I've never wanted to have an orgasm and vomit at the same time. Not my kind of kink. Something has gone terribly wrong. I don't know what it is, a gut instinct. I can feel it throughout my entire body.

"But I want you to know," he continues, "that as President, I will do the best I can to live up to my father's legacy and continue to keep Sterling as the most trusted name in the business."

I know I didn't hear him right.

Reid is President.

Reid is President?

Achoo!

Of what? The United States?

Achoo!

Reid is—

The toy inside me continues to send impulses to the most delicate tissues.

President.

President?

Achoo!

Me?

Am I President?

No. Reid is the new President of Sterling Brokerage.

Reid approaches me, and whatever it is he sees on my face seems to pain him. He closes his eyes and when he opens them again, all I see is regret.

"Sam," he says, standing in front of me. "This isn't how you should've found out. I'm sorry." Reid holds his hand out to me for a shake.

Now I'm supposed to shake the hand of the man who snaked my job. Who fucked me in all senses of the word. This morning when we woke up together, in my bed, he knew. He knew and didn't say a word. He kinked his way into my office with his silly idea of a phone-controlled vibrator and made the conscious decision to bring me to the meeting where I would be dethroned.

I plaster on a smile and rise from my seat. I shake Reid's hand and then Frank's, playing the role of Sterling's VP.

I sneeze again.

Five minutes ago, this device was about pleasure and exhibitionism. Now, it's become an implement for torture.

35

Sam

I removed that stupid vibrator and hurled it against the wall the moment I entered the en-suite bathroom of my office. Turns out it's exceptionally durable. So durable, in fact, that it bounced back and nailed me square between the eyes, and I've been huddled in the corner of the bathroom ever since. Crying. Ugly crying. Not the sweet, single tear sliding down my face. No, I'm bawling like a four-year-old who didn't get a cone from the ice cream truck.

The moment I shook Frank's hand, I was out the door of the conference room. I couldn't handle the looks on everyone's faces, their expressions filled with platitudes. "Poor girl," or "Women aren't cut out for this job," or, my personal favorite, "Bitch got what was coming." My whole world is crumbling around me. Everything I've worked so hard for over the last sixteen years of my life has been destroyed by the prodigal son.

A soft knock at the door draws me out of my self-pity. I shove a tissue up one nostril. "N-n-no one's home," I stutter between sobs.

"It's me, Sam," Ben announces. He peeks his head through the door. His face oozes pity. "Can I come in?"

I take the tissue out of my nose and grab a new one, giving a big, semi-truck blow. "O-o-o-okay," I wail.

Ben joins me and sits down on the cold ceramic tile. "I guess things didn't go well, huh?"

"No. Stupid island stranger swooped in and stole my thunder."

Ben quirks an eyebrow in question.

"It doesn't matter. All that matters now is that everything I've worked for has been flushed right down the toilet." I begin slamming the handle, flushing the toilet next to me.

"I'm sorry, I'm not following. What happened?"

"Reid Gallagher happened. Frank's son has returned to the Father Land to claim his seat on the Sterling Brokerage throne."

Ben nods. "So, Reid is taking over for Frank? Why Reid? What changed?"

"I don't know. Frank told me, he said," I continue to sob. "He said Reid had no interest in taking over the family business. I guess he changed his mind."

Ben shakes his head in disappointment. "Jesus. Okay. Time to get up."

"I don't want to," I cry.

Ben stands up and hovers over me. "Damn it, Sam. Get up now."

"*I don't want to,*" I yell. "You're not the boss of me. I'm the boss of you. You're fired."

There's a sudden pressure under my armpits, and I realize I'm being lifted.

"I should get a goddamn raise for the shit I deal with," Ben says, setting me back on my feet, unfolding my hunched and defeated body. He kicks at my heels, forcing me to walk forward.

When I dare to look up, I see myself in the mirror, and I'm terrified by the woman who's looking back at me. Her eyes are red-rimmed with mascara streaking down her cheeks and hair which looks like a nest for a large family of rats. I rub the bruised patch between my eyes. The one thing more mortifying than orgasming in a room full of people you know is the evidence left behind by the vibrator.

"You look like shit," Ben tells me.

"Way to kick me when I'm down, asshole."

"This woman in the mirror," he says, pointing to my reflection. "This is not the Sam Valentine I know. I don't know who she is, Medusa maybe, but she's not my boss."

I cry a little more. "Are you going to tell me something that's going to make me feel better soon? Cause if this is all you've got, I'd like it better if you'd fly off and colonize the moon."

Ben rolls his eyes, and the idea that I've annoyed him makes me feel marginally better. "How many times do I have to tell you the moon can't be colonized. It isn't even a real moon. It's an alien substation constructed to keep an eye on the human race." He grabs a washcloth on the rack and runs it under warm water. "NASA has proof."

I give a nod and bite my lower lip, trying not to laugh.

"Wash your face." He tosses the damp rag at me, walking out to give me time to collect myself.

I scrub away the evidence of my breakdown and reapply my makeup. When I walk out to my office, Ben is sitting in one of the Queen Ann chairs, his legs crossed. I sit at my desk, beginning to feel a bit more like myself.

"Why the sudden rush?" Ben asks.

Frank didn't go into detail. "He said something about health issues, I think? My mind was, um, someplace else when he was talking."

"Someplace else? During the biggest moment of your life?"

I shrug my shoulders. It's all the defense I have.

"The Big C?" Ben suggests.

"He didn't say." The idea that Frank may have cancer hadn't crossed my mind. I'm sure I'll have to talk to him at some point after this whole thing. Just thinking about having the conversation makes me itch.

"So, now what?" Ben asks.

"I have no clue."

"Well, you need to come up with something."

"It's out of my hands. Frank has every right to choose his successor, and that person isn't me." A plan to turn back time would be ideal, and the first thing I would change would be inviting Reid for Euchre. As for the whole ordeal in Barbados, before I knew who he was, I wouldn't change a damn thing.

"True, but it doesn't mean you have to make it easy for the chosen one," Ben says.

A small bubble of laughter escapes my lips. "Fine. What do you suggest, oh wise one?"

"I'm just spit-balling here, but I know a guy. He's, uh," Ben stutters. "He's a specialist in making problems go away."

"Uh-huh."

"Yeah, yeah. My cousin had a problem with a, uh, um, a neighbor's dog barking. I mean this dog just would not quit. All day, all night, a real nightmare, you know? So, he hired this guy, and he acted as a...a mediator of sorts. You know, between my brother and his neighbor."

"I thought you said he was your cousin?" I ask, calling him out on his bullshit story.

"That's what I said. My cousin. Anyway, this mediator talked to his neighbor and just like that," he snaps his fingers, "the next day? No barking."

"Impressive, but let me ask you something. Was the dog there the next day?"

Ben glances around the room. "My cousin said his neighbor thought the dog was more trouble than the mutt was worth and decided to give it to his aging mother. I guess she was lonely."

The vision of a puppy weighted down with a cinder block at the bottom of a desolate pond in the middle of Nowhere, USA comes to mind. "Aside from hiring a hit, any other suggestions?"

"Not a hit," he clarifies. "I'm not a monster. Maybe, some

kind of life-altering accident. He's out hiking, and oops, he falls off a shallow cliff. Paralyzed for life. What a shame, he had so much potential."

I'll admit that I give the idea consideration for the briefest of seconds. I mean, the man lured me into a meeting full of people while I had a vibrator going full blast and watched the hammer fall. Aside from hiring a hit, it doesn't get much eviler than that. I think of the time we've spent together, the connection, the chemistry, the little moments we've shared. Death seems a bit over the top.

And a bit permanent.

But appropriate...

No. No. No.

"Sam? Anyone home?" Ben asks.

I suppose I've drifted into my own little world. "Yeah, sorry."

He looks at his watch. "It's almost six. Mind if I call it a night?"

"Oh, sure. Have a good—what day is it?" I ask. It feels like the meeting was years ago already, so far in the past and I still haven't gotten over it.

"Friday. Any plans for the weekend? Might I suggest alcohol? And lots of it."

If a cartoonist were to draw this moment, they might have a light bulb illuminate over my head, but the bulb would be shining so brightly the sun could be rising right here in my office. "You're a genius," I proclaim, hopping up from my seat and rushing toward Ben.

Ben's eyes go wide with shock as he stands, looking like he's going to bolt. I tackle him with a big bear hug and rain kisses down his face. "I love you. You *wonderful* man."

36

Sam

During the cab ride home, I sent out a series of texts. The first one was to Tressa. She works for Grayson and only with particular clientele.

Me: "Hey, girl. U busy tonight? Need a favor."

Tressa: "Anything for you, doll face."

Me: "I'll call you in a bit with the deets."

My next message was to Lizzie.

Me: "We still on for tonight?"

Lizzie: "Wouldn't miss it for the world."

Me: "9 p.m.?"

Lizzie: "C U then!"

My last correspondence was sent to my new arch enemy. The Duke of Douche himself.

Me: "C U tonight?"

Reid: "Whatever you want. I'm sorry."

You're about to be.

Me: "At Whiskers. U have a bet to make good on."

Reid: "Right."

Reid: "Can I see you after? We need to talk."

He wants to see me? Sure. Not that there will be much talking. Eventually screaming though. Lots of screaming.

Me: "Sure. Congrats BTW."

As I get ready for Ladies Night, I call my parents putting them on speakerphone. I haven't talked to them for weeks. Right now has to be the worst time for me to call, seeing as my wounds are still fresh, but there is nothing as soothing as the sound of my mom's voice.

The phone rings, and I roam in my closet until I find the perfect outfit for the occasion. A fabulously short, red Valentino dress. It hugs me in all the right places and gives all the wrong impressions.

"Hi, sweetie," my mom answers. "How are you? We haven't heard from you in so long."

"I know. Work's been busy. I'm in the middle of this big deal. It's been eating up a lot of my time." It's not a total lie, dealing with Silas Keogh has been quite time-consuming.

"You're coming to the anniversary party, right?" my dad chimes in. I can imagine him yanking the phone away from my mom's ear. "Haven't gotten your RSVP yet."

I apply some light foundation and powder to my face. "Does your only daughter need to RSVP?"

"Nope," he says, laughing, and gives the phone back to Mom.

I get dressed as my mother goes on and on about how my cousin Janie is getting married next year.

"She's twenty-nine and on track for partner in her law firm. She's going to have it all," my mom says. "You can too, Sam."

I sigh my annoyance. This has been an on-going battle with my mother. She's an amazing woman. The best mom in the world, devoted wife to a thoracic surgeon. The pinnacle of success to Mrs. Valentine is being a wife and mother. Our opinions vastly differ. "Our definitions of 'all' aren't the same, Mom," I tell her as I apply mascara. "I'm happy where my life is right now." Or at least I was this morning.

"I know, sweetie," she says. "I just want the best for you."

My heart smiles for the first time since the meeting. Talking with my mom wasn't the most therapeutic experience, but hearing her say the words makes it worth it. "I know. I love you, Mom. I have to go now, I'm meeting Grayson and Lizzie tonight."

"Okay, have fun. Oh, and remind those two that your father and I expect to see their faces at the party too."

"Will do."

After we hang up, I apply ruby red lipstick to bring the whole look together, and I know I look hot. I hop in a cab to Whiskers, excited for the show Grayson and Reid have put together, and the surprise I have in store for Reid later.

When I get there, Whiskers is packed. I weave my way through masses of breasts until I find Lizzie in the center stage section, sipping a cocktail in one of the VIP booths. I slide in next to her, shaking my head. "You shouldn't be drinking."

The pink frozen drink rapidly disappears as she takes a long pull on the straw, glaring at me. "It's a virgin daiquiri."

"Sorry." I regret my rushed judgment on one of the most responsible women I know. She may be an emotional, hormonal wreck right now, but of the three of us, she's the most responsible. Pregnancy excluded of course.

"Don't worry about it," she says, "I would have done the same thing if the shoe was on the other foot." She raises her hand to get our kitten's attention and points to her drink, requesting a second round. "The problem with virgins is that they're nowhere near strong enough to meet my needs."

The other day in my office, when Lizzie had unexpectedly shown up, she said she wasn't sure what she was going to do about the baby. I didn't know if she was considering adoption or abortion. "Have you thought any more about telling Grayson?"

"I don't know," she shrugs. "I need to adjust to the idea of becoming a mother before I tell him."

"So, you're keeping it?"

"Yes, I'm keeping it. Why shouldn't I?" Her personality changes so quickly, I expect her head to spin.

"You should." I agree, fearful that Lizzie is carrying a weapon, and I may have spoken my last words.

She giggles like a schoolgirl. "I can't wait to see Reid and Grayson dancing on stage," she says, switching personalities again to become the scariest school girl I've ever come across. "They've been practicing all week. I've seen them backstage. I think it's going to be one hell of a show."

The lights above brighten and dim, informing the audience that the event is about to start, similar to a Broadway play, except Broadway doesn't do show-and-stroke.

"Ladies and Gentlemen," the DJ announces, multi-colored strobe lights bounce off granite and glass surfaces. "Welcome to Ladies Night, where the drinks are free, but the eye candy comes at a much higher price. The cost? Your self-respect. Please welcome, Whiskers' Panthers."

Men on the side stages walk the panther walk, wearing tight shorts which leave little to the imagination and nothing else. The men dance and shake, walk amongst the crowd, earning a few dollars tucked into their waistbands.

A younger man saunters over to our seats with dollar signs flashing in his eyes. Lizzie and I get out from behind the table which could have been moved, but we prefer to sit on top with our legs slightly parted. A second stripper makes his way toward us, and in the blink of an eye, we both have men working our bodies into a frenzy as they rub their oiled muscles all over us. My body hums with delight.

I glance over at Lizzie and see her tucking several twenties into the barely-there costume of the dancer grinding on her. She's glowing with delight; her smile so broad it could touch her ears.

This is precisely what I need right now. This is what Lizzie needs too. I am glad to be here, at this moment because even though Lizzie doesn't know what happened today, seeing her happiness is bringing about my own.

And the half-naked guy too. He's helping make me exceptionally happy right now.

37

Sam

The Panthers who started us off leave our table a couple of hundred dollars richer and two new dancers swoop in to take their place. They caress and dance with us, grinding and bumping in time with the music. The lights flicker once again, signaling the main event is about to start. After the last set of strippers leave, we settle back into our booth smelling of testosterone and baby oil. I take a few deep sniffs of the delicious scent, but when I look over to Lizzie, she appears a bit green.

"Are you okay?" I ask.

"Man, these guys stink. All I can smell is B.O." She cups her mouth and heaves. "I have to—" She doesn't finish her sentence, instead she bolts from the table and runs toward the bathroom.

My attention is diverted from my sick friend to the show when the DJ makes his announcement. "Ladies and Gents, you've come here for debauchery and muscle-clad men, and we don't want to disappoint. I know many of you here have fantasies of the unattainable. Well, tonight, the unattainable *has* been attained."

The crowd begins to holler, and the music becomes excitingly familiar.

"I think all of us have had a fantasy about this man. The greatest boy band superstar. Welcome, *Justin Timberlake.*"

The music turns up, and so does the crowd as NSYNC's *Bye Bye Bye* plays. Half the curtain draws open, and Reid stands with his back to the crowd, his feet shoulder-width apart, and his head bowed. Smoke billows up from around his ankles, and the blue light above him collides with the smoke, keeping him shrouded in mystery.

"But no fantasy would be complete without the star of the boy band who started it all, *Jordan Knight.*"

Bye Bye Bye fades out and *Hangin' Tough* by New Kids on the Block amps up. I look around as the hoots become lower-pitched than J.T.'s debut. Women in their late thirties and forties are screaming with delight and fanning themselves as the other side of the curtain raises.

Grayson stands with his back turned and is holding the same pose as Reid. The smoke swirls around his feet and red lighting rains down on him. The colors collide from both sides of the stage and create a purple backdrop.

I must hand it to Grayson—this was pure genius. He's managed to capture the teenage crush of nearly every patron in this club tonight.

Lizzie slides back into her seat, and her eyes look teary from what I'm guessing was intense retching. "Feel better?"

"Definitely," she replies, rubbing her belly. She glances around at the spectacle caused by Grayson and Reid. "Impressive."

"Very."

"Now we need a couple of volunteers from the audience," the DJ announces. The crowd begins to scream, and every woman starts to wave their hands in the air.

"Oh no, Jordan, I think you're going to have your hands full tonight. No need to show the girls, honey, it's about you, not us," the DJ says, pointing to a woman flashing him.

"You, in the hussy-red dress," he says, pointing to me. "I think you need J.T. to show you some love tonight."

I shake my head, somehow not surprised that I've become the volunteer for "J.T." But, I play the part. I make my way up to the stage, feigning excitement. Somehow, Grayson devised a plan that would make the winners of a card game pay the stakes along with the losing team. Fucking brilliant. If I'm to be completely honest, I am excited. I hate that I feel that way. It reeks of the deepest betrayal of one's self. Only a few hours have passed since the fatality of my promotion, but seeing Reid here, like this, elicits a primitive reaction. I'm damn near helpless.

Is that the seam of a cod-piece I see? Yummy.

"I see someone perfect for Mr. Knight," the DJ announces as a stagehand places a chair for me to sit on.

Lizzie receives the same treatment with a chair and is sitting directly behind Grayson. She doesn't look too pleased about it either.

The DJ plays songs by NSYNC and NKOTB as our Euchre competitors give us lap dances and force our participation. I'm pleasantly surprised by Reid's agility and talent for dance. His hard muscles rub over my soft curves. My, oh my, has he got *The Right Stuff*.

Both men rip off their shirts in one swift motion at the same time, eliciting whistles from the crowd. Next, they yank off their pants, leaving them naked, save for the cod-pieces that are swinging in mine and Lizzie's faces.

Grayson works over Lizzie in a manner I consider surprisingly intimate for two friends. Obviously, they've slept together, so there is some chemistry. However, if they're in the friend-zone right now, I wouldn't expect to see Grayson massaging Lizzie's tits with that much enthusiasm.

Lizzie's entire body goes rigid as Grayson repositions her on his leg, bouncing his leg to give her a ride. Her body goes completely slack. Slack in a way that happens with a specific type of satisfaction. It would seem Lizzie and I have both trodden the fine line of exhibitionism today. From the corner of my eye, I see Grayson speaking to Lizzie, and she vigorously shakes her head. She scrambles off his leg and takes back her seat, gesturing for him to continue.

A mix of both bands' most famous songs are blended together for the grand finale. With the last beat and their backs to the audience, both men rip off the cod-pieces and give the Full Monty. I guess they technically fulfilled the details of the bet. I almost hate to admit that I'm turned on and enjoying the sight of Reid's partially erect cock at mouth level, the head so close it brushes against my lips. His penis is beautiful. I got to play with it this morning, but it feels like years ago. So much has happened since then. The roaring of women behind me brings my mind back to the boardroom. Never has an opportunity so graciously presented itself.

Lizzie storms off the stage, leaving Grayson standing there naked and exposed to everyone. Lizzie's actions are a sort of karma, I suppose. Grayson tried to manipulate the bet. Lizzie has ensured that he fulfills it. The Full Monty. From what I can see, Grayson has nothing to be ashamed of. Wow.

Reid pants heavily as the crowd hoots and claps. It seems the righteous thing for me to do is to follow Lizzie's lead and introduce Reid to my own brand of karma. In a quick gesture, I open my mouth and swallow his cock whole, down to the hilt. He grabs the back of my head, resting his cock on my tongue. The crowd falls eerily silent. I look up at Reid, forcing myself to have big doe-eyes to convey my so-called innocence.

He gazes down at me, and I can see the instant he realizes what I did. His eyes go wide, he pushes forward, and I swallow him to the back of my throat. He jerks back, slipping from my mouth and covering his manhood with his hands before he rushes off the stage, seeking cover.

I turn to my audience, wipe the saliva off the corners of my mouth, and give a big smile. The crowd erupts with cheers, rising to give me a standing ovation.

I take a bow, as is proper.

38

Reid

I pace in the dressing room backstage. I can't believe she did that. I'm pissed. No, I'm *livid*. I'm also the most turned on I've ever been in my life. *Fuck.*

I can smell her before I see her. Lavender and sex—that's how she always smells. I think that's how she manages to have men pander to her every demand. I slip into my jeans and turn to look her in the eye.

"What the hell was that?" I roar. I don't think I've ever been so angry. Not when Amanda died. Not when Frank couldn't be bothered to attend the funeral. For some reason, this woman is bringing out a completely foreign side of me, and I don't like it.

Sam stands there and stares, her arms folded. I think she's waiting for me to figure it out on my own. Don't worry, sweetheart, I get it.

"It's payback for the vibrator." The blue-tooth controlled vibrator. It must be the stupidest decision I have ever made. When I bought it, I thought it would, hell, I don't know what I thought. It seemed like fun, and maybe it would make the news of losing her promotion a little easier to take. Was this really about a vibrator? Or was it something else? "The vibrator and…"

I wait for her to fill in the blank, but she's too stubborn for that.

"And nothing," she finally answers.

"Nothing. Nothing else?"

She shakes her head.

I grab my leather jacket off a chair and slide into it. "I guess we don't have anything to talk about then."

I'm almost to the back exit when Sam speaks up. "How could you?"

I stop in my tracks, my heart sinking to my stomach. I walk back toward the dressing room and meet her on the threshold. She looks hurt, and I hate myself for being the one to make her feel that way.

"You knew," she says. "This whole time. You knew, and you didn't have the decency to tell me."

I rub the pad of my thumb across her cheek, reveling in the feel of her skin on mine. "It wasn't supposed to be that way. Frank was supposed to tell you. I'm sorry, sweetheart."

"Frank didn't tell me. You could have told me last week, last weekend, hell, even this morning. Anytime would have been better than for me to find out like that."

I haul her to me, our bodies flush. "You're right. I thought it would help take the edge off. Make the news easier to take. It was wrong. *I* was wrong." I bury my face in her neck, her silky soft hair tickling my cheek. "Forgive me. Please."

She deflates in my arms. "I guess I should apologize too. No matter what you did, you didn't deserve that," she says, pointing toward the stage.

I let out a small laugh. "You mean a blow job in front of a hundred wild women?"

"Men too. But, yeah. I'm sorry."

Yelling from several feet away catch our attention. We both turn to find Grayson and Lizzie in the other dressing room.

"What the fuck is going on?" Grayson shouts.

"*Nothing*. Everything is great," Lizzie yells back. "It's *none* of your business."

Grayson stomps to the door of the room. "The hell it isn't," he roars as the door slams shut.

"What's that about?" I ask Sam, pointing my thumb toward the closed door.

"Nothing I want to be a part of. So, anyway," Sam leads me by the hand to the bar area. "I booked us a suite a few days ago. Do you want to make up?"

"Depends."

"On what?"

"Which room."

"Guess you'll just have to take a chance if you want to find out," she says as she plucks a gold skeleton key from her purse.

After that show of exhibitionism on stage tonight, the chance to sink my cock into her hot, tight pussy has never been so inviting.

We walk through the back halls of the club, and I read the plaques on the wall with the designation of each room.

Toys Galore

Shipwrecked

Blackout

S&M

Sam slows down as we encounter the door for the S&M room. "Are we going where I think we're going?" If this is Sam's idea of taking it slow, I'd hate to think what her concept of too fast might be. Besides, after what happened in the boardroom today, I'm not in any kind of rush for whips or chains or anything.

She snickers, grabs me by the hand, and we pass a few more doors. A gold-plated plaque with *The Bubble Room* scrawled into it defines the character of this room.

Sam pulls the key back out of her purse and unlocks the door.

"The Bubble Room. I've heard about it, but I thought the

room was a myth. Like Atlantis or The Titanic." It's beautiful, swathed in light blues and creams with gold accents and a king-sized bed draped in ivory linens. I've spent every day for the past week at Whiskers rehearsing with Grayson. I've overheard a few conversations about some of the rooms upstairs, but I figured the anecdotes were blown out of proportion.

"The Titanic was real," Sam says, tossing her purse on the bed.

"I'm fucking with you. Listen, I need to talk to you about the Keogh thing." Some things from the meeting this morning keep coming back to me. Sam wanted me to be a part of the Keogh/BLH negotiations. I can't do it. It would be a massive conflict of interest, but the bigger issue is Silas Keogh. I don't want anything to do with that piece of shit. At all. Ever. "I'm not sure—"

She cuts me off. "No. No business talk. Only dirty talk."

Fuck, I love it when she talks dirty. I kick off my shoes and hop on the gigantic bed. "Fine. No business." I glance around while Sam lights several candles around the room. "What about this room makes it *The Bubble Room?*"

"Excellent question." She picks up a small bottle on the nightstand and pulls out a wand, blowing a plethora of bubbles toward me. "And..." she lifts a bottle of champagne from the chiller.

She takes her time unwrapping the cork, rubbing her thumb across the top like the head of a cock in a slow, sinuous gesture. She slides her free hand down the cool glass of the bottleneck, stroking it.

"Shit," I breathe out. Who knew champagne could be so erotic?

She tilts the bottle toward the corner of the room, away from me. The cork pops and the bubbles spray free, releasing the tension. She runs her tongue across the lip of the bottle, licking up the suds.

Holy fuck, that's hot, my cock pulses as I watch her. Not able to take it any longer, I stride toward her, taking the bottle from her hands and setting it back in the chiller. "There are about ten different things I can think to do with that champagne right now. Not one of them involves you wearing clothes."

She stretches behind her and begins to slowly unzip her dress, pushing the straps off her shoulders and letting the dress slide down her perfect body until it pools on the floor. She's standing in front of me in her bra and panties and the highest pair of shiny red heels I've ever seen.

She's a fucking dream. "You, Samantha Valentine, are the most disturbingly beautiful woman I have ever seen." And I mean it.

She smiles. My words might seem like an insult, but I know she understands what I mean. She knows me in a way nobody on Earth understands, and I get her too. She's kind, funny, sexy, and above all, challenging. These past two weeks have been the best I've had in a long time. I never thought in a million years that I would fall so quickly or easily after losing Amanda, but here I am.

Sam tugs at the button of my fly and escorts me toward the bathroom, laughing. "You have no idea how disturbing I can be."

39

Sam

Initially, I hoped to book the S&M room, with whips and a St. Andrew's cross, I could undoubtedly release some aggravation. However, with such short notice, and it being Ladies Night at Whiskers, the original plan was a no go. Ladies Night doesn't seem like the kind of event where such proclivities take place. However, there are plenty of men with power who love themselves some corporal punishment and just as many women who enjoy doling it out.

After talking out my thoughts in more detail with Tressa, we decided that The Bubble Room would fit my needs. Under the guise of forgiveness, I've lured Reid into my trap. It sounds cold-hearted when I put it that way. Maybe it is and maybe I am, but I think I was beginning to truly fall for him. For him to humiliate me in front of a room full of people, people who answer to me, who seek out my advice, who respect me—well, that is unforgivable. I may never get back what I lost, my promotion, but at least I'll feel a little better.

After stripping down to my bra and panties, I grab Reid by

the top of his pants and guide him toward the bathroom. He says I'm the most disturbingly beautiful woman he's ever seen.

I can't hold back my laugh. "You have no idea how disturbing I can be."

Once inside the massive shower stall, I unzip Reid's pants and tug them off his hips, dropping to my knees as I do. He's naked and glorious with an erection. I can't stop myself from licking my lips and giving a little flick of my tongue, craving the taste of him. I hate that I crave him.

"Not yet." He heaves me back up to a standing position.

With the height of these heels, we're almost nose to nose. Reid's cock notches at the V of my legs, teasing me. I'm aching for him. I hate that too. He dips his head into the crook of my neck and begins to suckle, and I'm nearly spineless.

"There are a few extraordinary features in this shower you won't find anywhere else in the world."

"That's nice," he mutters against my neck.

"No, I'm serious. You wanted to know what makes this room The Bubble Room. Well, this is it." I step out of his grasp and turn a knob on the opposite side of the hot/cold levers.

The lights on the other side of the glass door dim, and inside the shower steam rises. Soft, multi-colored lights beam down on us as bubbles fall from seemingly nowhere. It's like tripping on LSD.

Reid's eyes dilate, as I'm sure mine do, an intended side effect of the psychedelic effervescence of the bathroom in this suite.

"Wow. This is amazing," he says, capturing the falling bubbles.

"I told you," I tease. "Nothing else like it in the world."

Reid tugs me closer to him, my breasts gliding against his slick chest, the lace of my bra giving the perfect amount of friction against my nipples. He stares down at me and pushes my dampened hair off my shoulder.

"Yeah," he breathes. "Nothing like it in the world."

Reid's roaming hands run along my shoulders as he pushes off the straps of my bra. One hand cups my cheek, the other deftly unclips the clasp on the back, the garment becoming lost within the steam and bubbles. He bends at the knees and trails kisses across my chest. The path continues down my belly, giving no attention to my breasts which are achingly full, desperate for his touch. I hate that now too.

Just below my navel, he lays a slow, wet kiss as he hooks his fingers into the sides of my panties. Chills run down my spine and settle in my core.

He skims them over my knees and nuzzles into the bare flesh of my sex, inhaling deeply. "I love the way you smell."

That might be the sexiest thing I've ever heard. Now, I have to hate those sexually charged words. Bastard.

Reid pulls up one leg and slides off the shoe and then the other, resting my leg on his shoulder. "Do you know what else I love?"

"What?" I rasp.

"This beautiful, delectable pussy." He runs his tongue through my cleft until he finds my most tender spot, giving rough suction, as he glides two fingers inside my channel.

I stop breathing, an orgasm coming fast and hard as he pumps his fingers inside me and continues to lave at the delicate bud. I tug at his hair, trying to keep my balance, the act earning me a moan against my clit. "Oh, my God. Reid," I cry, feeling the wetness on his fingers as I come.

Reid abruptly removes his hand and mouth from my sex and stands. Gripping my ass, he hoists me up, compelling me to wrap my legs around his waist.

The steam is thick, I can barely see his face right in front of me. I'm smashed against the cold tile of the wall, the shaft of his cock pressed against my pussy. I wiggle, aching for friction. The right friction. The friction I now hate to love.

"You are the most amazing woman I have ever met. You drive me crazy." He pushes against me, rubbing like I want.

"Aggravating as hell."

These are not the words I want to hear. These are words just before a declaration, and I don't want to be around for that declaration because I'll have to hate that too. I might end up hating myself in the process. "I think the lights are getting to me. I need to step out for a minute."

"Are you okay?" he asks, setting my feet on the ground.

I rub my fingers along the stubble of his jaw. "Yeah," I assure him. "I just need some water."

Plucking up my shoes as I stride out of the shower, Reid falls in step behind me. Steam billows out of the stall, and I appreciate the magnificent artwork of the male condition before me. Every muscle is highlighted, and my mouth begins to water. "Stay. I'll be right back."

He nods and steps back behind the enclosure.

A complimentary robe hangs on the door and I cocoon my body and heart inside its high-grade terry cloth and step into the clear, well-lit bedroom. After a couple of sips from a bottle of water from the mini-fridge, I allow myself a deep breath. A quick glance at the clock tells me Tressa should be here any minute.

"Girl," Tressa announces as she strides through the door. Speak of the devil. The Latino bevy of the Chicago Drag Queen scene has arrived. She's dressed in a champagne sequined gown which gives her sienna skin an even brighter glow. "You wouldn't believe what it took to get here," she says with a Latino lilt.

Not for the first time, I find I'm struck by what a beautiful man she is when she's all decked out. Her stature is short, but with her heels and her hair styled into a modern version of the Beehive, she's quite imposing.

She tosses her purse on the couch next to the balcony. "Since school's back in session, Mommy's focused on the kids, and Daddy is more than happy to give me his money." She peels off one four-inch pump and begins to rub her feet. "But it's hell on the feet."

"You need to hurry up," I tell her, a sense of urgency hitting me. The last thing I want right now is for Reid to come out here and see me with Tressa. I start unzipping her gown. "He's in the shower right now."

She swats my hand away and finishes undressing, except her thong. I can only see her from the back, but man, she must work those buns six days a week. I could bounce a quarter off that ass.

"Did you start the bubbles? Is it steamy in there? I'm not going to make it far if you didn't."

"Yes," I hiss, losing my patience.

I scramble around the room, shoving myself back into my clothes, slip on my shoes, and grab my purse.

As soon as Tressa's hand turns the knob, Reid calls out, "Are you coming back?"

I holler over Tressa's shoulder as she pushes the door open, "Coming!" I hook my fingers into the waistband of Tressa's undergarments, yank them down to her ankles, and shove her into the bathroom.

40

Reid

A drag queen? A goddamn drag queen. I knew Sam was pissed, but a drag queen? My mind is still reeling. Thanks to the steam in that shower, I couldn't see his face. Instead, I found out when I had a handful of dick. The screaming didn't help matters. Mine or his. As soon as I heard the low-pitched howl, I lost it. Socked him right in the eye. He got me with a refined uppercut. When we found ourselves tousling on the floor of the shower, we both separated quickly. My body was making way too much contact with another man's junk. I don't know that he had as much of a problem with it as I did.

I arrive at the office late on Monday. I crave Sam's warm smile and wicked gleam, but everything is still so fresh, I want to give her the space she needs. It took every ounce of restraint to keep from calling her over the weekend. I'm not sure if I wanted to make love or spank that pretty ass red. I can't help but laugh. I've never had a thought like that cross my mind. What I shared with Amanda was precious. She was beautiful, devoted, and sweet. I never imagined I could fall for another woman. I was certain no one could compete with what we had.

However, there is no competition, Sam and Amanda are as different as night and day. Sam is sex and spunk wrapped in a sexy red dress; love mixed with pain. Just like I did with Amanda, I've fallen fast and hard. Even though I found myself in a shower with a drag queen, I can't say I didn't deserve it. What I did, how I handled it, was wrong. Sure, I'm not the only guilty person in this situation, but Sam was right. I had plenty of chances to tell her, and I made the decision not to. Everything was going so well, I just wanted it to last a little longer. Let us stay in our safe bubble right up to the last second.

When we were in that steamy shower, the lights, the bubbles, her beautiful face, I knew. It hit me like a ton of bricks. For all her flaws, her competitiveness, her big heart, I love this woman. I wanted to tell her right that instant. I couldn't imagine another second passing without proclaiming my feelings, but she stopped me. Then I found out why.

I still can't get over it. It was cruel.

And creative.

I sit across the hall, staring into Sam's office where Ben is a sentinel. I want to go in there and see if we can't call a truce. She had her payback, now let's go back to where we were. Put it all behind us. However, there is one tiny detail I can't ignore. A detail that I wanted to talk about last week, but Sam didn't want to discuss business. That thought has the wheels turning.

I need to talk to Frank.

"Is Frank in?" I ask Delores, stopping at her desk.

"Yes, sir, he is. How's your day going? Do anything fun over the weekend?"

"Better, now that I've seen you. You look beautiful today," I deflect, giving her a huge smile.

She casts her eyes downward and plays shy. She's not. "Congratulations on the promotion by the way," she says, although I'm sure she knew my fate the moment Frank clutched his chest. "If I may be forward, I think you're better suited for the position than Ms. Valentine."

For whatever reason, Delores has it in for Sam. "Oh, yeah? Why's that?"

She shrugs her shoulders. "I don't think her lifestyle fits well with so much responsibility. She has a *reputation* you know."

"I see." I think back to that moment behind the waterfall in Barbados. Sam said the standard for success was different for men than women. At the time, I thought she was kind of paranoid, but now I get it. "Ask yourself this, Delores. If we were talking about a man with the same reputation, would your opinion change?"

She blanches. At least she has enough sense to realize her judgmental ways. Maybe.

"I'll talk to you later."

"Yes, sir."

I walk into Frank's office, not bothering to knock.

"Son," he cheers. "Come in. How are you? How are you, my boy?"

"It's looking up." I sit across from his desk and cross my legs. "Closed on my new apartment today."

"Wonderful. When do you move?"

"This weekend." And it isn't soon enough. When I moved back from Barbados, I didn't bring anything with me but clothes. I'd sleep there tonight if I could, but I need to shop for furniture and housewares first.

Frank's face flashes with sadness. "Well, I'm sorry that you're leaving. It's been nice having someone to talk to."

Frank makes it sound like we had wonderful dinners every night with stimulating conversation. Real father-son bonding type of shit. It's a figment of his imagination.

"I know Stella will be sorry to see you go," he adds.

That I believe.

"That was a shitty thing you did to Sam." I switch topics quickly before he becomes too comfortable.

"Hmm? What was?"

"I thought we agreed you would tell her." I knew he wouldn't tell her. I could have pushed it on him harder. Then again, maybe I preferred the truth stay buried for as long as possible.

"I did," Frank says adamantly.

"That's right. You did. At the same time as forty other people. She was fucking *blindsided,*" I yell. I'm losing my temper, and I'm not sure who I'm angrier with—me, Frank, or Sam. Regardless, Frank deserves it.

Delores appears in the doorway. "I'll give you men some privacy," she says, closing the office door behind her.

Frank lets out a sigh, rubbing a hand over his bald head. "I know. You're right. I wanted to tell her, I was just—"

"Chicken-shit?"

"No. Concerned. Concerned how she'd take the news. You know, she's wrangling that BLH/ Keogh deal. I didn't want it to backfire. That money could keep us in the black."

In the black? "You didn't say anything about Sterling having money troubles."

"Oh, no. We're not. It's just that, with me stepping down, Sterling may hit some rough waters. It doesn't take much for people to get scared. This would be a nice cushion."

"Whose idea was it that I should become a part of these negotiations?" Silas Keogh is the bane of my existence. Just thinking about him makes me want to punch a fucking wall. We have a long history and a shared mutual disdain for each other. Frank knows this.

"Sam's," he answers matter-of-factly.

"Does she know?" I'm curious to see if Sam's anger toward me runs deeper than the stunt I pulled on Friday.

"I couldn't say."

Trying to make progress with Frank is like herding cats. I've gotten absolutely nowhere and my mind is reeling with uncertainty as I walk back to my office. I'm willing to bet money that Sam knows about Amanda and Silas. This is a game-changer. This means Sam knew what was going on all along.

She played the victim when she had been planning to run me off from the very beginning.

I send a text to Grayson.

Reid: "I saw a flyer for women's mudwrestling on Wednesday. You in?"

Grayson is Sam's friend, and over the past couple of weeks, I've gotten to know him quite well, mainly because of rehearsals for our Ladies Night event. He's a good guy and treats his employees like royalty. He's not what I expected from the owner of a strip joint.

Grayson: "Absolutely."

Reid: "Great. I'm going to need a favor."

Grayson: "Anything."

If there's one thing I know, it's that Sam isn't the kind of woman to go down without a fight, and a fight is precisely what she'll get.

41

Sam

"**I** can't believe I agreed to this," I mutter as Grayson and I charge through the throngs of people milling around in a dingy bar. Grayson texted me on Monday asking if I wanted to go out tonight. I thought, What the hell, I don't have anything better to do. It's not like I'm going to be entertaining a certain job-stealing, egotistical jerkoff because I hate him.

I also miss him. I liked him. Like really liked him, but it doesn't matter. I'm here now, and I'm about to watch some girls get down and dirty in the mud. On a Wednesday. Hump day. Sadly, this is not a day that I will get to be humped. We find the perfect table, situated front, and center, giving unobstructed views of two women in bikinis tousling around in a large kiddy pool filled with mud. Grayson orders a pitcher of beer.

"Sure you don't want a Cosmo?" I tease.

He glowers at me. I guess he has to play macho tonight. I shrug my shoulders. He doesn't scare me. I fiddle with my phone, hoping for a text or email from Reid. Nothing. I haven't heard a word from him since last Friday. Not even at the office.

His door has been closed every time I look. It's a pretty safe bet that he's avoiding me.

"You're not going to find what you're looking for on your phone. What you seek is about to be sprayed down with a hose filled with ice-cold water," Grayson says, accepting the pitcher of beer and pouring two glasses.

"That's what you're looking for," I scoff, returning to my phone, considering sending Reid a text. I'm realistic enough to acknowledge that I'm not entirely innocent in this situation. Hiring Tressa may have been a step too far. Honestly though, how far is too far when someone steals your promotion? A promotion they knew you were promised and knew you weren't going to get. Of course, let us not forget the vibrator. That took it to a whole different level.

Grayson leans over the table and snatches the phone from my hands. "Hey," I whine, lunging toward him to get it back.

He shoves it into the pocket of his suit jacket. "You can have it back when we leave."

I sit back in my chair and fold my arms, giving Grayson my fiercest glare.

"Stop it. The good part is coming up."

I turn my attention to the pool twenty feet in front of me, and the MC makes an announcement.

"Ladies and gentlemen, the moment you've been waiting for. Undefeated for three years and counting, and certainly our *biggest* attraction. Give it up for the one, the only *Ginger*." The crowd cheers and the curtains behind him sweep to the side on cue.

The largest woman I have ever seen emerges into the lights. Her forehead protrudes over her brow line, and I wonder if she has a glandular problem like Andre the Giant. Her outfit reminds me of a high school wrestling uniform and what must be a specially-made sports bra beneath it. Her hair is frizzy and red, seemingly as angry and imposing as her demeanor.

"Holy shit," I gasp.

"Just wait," Grayson tells me.

The MC walks up to Ginger, and she towers over him. "Ginger, I hear you have an ax to grind tonight. What's the story?"

Ginger takes the microphone from the MC. "A friend of mine was recently betrayed by someone very special to him."

My heart sinks to the pit of my stomach.

"Oh, man," the MC says, shaking his head. "What happened?"

"My friend was ashamed. He didn't tell me a lot, but he did say he trusted her with his whole heart, and she betrayed this gift with..." She pauses for effect, "a drag queen."

No. Way.

My heart instantly starts to hammer in my chest.

"That's terrible. What a lousy thing to do," the MC says. "Tell me, Ginger. Is this woman here tonight?"

Ginger turns and points her index finger at the crowd, slowly scanning the room until she finds me and stops. "She is."

All heads turn in my direction, their eyes assessing and judging me. I turn around, hoping there is someone behind me, and Ginger is actually pointing to them. Unfortunately, for me, I'm surrounded by men. I slink down in my chair, embarrassed and utterly terrified.

"A drag queen?" Grayson asks, turning toward me.

I stare up at him and blink, giving a sheepish grin. My mind is in a state of shock that has me trying to become one with the metal seat.

"She's pointing at you," he verifies. Grayson lets out a low whistle. "Whatever you did, it must've been bad," he mutters, shaking his head with disappointment.

I swallow the rising vomit.

"Sam, I'm talking about you." Ginger is calling me out to the crowd, the spotlight focusing on me, and I'm beginning to drip with sweat.

"Did I miss anything?" I hear the words spoken from a too familiar voice.

I turn my head to find Reid pulling up a chair.

"Just in time," Grayson tells him, stretching across the table for a handshake.

Fucking traitor.

"What's the matter, Sam?" Reid asks, bending over to stare down at me from above. "Scared?"

Hell yes, I'm scared. Ginger will tear me to shreds. Still slouched, I look toward the mud pool and see Ginger wave to Reid with her fingers, hunching her shoulders to appear demure. Nothing in this entire world could make that woman demure.

Grayson's act of treason on our friendship, and Reid going out of his way to pay me back for the entire Tressa debacle begins to fan an ember of anger. As unjustified as my emotions may be, I'm pissed. I swiftly sit up, my back ramrod straight, take a deep breath, embrace my anger, tamp down my fear, and stand. I give Ginger a tilt of my chin, telling her that I accept her challenge. The stark white power suit I chose this morning was meant to give me the courage I needed to face Reid in the office. That moment didn't happen as I planned. I remove my jacket and toss it at Grayson, he catches it and gives me a smile, no doubt delighted to see how this will go down. I remove both white heels and fling them at Reid, one at a time. "I don't back down from a challenge. Not even one as asinine as this."

42

Sam

The rumble of the crowd approaches deafening levels as I walk to the pool and stand directly in front of Ginger. I'm so close, I can see the three hairs splitting out of the mole on her chin. Hairy mole or not, I can't deny the fact that she is going to slaughter me. Every instinct screams at me to sprint to the back door illuminated by the green exit sign fifty feet away.

"Sam, Sam, Sam. Tell me it's not true," the MC says, shaking his head and positioning the microphone in front of my mouth for a response.

"Oh, it's true, Mike." I don't know the guy's name, but he has a microphone, so Mike seems appropriate. "And I'll tell you something else. Andrea the Giant over here," I point toward Ginger, "she doesn't know shit."

The crowd bellows their approval.

Ginger stomps her feet on the ground like a bull about to charge. I will not show fear. I stare into Ginger's deep-set green eyes as we step into the pool, my feet instantly caked with goop. We circle each other, both of us waiting to see who strikes first.

My eyes are trained on the Amazonian in front of me. Before I can process what is going on, I'm weightless. I've been hoisted at least eight feet in the air, and the room is spinning.

Scratch that.

I'm spinning.

"And she's *in* the *air*." Mike is a little too happy. "Oh *man*."

Ginger may be large, but she is quick. The change in gravity was instantaneous, requiring several twirls around the bar to realize what was happening. One second, I'm standing in cold mud, the next she plucked me from where I stood by my armpit and groin and began spinning me around with impressive centrifugal force.

The ground comes at me too quickly as I dive toward the pool of mud, Ginger keeping a tight hold around my waist. I slide into the muck on my belly, my face pushing the silt toward the edges.

"Ginger is holding nothing back tonight," Mike announces.

My vision blurs, and I quickly swipe at my eyes, rolling over to better assess the threat. The threat is real and stomping toward me, the mud jiggling with each step Ginger takes. I flail my arms as she bends over, trying to grab at me, and I flip over, back onto my belly, scrambling between her legs, and fighting valiantly to get to my feet.

"I don't know about you guys, but I think it's getting awfully hot in here." Mike grabs the hose and squeezes the trigger, spraying freezing water directly onto me and my opponent. The crowd roars with excitement.

My blouse is drenched and torn at the buttons, my bra exposed and my nipples hard. The little bit of coverage I have from my shirt seems to be more of a hindrance than helpful. I grasp the edges of my top and rip the buttons off and whip the sodden, destroyed, silk garment to the ground. The whistles from men in the crowd do nothing to deter me. I find the laser focus needed to defeat my giant. My Goliath.

Ginger and I are at opposite ends of the pool, circling each other, looking for the perfect moment to pounce. Her left ankle rolls slightly, and her balance waivers the tiniest bit. It's the opportunity I need, and it may be her only weakness.

With my chin tucked into my chest and my shoulders poised to take aim, I barrel straight toward her. My shoulder crashes into her surprisingly firm stomach, and spikes of pain radiate down my arm. I ignore the burning ache and wrap my arms around her as tightly as I can. Ginger lets out a breathy *harumph* as we both lose our balance, sending us plummeting to the concrete floor, the mud doing little to soften our fall.

Ginger wiggles, trying to gain an advantage, but I'm straddling her, and I know my one-hundred and twenty-seven pounds won't be enough to subdue this mammoth. I stand, keeping my knees bent, trying to maintain a balanced center of gravity as I grab her arm and twist it toward her back, forcing her to roll over. Her face is hovering above the muck, and I drive her head right into it and sit on her back, reaching over to pull one of her legs backward toward her filthy butt.

"One," Mike begins to count. "Two," And the crowd begins to count with him. "Three," he hoots. "For those of you betting on the underdog, *this* is your night." He joins me in the middle of the mud pool, muddying his shiny showman shoes. Ginger groans at my feet. Mike raises my hand, "Ladies and gentlemen, our victor!"

The crowd cheers and I hate that I can't enjoy this moment for the monumental achievement it is but knowing Reid set this up, and enlisted Grayson to help, takes the air out of my party balloon. I yank my wrist from Mike's hand feeling a desperate need to get the hell out of here and make my way back to the table where Grayson and Reid are sitting.

I stand before both men, giving them a hard stare. No. I won't let anyone ruin this. I won. No matter what Reid says or does, it cannot take this victory away from me. I kicked a *giant's* ass.

"That was fucking *awesome*," Grayson picks me up and

swings me around, my grubby clothes ruining his shirt. I want to celebrate with him, he's my best friend, but he's recently enlisted with the other side. Whether or not he knows there are two sides doesn't matter. By default, he picked Reid.

When he sets me down, I stumble a bit, still trying to recover from the roller coaster ride that was Ginger. Grayson sets me right, and I take a deep breath as I guzzle down the beer straight from the pitcher, the drink soothing my nerves and spilling down my neck as I drink too fast. I snatch my suit jacket off the back of my chair and sling it over my shoulder with one finger.

"You're an asshole," I declare, pointing at Grayson.

I don't bother acknowledging Reid as he takes a sip from his beer bottle, smug satisfaction written all over his handsome face.

Oh, it's on.

43

Sam

It's time to talk to Frank. I can't keep avoiding this, and I deserve answers. As much as I blame Reid, ultimately, the responsibility was Frank's. He had the moral burden to tell me before I stepped into that meeting. With a vibrator in my panties.

"Good morning, Delores," I greet. She's keeping guard outside Frank's office. "Is he busy?"

She peers up from her computer and raises an eyebrow before going back to typing. "He is."

I'm not in the mood to deal with her today. After I got home last night, I took the longest bath of my life. The water was filthy, and my muscles ached so badly I could barely sleep. I tossed and turned all night. Missing Reid in my bed, snuggling into his warm chest, feeling him inside me. A deep breath and my back would twinge, which only reminded me of how we've gotten here. Maybe Ginger tossing me around the pool knocked some sense into me because I began to see things very clearly. War has been declared. The most effective way to win a war is to start from the beginning. So, this thing with Frank will be figured out today.

I stride into Frank's office, not giving a flying fuck what Delores says, and find Frank on the phone.

"I'll be fine. A few more days," he says to someone on the line. He looks up to see me, and his eyebrows lift into his hairline. I'm sure I don't have a jovial quality to my face at the moment.

"I'll call you back. Fine. Tomorrow," he adds brusquely.

"Sam." It's the first time he's ever called me "Sam" in the entire time I've worked here. "What can I do for you? Please, come in."

I take a seat in front of him and cross my ankles, keeping my spine straight and strong. "What happened?" There's no need to explain precisely what I'm referring to. He's a smart man, he knows.

He clears his throat as he picks up a cigar from a box perched on the edge of his desk. He offers one to me, and I decline.

To sit conveys weakness and that is not the impression I want to give. I decide to stand, making me the taller one while he sits in his fancy leather chair. By doing this, I believe it shifts the power to me, or so I tell myself. I make my way to the liquor on the bureau behind him and pour three fingers of scotch, taking a large swallow. It's smooth and smoky. Frank has excellent taste. I lean against the chest and stare him down as he clips off the end of his cigar.

He takes his time, lighting and puffing until the tip glows orange. "I know this wasn't what you expected."

This isn't a conversation. I want to know the story, so I take another sip of my scotch.

He takes the hint. "I had a heart attack."

I don't know what I was expecting, but to hear that my mentor is mortal is a shock. He had mentioned in the meeting that he had some health issues, but to hear the specifics makes it... real.

"I was scared," Frank admits. "Reid and I hadn't talked

for almost five years. I thought I was going to die. I...I wanted, needed, to make amends somehow."

I take a deep breath, saddened at hearing my boss's confession. "I'm sorry, Frank. I had no idea."

"I know you didn't. Only Stella, Reid, and Delores knew. Delores was here when it happened. She's the one who called nine-one-one. Anyway, I had a heart cath. They put in a few stents, and I was all better, or, so I thought."

He undoes the top four buttons of his shirt and pushes the collar to the side. There's an IV right beneath his collarbone. "Turns out, I had some issues with my kidneys. I didn't know. The Cath was emergent, they didn't have any lab work back yet when they took me. The dye that they used hurt my kidneys. They don't work anymore. Now, three days a week I'm hooked up to a machine to clean my blood."

It's starting to make sense now. "So, that's why you bumped up your retirement?"

He lets out a deep breath. "Yeah. Dialysis is exhausting. I'm not going to be able to keep up much longer."

No wonder he's been looking awful the past few weeks. "Why didn't you tell me about this before? Why wait for a meeting, in front of the entire company, for me to find out that I'm not taking your place? The whole thing was shitty, Frank."

He takes another puff of his cigar. "You're right. I'm sorry, Sam. I should have told you sooner. I wanted to, believe me. I was afraid that you would quit. Reid might be taking my place, but he can't do this on his own. He's going to need you. Sterling needs you."

Shit. "You're probably right. I would have quit." And had I quit, the BLH/ Keogh deal would have dissolved. "I don't like the way you dealt with it, and I hate that you're sick Frank, but I understand. I don't like it, at all, but I understand."

He continues to puff on his cigar. A cigar he shouldn't be smoking in his condition, but Frank is a big boy. He knows what he needs to do.

"How's the Keogh deal coming along?"

"Reid's on board." I assume since we haven't spoken about it yet. "He's having a dinner meeting with Bennett tonight. I think he needs some convincing that Reid can handle the job."

Frank's son has become an obstinate pain in my ass. Ben helped me try to arrange a time with Reid to discuss the ins and outs of the deal, but Delores said he was too busy, now that she was organizing his schedule. The VP and soon-to-be President of Sterling are not on talking, or even being in the same room, terms. It's embarrassing. Explaining to Tate why I felt it was essential that someone else represent BLH was equally embarrassing. So much failure in the span of a week is not good for one's ego.

"Don't worry about that, Samantha. If anyone can convince him, it's my boy."

I'm Samantha again. He must be feeling better about the whole thing now. "I hope so." It bothers me that Tate is hesitant to accept this change. "Any idea why Bennett might not want to work with Reid? Anything I should know about?" A sense of déjà vu sweeps over me.

Frank takes one last puff on his cigar and stubs it out in an ashtray. "Nope."

44

Reid

Andrea the Giant. She called Ginger "Andrea the Giant" to her face. Fuck that takes guts. I ran into the larger than life woman at a convenience store on my way home Monday. After talking to Frank, I was confident Sam was hell-bent on making me miserable. So, the next logical step when someone strikes is the counterstrike. Ginger was my weapon of choice. Grayson was all too happy to help. He didn't want to know the specifics but was giddy with the prospect of Sam mudwrestling other women. I might have left out the part about Ginger on purpose. I don't think he would have gone for it if I told him.

I've managed to stay out of Sam's line of sight for today, but I need to get this thing with BLH underway. Delores set up a dinner meeting with Tate Bennett at Agostino's, some posh Italian restaurant. The host escorts me to the table where the server and Bennett are waiting. Not a good sign, the client should never be the one to wait. Bennett's already drinking a beer, so I order one as well.

"Mr. Bennett, it's a pleasure meeting you," I tell him as we shake hands.

"Same to you Mr. Gallagher. I hope you don't mind," Tate says, "but I took the liberty of ordering for us. I have somewhere to be by nine."

What kind of man orders another man's dinner? "Of course not." I sit back in my chair. "So, tell me your thoughts."

He takes a swig of his beer. "Can you be more specific?"

He knows what I'm asking. I want to know his thoughts on me taking over for Sam on this side of the account, but I'll play the game. "A decision had to be made. We believe it's best for you if I take over BLH's side of negotiations. What are your thoughts and concerns? The more I know, the better I can represent you."

The waiter comes back and drops off my beer and a platter of something which resembles ravioli. Bennett forks a few pieces onto his plate. "I hope you don't have a shellfish allergy. They're crab-stuffed."

That's precisely why a man should never order for another man—the possibility he will try to kill him with food. "Nope, no food allergies."

"Good. As for my concerns, I have a few. It should be noted that Keogh was the one who brought this idea to sell to Sam."

Sam? It seems informal for a client to refer to his broker by her first name, but maybe it's by design. I can imagine Sam insisting on being called by her first name to give the impression of accessibility and friendliness. It's a solid approach, one I used myself back in the day. Apparently, Mr. Bennett and I will not have that kind of relationship.

"And," he continues, "to sell specifically to BLH. Keogh says he's looking to make some cutbacks and wants to save jobs, and that's why he wants to sell to us. It's one of BLH's core foundations to keep employees happy and provide a livable wage because, without them, we would be nothing. We recognize that."

Every company makes that claim.

He cuts into a portion of ravioli. "I know you're thinking,

'that's what every company says,' but in this case, it's true."

"Understood." I take a bite of my ravioli.

"I'm glad we got that out of the way. Now, tell me a little bit about yourself."

This almost feels like a job interview, but I suppose it would be wise for a man to have a better understanding of the person negotiating billions of dollars on his behalf. I launch into the rehearsed answers: top of my class, selling real estate in New York, successful past deals—the usual song and dance.

"And what have you been doing for the past few years?"

The way Bennett says it, the hard look on his face, tells me he must have investigated my background. No point in trying to deny anything. I'm just going to be honest—I have nothing to be ashamed of. "When my wife died, I had a tough time dealing with it. So, I picked up and started over. In Barbados."

"I'm sorry to hear that," Bennett says, looking like he means it.

I tell him about some of my hobbies and interests in an effort to humanize myself, make myself approachable and trustworthy.

"You like racing?" he says, picking up on the detail about my Ducati. The Ducati that I will forever kick myself for leaving in Barbados. At the time, I decided I was better off leaving everything from my former life behind, starting fresh. A therapeutic cleansing of sorts. Sold it for my plane ticket back to Chicago. Sad, but true.

"You know, Sam's into racing too? Maybe she can take you out sometime? You should ask her."

I had almost forgotten about that. When Sam and I had ridden my bike to the beach, and she told me she had an Aston Martin Vulcan, I about came in my pants right then and there. A twinge of jealousy surfs down my spine. "You seem to know Sam pretty well."

"I do. We're good friends," Bennett answers.

"How good?" I hate that I'm jealous. I don't know why the

idea of her being with another man pisses me off so much.

"It doesn't matter, it's in the past."

Fuck. Is there a single man left in Chicago who she hasn't screwed?

The waiter drops off our main course, and I'm grateful for the few minutes reprieve to harness my anger. It smells delicious. Linguini with clam sauce? I can't complain. Not about the food anyway.

"What made you decide to come back?" Bennett asks, his tone bouncing back to friendly.

"Guess I thought I needed to get back into the game of life. I couldn't hide out there forever, and after Frank's heart attack, I knew it was time."

"So, your father becomes ill, and you don't want to have any regrets?"

He hit the nail on the head. "Pretty much."

"I bet it doesn't hurt that he promised you his company, does it?"

I wipe the corners of my mouth with my napkin, set it next to my plate, and stand to leave. I've had enough of this guy's shit. "I don't think this is going to work. We'll have to find someone else to work with you."

"Sit," Bennett says, not looking up from his food, swirling the noodles with a fork and spoon.

I do as he asks, not because I want to, but because this deal needs to work. I can't blow this. This will be my first act as President of Sterling. It's a statement. A strong statement that my employees and future clients will judge me by.

"You rile pretty easily. You're going to need to get that under control if you have any hopes of warring with Keogh," Bennett says. "He's your biggest motivation and your biggest weakness. He's a real son of a bitch, but you knew that already, didn't you?"

45

Sam

Silas Keogh has been insistent on meeting face to face, which I dubiously accommodate, and meet up with him in the Keogh Tower bar after work on Thursday.

"This is ridiculous, Sam. I don't know where they got these numbers, but Keogh Tower is worth three times this amount. The name alone is worth its weight in gold."

Christ, his ego is big. I don't know how his head ever made it through the doors. His belief as to the worth of Keogh Tower is grossly overestimated. "It is, for sure, but you're looking to sell. Not to mention, to a specific buyer. BLH is the one with the advantage. You have to know that."

Keogh scribbles down a number on a piece of paper and passes it to me. I peek at it. It's still too high, but more in the realm of possibility.

"Okay," I nod. "As we discussed before, I'm having Reid Gallagher take over BLH's negotiations from here on out. So, I'll take this to Reid and have him talk to BLH. See what we can't come up with." I called Silas yesterday and discussed the decision to split up my duties with another member of the Sterling team. First, he seemed peeved, but when I told him Frank's son was the person taking over that side of negotiations, he broke out into a deep maniacal laugh. The throaty gruff of his borderline insanity was unnerving.

"How is Reid?" he asks.

It's interesting that Silas refers to Reid by his first name, which seems terribly cozy for someone he's never met. "Okay, I guess. He's adjusting, we're all adjusting. It's a lot to take in with Frank stepping down sooner than planned. Can I ask you a question, for the sake of full disclosure?" My meeting with Frank left me with a sick feeling, and Silas's reaction to Reid taking over is not helping. I figure I might as well ask the man himself.

"Go on," he says, nonplussed.

"There's history between you and Reid." I state it as a fact, but it's more like instinct. "What's the deal?"

He looks down into his glass. I'm not sure what he's been drinking, the tumbler was sitting in front of him when I arrived. His face looks pained, and for the first time, I see a man and not a billionaire.

"Several years back Reid worked for Keogh Real Estate. We had a disagreement. It ended on bad terms. He quit, and I was grateful."

Waging War 101: Know your enemy's history. I've failed that course with flying colors. I've been so preoccupied with trying to annihilate Reid, that I've fumbled the most basic steps. I'm seriously disappointed in myself. "Do you think you have it in for Reid?" I'm eager to get to the root of the issue, make up some of my missteps. "And by that, I mean, do you think we can make this relationship and all further negotiations work? Or is this going to be some kind of nightmare where you two fight to the death?"

He lets out a sardonic laugh. "I'm already dead. I think part of Reid is too." He tosses a twenty-dollar bill on the bar and walks away.

I'm not sure what happened, but I don't have long to dwell on it when my phone rings, Lizzie's face popping up on the screen. When I answer, she's all sobs, and I can barely make out a word she's saying. All I catch is that she's at Whiskers and the words "Grayson," "pregnant," and "bleeding" jumbled with wailing.

"I'll be right there. Don't go anywhere."

I flag down a cab, and with rush hour traffic, it takes close to forty minutes to arrive at Whiskers. I wave to Brutus as I exit the car and run toward the door. "Hey. I'm looking for Lizzie. Any idea where I can find her?" Starting with Brutus is my best shot. I don't want to go around bringing attention to Lizzie or me when I don't know what happened, or if Grayson knows anything yet.

"In her office. Stacey called and told me to tell you where to find them. Lizzie doesn't want anyone to know anything. Whatever that anything is."

"Thanks, Brutus." I give him a quick peck on the cheek and run through the doors.

There are several stares as I rush in, and I slow my run to a purposeful walk and climb the steps. As I stride down the hall, I stay vigilant for any signs of Grayson, but there doesn't seem to be a single person in sight. When I open the door to Lizzie's office, I find her on her couch, pale as a ghost and sweating like a pig. Stacey, one of the dancers, is sitting next to her and rubbing Lizzie's back, cooing encouraging words.

"It'll be okay," Stacey says. "God has a plan."

I'm not sure those words are bringing any comfort to Lizzie as she begins to hiccup between sobs.

"What happened?" I bend at the knees to glimpse into Lizzie's eyes, and she looks scared out of her mind.

"She started having cramps," Stacey says. "Then she started bleeding."

"Shit," I mutter. I sweep away the sweat-drenched hair along

Lizzie's forehead. "Sweetie, we need to take you to the ER."

Lizzie nods, her entire body shaking as she bawls.

When we arrive at the hospital, we sit in the waiting room for over an hour. The person at the front desk said something about the sickest going first. To which I said, "She has a baby dying inside of her. It doesn't get more serious than that."

The secretary replied, "Tell that to the guy whose wife shot him in the balls."

As much as I wanted to, I couldn't find a valid argument to that. Ball-less guy wins this round.

Lizzie sits in a chair and stares at the TV broadcasting *CNN*. "So much hate in this world. Do I want to bring a baby into this shit?" she asks, but not to me. I'm not sure she realizes I'm here.

"Hey." I give Lizzie's shoulders a light shake and force her to look me in the eyes. "It'll be all right. Everything will be fine."

She nods and closes her eyes as she leans back, laying her head on my shoulder. "Grayson was going to be a dad. Now he's not," she whispers.

"Did you tell him?"

"No, and good thing too, seeing as how—" she breaks off and starts to cry again.

An eternity later, a nurse calls her name. As I get up to go with her, the nurse stops me. "Ma'am, we're going to help her get changed, start an IV. Once we get her settled, we'll call you back."

Lizzie slides into the wheelchair in front of the nurse and gives me a small wave as she rolls through the double doors to the other side.

This is as good an opportunity as any. I dial Grayson.

"Hello?"

"Are you in the middle of anything?" I'm trying to sound normal, but I'm not sure it's working.

"Just the usual. What's up?"

"I'm at the hospital. With Lizzie."

"Is everything okay?" he asks, his voice cracking.

"I'm not sure. I thought maybe you should be here."

"Yeah. Yeah. I'm on my way now."

"Good. Text me when you get here. I'll meet you outside the ER doors. I need to talk to you about something first."

He agrees, and we disconnect as Lizzie's nurse calls for me to come back. When I walk into the curtained off room, Lizzie looks small and fragile dressed in a blue striped gown and hooked up to tubes and wires.

"Hey," I greet, giving her a kiss on the forehead.

"I'm going to take a nap. I'm tired."

"Whatever you want, sweetie."

Lizzie closes her eyes, and her head lolls to the side of the plastic pillow.

The nurse turns down the lights and hands me the call button. She shows me how to get a hold of the staff and how to work the TV. "Brian, the physician's assistant, will be in shortly."

I tell her thanks and settle on a rerun of *Gunsmoke*. Lizzie's light snoring tells me she's asleep.

My phone vibrates in my pocket, and I find a text from Grayson.

Grayson: "I'm outside."

Me: "I'll be right out."

46

Sam

Outside, I find Grayson leaning against a wall next to the ambulance bay. I wave my hand toward a bench by the ER doors because news like this shouldn't be told when standing.

"What's going on? Lizzie all right?" he asks, taking a seat on the bench.

"I don't know how to say this."

His eyes go wide, tears forming.

Oh my God. "She's fine. She's alive," I clarify, realizing the impression I must have given. "But things are still..." I can't find the words. "I'm just going to come right out and say it. She's pregnant."

Grayson turns pale, no doubt stunned by the news. After a few minutes, he turns to look at me. "Is it..."

"Yours?" I fill in. "Yes."

He scrubs his hand down his face and starts pacing. "Why didn't she tell me? Jesus. I have the right to know. God, she must've been so fucking scared. Shit."

"Please, sit back down," I beg. "That's not all." Once he's

seated next to me, I continue. "She started to have some cramping and bleeding tonight. I brought her to the hospital and called you. I'm not sure if the baby's going to make it."

"*Fuck*," he roars. "I lost a baby that I just found out existed five seconds ago? Is that what you're saying?"

"Yes. No. Maybe. We don't know anything yet. She's in a room sleeping. She's exhausted. Right now, they're running some tests. Hopefully, we'll have a better idea soon."

Grayson gives a violent shake of his head and storms past me and into the ER waiting room. I follow close behind, and my heart breaks as he speaks to the receptionist. His tone is clipped, but the secretary must recognize it for what it is—anguish. She presses a button and points down a corridor as the double doors open.

He walks like a man with a purpose as he navigates the maze of hallways to Lizzie's bed. I know where we need to go, but I don't interfere. Grayson needs to do this.

When he reaches Lizzie's curtain, I stop him. "She doesn't know I called you. I know this is a lot to take in. Try and remember Lizzie is just as scared. She needs you to be strong right now," I whisper.

Grayson takes a deep breath as if he's reining in his anger and nods. As we're about to walk into the room, a tall, young man in scrubs swoops past us, and we follow.

"Elizabeth Anderson?" the tall man asks.

Grayson and I huddle in a corner, trying to stay out of the way.

Lizzie looks to me and Grayson, wringing her hands as she confirms that she is the woman the tall man is looking for. He holds out his hand and gives Lizzie a weak shake accompanied by a weak smile. "Nice to meet you. I'm Brian. I'm a PA for Emergency Services. I understand you're having some bleeding."

Lizzie nods.

"And you believe you're pregnant? When was the first day of your last period."

Lizzie's eyes widen and dart to Grayson. Grayson's face stays impassive.

"Um, July eighth," she answers nervously.

"We did some blood work to confirm, and you are pregnant. We also checked some hormone levels to give us a baseline. First, we need to get an ultrasound. After that, we'll have a better idea of what's going on. Since you're still in the first trimester, it is possible that you could be having a spontaneous abortion."

"She's not having an abortion," Grayson barks, and the look he's giving the PA is lethal.

"No sir, that's not what I'm suggesting," the PA says, his tone practiced and soothing. "The term abortion, at least in medical terms, doesn't take intent into consideration. Rather, it's a term meaning the body is attempting to end the pregnancy for one reason or another. We don't always know why. I hesitate to bring it up until we know more, but I feel it's important that we're aware of the possibility."

Grayson closes his eyes like he's trying to accept what Brian said.

Brian gives a few more words of compassion and explains the limits of his ability to treat Lizzie and the baby. Once he leaves the room, it becomes eerily silent. Silence filled with tension.

"I'll give you two some privacy," I tell Lizzie.

She starts to bawl again. Grayson swoops in beside her and grabs her hand, kissing her knuckles, trying to reassure her.

I give Lizzie a peck on the forehead. "I'm only a phone call away."

On the other side of the cart, I drop a small kiss to Grayson's cheek and squeeze his shoulder. "Take good care of her."

"Of course," he replies, his eyes pinned to Lizzie.

I leave the hospital and take a cab home. It's been a long day, and I find I'm not immune to Lizzie and Grayson's pain. I will be sad, devastated even, if something happens to the baby. My first instinct is to call Reid and share my heartache for my two friends. To hear his voice. Invite him over and let him make it better, but I can't do that. So, I do the next best thing.

"Hey, Mom," I say when she answers the phone.

"Hey, sweetie. It's almost eleven-thirty, what's wrong?"

"Oh, Mom," I burst out. "It's all going wrong. I don't know how to fix it."

"What do we need to fix, sweetie?"

I spill the beans. Everything. I don't leave out a single detail. Well, that's not entirely true, it's more of a "G" rated version than the "X" rated truth.

"Oh, my," she says, after a few minutes. "And Frank? How's he doing? Will he be okay?"

"I don't know, Mom. I don't know a lot about dialysis. He says it's too exhausting to continue working. I don't blame him, you know, but it doesn't make it hurt any less."

"Of course you don't, sweetie. A successful career has been so important to you. You've always had these lofty goals. Come to think of it, I don't know that you've ever failed at anything in your life. This must be quite a shock. This young man Reid? How do you feel about him?"

How do I feel? I feel like my life sucks. Nothing is as good as it was when I was with him. Food tasted better, the air was fresher, the music more melodious. Everything was better. Now, we're on opposite ends, and every molecule in my body wants to destroy him while making love.

My lack of an answer must have been the response she needed. "Go with your gut. It's gotten you this far. No reason not to trust it."

After I hang up with my mom, I sit in the tub and take a nice hot bath, needing to relax, but it's impossible. I've never been one to harbor a grudge, but I can't get past what Reid did. How he did it. Why he did it. The more I think about it, the angrier I become. And, interestingly enough, the more turned on I am.

My hand wanders into the water and between my thighs, I imagine it being Reid's. He drops kisses along my jaw as he brings me to the brink and back again. By the time I climb in bed and snuggle under the covers, I find myself less satisfied than I had been in the tub, aching for Reid to be next to me.

Next to me, or six feet below a headstone where he can't cause any more problems. Decisions are hard.

47

Sam

Lizzie was sent home from the hospital early Friday morning, prescribed bed rest for the next few days until it can be determined whether she's still pregnant. She spent a day with Grayson, but called me on Saturday, saying she felt stifled and wanted to stay with me.

"I procured bagels and Chinese as requested," my mom announces as she walks through the door. She looks perfectly put together with her glossy blonde hair hanging loose and her blouse, jeans, and jacket combo. Fashionable yet age-appropriate. Way to go, Mom.

At five-foot-three, my mom is adorable. I get my height and analytical thought process from my dad, and my blonde hair and pouty lips from my mom. Somehow, I lucked out and got a perfect blend of both of my parent's best assets.

At this point, I'm willing to put money on Lizzie still being pregnant because who wants bagels and Chinese for brunch?

My mom sets the food down on the coffee table in front of the couch where Lizzie and I are lounging. "My poor, poor

Lizzie. How are you feeling?" she asks, running a gentle hand through Lizzie's hair.

"I'm fine. Nervous, but fine," Lizzie answers.

"I don't blame you," my mom says as she opens the container of lo mein. "And Grayson? How's he holding up?"

I'm heavily invested in Lizzie's answer. I wanted to ask the same thing, but Grayson doesn't seem to be talking to me right now, and I didn't want to pepper Lizzie with a thousand questions when I picked her up from Grayson's apartment.

"As well as to be expected," Lizzie says, shrugging her shoulders. "He seems to have gotten over the initial shock. Now, he's grappling with the idea that we might lose the baby, but he's trying to be strong."

"He doesn't want to upset you," my mother says as she walks toward the kitchen.

"Probably," Lizzie agrees.

My mom comes back to the living room with plates and begins to spread cream cheese over a bagel. I shovel some lo mein on a plate.

"How did you end up at Sam's?" my mom asks, continuing with the interrogation. "Knowing Grayson, I'm surprised he didn't try to keep you under lock and key."

Lizzie bites into her bagel. "Oh my God. This is delicious," she moans around a mouthful of food, forking a heaping pile of Mu Shu pork on top. "He tried, but the key was my finger, and the lock was a diamond ring."

Lo mein dangles from my mouth as my jaw hangs slack in surprise. "What?"

"Yeah."

My mom and I look down at Lizzie's left hand at the same time. No ring.

"It was sweet," Lizzie says. "There was sparkling cider and candles, Frank Sinatra crooning in the background. He even got down on one knee, but I couldn't do it. I love him. I do. Just not like that. It wouldn't be fair to either one of us if we rushed into a relationship that was a bad idea in the first place."

"So, what's the plan?" I ask, following my mom's lead.

"Well, if I'm still pregnant, I don't know. I think I'm going to find someplace cheaper to live. Save some money."

I can't imagine it. Lizzie living in the suburbs, away from the chaos of the city? She loves the city. "Don't jump the gun. It's not like Grayson is going to let you and the baby go without."

"I know he wouldn't, but this is something I need to be able to do on my own. I don't want to depend on Grayson for anything."

"Maybe you don't need to move. Get a roommate and split the bills. That'll save you some money."

She takes the last bite of her pork-topped bagel and seems to give thought to my idea. "Yeah. Maybe. For a little while anyway. That might work."

My mom pipes up. "Yeah. Find yourself a dreamy looking, dark blond swimmer to be your new bunk buddy."

"What?" I ask, confused. "Where did that come from?"

"On my way in, I saw your new neighbor moving in next door," my mom answers.

New neighbor? "I didn't realize the Britten's moved."

"Oh, my," my mom gushes. I don't think I've ever seen her gush over a man who isn't my dad. It's freaking me out. "He is handsome. Tall. Sharp jaw. You should go introduce yourself. You two would make the most adorable babies."

I roll my eyes. I don't think she'll ever give up the dream of me getting married and giving her a hundred grandbabies. Not that I'm necessarily opposed, it just isn't something I care enough about to go out of my way to find.

"Let's go introduce ourselves!" Lizzie suggests, excited and clapping her hands. "We'll take him some bagels and welcome him to the building."

My mom starts to pile food onto a plate. "Great idea."

"Fine," I concede. "But, you're on bed rest, so you have to stay here."

Lizzie wrinkles her nose. "I can walk the few feet next door. It's the same distance as the bathroom."

When the three of us step into the hallway, we're nearly plowed over by two men dressed in coveralls, hauling a couch. We follow them as they walk into the apartment next door.

Mom knocks on the opened door. "Hello, anybody home?"

The movers set the couch against a wall in the living room. This apartment has the exact opposite layout of mine. I've spoken with the former tenants, the Brittens, several times, but I've never been in another apartment in the building. It's spooky.

"I'll be right out," shouts a man from the back, I can barely hear him through the ruckus of the movers as they scratch the hardwood floors with the feet of the couch.

"Just wait till you see him," my mom whispers excitedly, wedding bells floating in her eyes.

Two other men weave around us, carrying a bed. I catch a glimpse of naked shoulders, but the movers block my view, taking the mattress into the bedroom.

"Sorry, it's crazy around here right now," the man says.

As the movers slide past him, he tugs on a black T-shirt, and I get a marvelous view of sculpted abs. Yum.

When his head pokes through the top of his shirt, my heart drops or flutters—something funny happens.

"What are you doing here?" I grate out. Reid Gallagher cannot be my new neighbor. I forbid it.

"Nice to see you too, neighbor," Reid says with a devilish smirk.

"You two know each other?" my mom asks, looking more excited with each second that passes.

"Oh, yeah," Lizzie chimes in. "Mrs. Valentine, I'd like you to meet Reid Gallagher. Reid, this is Sam's mother, Victoria Valentine."

Reid grabs my mother's hand and gives a kiss to the top of it. "It's a pleasure to meet you, Mrs. Valentine. I certainly see where Sam gets her looks."

Bastard.

My mom blushes. "Oh, so you're the Reid she's been telling me about?"

I want to scream. She makes it sound like I call her every day and burble about the new guy at work. I don't. I talked about him once, two days ago. *One* time.

"All good things, I'm sure," Reid says hopefully.

"Nope," I answer.

Reid and I begin a stare-off.

My eyes are saying, "What the hell are you thinking?"

His eyes are saying, "Being a pain in the ass."

My eyes reply, "I want to claw your eyes out."

His eyes respond, "I want you to claw my back 'til I come."

"Reid," my mother interrupts, "you're into racing?" She pulls out a framed photo from a pile on Reid's kitchen counter. He's sitting on a Ducati wearing a helmet with the visor flipped up.

"I am," Reid answers without taking his eyes off me.

"What a coincidence," Lizzie says. "Sam, don't you have a race tonight? Maybe Reid can tag along."

My eyes tell him, "Over my dead body."

"I'd love too," Reid says, accepting Lizzie's invitation.

If it weren't for the life growing inside of Lizzie, I would kill her.

48

Sam

I love my car more than my own life. It cost more than my apartment and is an exclusive—only twenty-four Vulcans exist in the entire world. It's my pride and joy. When I bought it, I had to purchase a large section of parking under my building to ensure its safety. It's securely tucked away in a garage inside a garage.

Despite Lizzie's backstabbing, I told Reid to meet me at my car stall at seven o'clock sharp. I mulled over the entire situation for several hours and decided to call in a few favors. Reid stole my job, got me off in a boardroom full of people, and had me in a pit of mud with a woman twice my size. Now, he's moved in next door? There is no way I'm just going to lay back and take it.

Reid makes it with three minutes to spare. He looks delicious decked out in all black, riding boots, and a matching leather jacket. I bite back a moan.

With the tick of his jaw and the lust in his eyes, I'd say he feels the same way. We're dressed the same, except I accessorized with a red scarf tied around my neck and red heels. To the naysayers who think it's impossible to race such a beast in heels, I believe that nothing is impossible.

"Listen, I want you to know that I'm not stalking you or anything. This apartment came on the market, and I jumped on it. It's a great building. Excellent location—"

"Okay." I have no interest in having this discussion. I click the remote to the garage door and the car comes into view.

Reid's mouth hangs open as he steps toward the car. "She's exquisite," he rasps as his hand runs along its carbon fiber curves.

"He is," I agree.

Reid laughs. "She's a he? Seriously?"

"Absolutely." I open my door and slide into the driver's seat. He follows suit, folding into the passenger side.

"It's surprisingly roomy," he says, stretching out his long toned legs.

We pull out of the garage and onto the street. I focus on the speedometer. It doesn't take much effort to hit a hundred, and I need to keep myself in check. For now.

"You know, I kind of thought you were bullshitting me when you said you had a Vulcan."

I glimpse over at him, and that boyish smile softens my heart as he fiddles with the accessories on the dash.

Nope. Nope. He's still an asshole.

"What's his name?" Reid asks.

"Hmm? Who?"

"You said the car was a 'he.' What's his name?

"Oh, right. Spock."

"A Vulcan. Nice."

The ride through the city is quiet inside the car but bustling on the avenue. Street performers, tourists, bars, shopping— these are just a few of the reasons why I love this city.

As we head onto the highway, I let Spock open up and hit close to ninety miles an hour. Much faster will raise suspicion and a ticket with outrageous fines.

"Correct me if I'm wrong, but aren't these cars track-only?" Reid asks. "Is Spock even street legal?"

I shake and nod my head, considering his question. "I suppose it depends on the definition of street legal."

"Is that going to be your defense when you end up in court? Okay. Street legal—to drive on the street with the proper permits, licensing, registrations, and modifications."

"Well, with such a narrow definition, I'd have to say no— definitely not street legal. However, it has been modified to make it less...noticeable. I added turn signals. Headlights."

"There is nothing about this car that isn't noticeable, sweetheart," he says, laughing and running a finger down my cheek.

I hate that I like it.

"How does someone like you end up with the baddest car ever made?"

"If by 'someone like me' you mean awesome, hardworking, and fears nothing? Then the answer would be that I pinched every penny and spoiled myself for my thirtieth birthday. A girl's got to have a little speed in her life."

Spock and I navigate the streets of a small village less than fifteen miles from the Wisconsin border. Caramel, Illinois was once a bustling town with stores that lined Main Street. In the forties, its entire economy hinged on one business. A candy factory, Brandy's. In the late eighties, Brandy's declared bankruptcy, a victim of Black Monday. The company was never able to recover. When it sank, it took the entire town with it. Now, all that's left are crumbling homes, an overwhelming homeless population, and a gas station. The kind of gas station, I might add, when you stop for an emergency bathroom break, you choose not to wash your hands because even if you peed all over your fingers, your urine is still cleaner than anything in that bathroom.

"Where are we?" Reid asks. His eyes are wide as he takes in the dilapidated scenery. Two men are making a not-so-obscure drug deal on the corner.

We idle at a traffic signal, the street light at the corner illuminates the men's activity, hiding nothing. One man has a spoon at the ready, the other whips off his belt and wraps it around his bicep. Their addiction is as explicit as the track marks on their arms.

The light turns green, I give a gentle tap to the accelerator, and point toward the shadowed horizon. Reid squints his eyes and shakes his head.

"The race track," I boast.

Within a few seconds, I turn onto the deserted road which leads to the once-famous candy makers.

"Brandy's?" he asks, disbelievingly.

"Why not? It's perfect. Miles and miles of unobstructed roads. Johnny law doesn't give a shit around here. He's got bigger problems."

"Bigger problems than what?" Reid asks.

I pull up next to a souped-up Mazda parked near a rickety smokestack and put the car in park. "Drag racing," I reply, my eyebrows dancing with delight.

His face lights up like a fourteen-year-old boy who's just seen his first pair of tits. "Shit. My dick just got hard," he rubs at the crotch of his pants. Seems like a stupid idea—from my experience, rubbing it only makes it harder.

I open the door, and people corral around me. More accurately, Spock. Most of them are familiar faces, some are newbies out to prove something. I high-five people and give small hugs as they call out my name, and I make my way through the crowd.

"Baby girl," a baritone voice calls out.

I turn around to see my favorite person in the underground racing world. "*George*," I squeal, running, and launch myself at him. He catches me and swings me around. George sets me down but keeps his arms wrapped around my waist.

"I ain't seen you 'round here in a dog's age," George says.

"Yeah, I know. After the last raid, I thought it best to lay low. Spock doesn't exactly blend in with the other cars, you know?"

A loud cough comes from behind us, interrupting the conversation. George and I turn to give our attention to Reid.

"George, I want you to meet my friend Reid. Reid, this is George."

George is a big guy, the size of a linebacker. That's because he is a linebacker. We never make mention of his identity down here because what we're doing is illegal. We love having him, and we're not going to screw it up.

Reid's jaw drops. "George? George—"

I jab him in the ribs to stop him from breaking the unspoken rule of our underground world, but I do whisper in his ear and confirm his suspicions.

The three of us walk around and get the skinny on the racing for the night. George keeps me close to his side, and Reid follows behind. I know I'm not giving a good impression right now. George and I aren't an item. Like Nick the Barista and Jerry the whiner, George is one of my good-time guys.

"Last time, you whipped me so good, I had marks for two weeks. On a dark man, that says something," George says, none too quietly.

I can hear Reid behind us, muttering about not being jealous. I refuse to give in to his jealous tendencies. We aren't together, and after tonight he'll have no desire to be.

49

Sam

Everyone appears to be vying for the chance to race against Spock. They won't win with a max speed of three-hundred and twenty miles per hour. Regardless, they want the opportunity to tell the harrowing tale of losing to the fastest car on earth.

Reid glances around. The ambiance of the underground culture is an experience unto itself. "What's your take on this?"

Several people pool their money and place their bets. "I don't race for money. I race for glory. Besides, not a single car here will be able to out-do Spock. It's a fool's bet to put money against me."

He nods, and we both watch as several cars take their turns running in this hidden gem of illegal street racing.

"So, you and George, huh?" Reid asks, keeping his eyes on the race. He's leaning against my car, several feet between us.

I shrug my shoulder. "We have." I choose not to go into detail.

Reid lets out a deep breath and has the decency to look ashamed. That's right, Reid Gallagher, shame on you.

"You're up, baby girl," George says, coming back to us after placing his bet.

I shake hands with my competition. A short man with bright red hair and a patchy beard. If I squint hard enough, I could almost swear he's a leprechaun.

"I've heard so much about you," the leprechaun tells me. "I can't believe I get to race against a Vulcan. Lady, you just made my day."

I can't help but smile at his jubilation, it's almost infectious. "Happy to make you happy. You ready to lose?"

"Like never before." He hops into his sun-yellow Mustang and revs the engine.

I slide into Spock's driver's seat and put on my helmet. George helps me buckle in and ensures the restraints are extra tight.

"You got this," George yells over the roar of the crowd as he taps on my helmet.

I nod, and George closes my door.

A young woman in her early twenties stands between the two cars. Her pin-up style fits remarkably well with her curvy hips. She unties the scarf around her neck and raises her arms.

The leprechaun and I rev our engines. He doesn't stand a chance.

The pin-up throws both her arms down, and I give a gentle tap to the gas, letting the short man gain a little distance. I keep my horsepower low because I don't want the noise that comes with tapping into Spock's full potential. It'll only invite trouble I'm not ready for. Yet.

The leprechaun gains a few car lengths. The head start was a nice gesture on my part, but it won't last. It isn't meant to be. I press harder on the accelerator and quickly gain speed. Within seconds we're nose to nose, and before I know it, I'm passing him. The needle on the speedometer tilts toward two hundred. Gotta give the people what they want.

As we cross the finish line, Spock hits two-hundred and

twenty miles per hour. The crowd and lights are a blur of colors, similar to the view I enjoyed on the back of Reid's Ducati. I lift my foot off the gas and apply pressure to the brakes, the smell of rubber invading the cabin of the car. When I come to a full stop and open the door, I throw my helmet onto the passenger seat. Scores of people crowd around me hollering, laughing, cursing, and paying up.

Reid jogs toward me, jumping and throwing his fist in the air. His eyes are bright with excitement, adrenaline flushing his skin. He gives me a brusque kiss on the lips. If enthusiasm had a flavor, it would be cherry lip balm.

He yanks me into his arms and gives me a hug. "Holy *shit,*" Reid howls over the noise. "That was *awesome.*"

George parts the crowd with his massive frame, counting his money while he walks.

"Reid, do you think you could grab me a bottle of water?" I point to a homeless man propped against a cooler.

"No problem," he says, still bounding with excitement. He plants another kiss on my cheek and makes his way through the crowds of people.

"Here's your cut," George says as he hands me a folded wad of cash.

I wave it away. "Nah. Give it to the guy in the Mustang."

George shrugs his shoulder and shoves the money in his pocket.

"Is everything set?"

"Yeah, baby girl, it is. You sure you want to do this?"

I let out a deep sigh. I talked to George this afternoon and gave him a cliff notes version of my problem, conveniently leaving out anything specific.

"Here you go," Reid says, returning with my water.

I grab it and guzzle it down. Racing seems to wick the water out of the body. "Thank you." I toss the bottle into a nearby trashcan like a lay-up. "You want to ride with me while I drive the car back around? I have one more race."

My second race for the night is upon us. I made arrangements with George to let me in on the last spot of the night.

"Normally, they only allow one race per event," I tell Reid. I surprise myself with my ability to make our activities of the night sound legal. It's not. At all.

We lean against the bumper and share a bag of chips. "So why is tonight an exception?" Reid asks.

"By request. Said everyone loves racing against my magnificent car."

He laughs. "*Magnificent* doesn't do it justice. This had to be the best birthday present you've ever gotten."

I pop a chip in my mouth. "It is." I pause, give a hard-thinking look and follow it up with a bright-idea look. "Do you want to..." I pause. I give a wave of my hand. "Nah, never mind. I don't want to put you in an uncomfortable position."

"Don't hold out on me. What?" Reid asks, his eyes pleading, hopeful.

"You wouldn't want to—"

"Hell yeah. I mean want to what?" he asks. I know he's playing stupid, and it's adorable.

"Drive my last race?"

He bends over at the waist.

"Are you okay?"

"I just got hard again."

I laugh as I help Reid into the car. "Try this helmet. If it doesn't fit, I have another one."

He tries it on and gives me a thumbs up. I assist him with the buckle and tug his straps tight. "Remember, Spock's potential is beyond your comprehension. Don't go over one-fifty. You won't be able to handle it. Press lightly on the accelerator. See this nob?" He nods his head. "Don't touch it. It adjusts the horsepower. Bad things will happen if you let all eight-hundred horses loose. That red button there starts the engine."

He gives another thumbs up.

"Go get 'em, tiger." I shut the driver's side door then walk to stand over by George.

A Ford Focus pulls up next to Reid, and they give each other a salute of solidarity. The pin-up girl returns to her position with her scarf in hand, and both drivers rev their engines. The roar from the cars has no barriers and seems to fill the night sky like a thunderstorm. My heart whacks in my chest, bruising and nauseating.

"No turnin' back now," George reminds me.

The pin-up girl throws her arms down, and tires squeal as both men take off. My stomach roils, and I turn toward a pillar and watch in horror as my dinner splatters onto the cracked and decaying concrete floor next to a homeless woman. "Sorry," I mutter, wiping my mouth.

"Damn. That's nasty," the woman mumbles as she picks up the cardboard she was sitting on and walks in the opposite direction of the race.

George puts his arm around me like he's trying to make me feel better. "I don't know why you have to do it, but I know you wouldn't do this if you didn't have a good reason."

George doesn't know me as well as he thinks. There isn't anything remotely noble about my motivation.

We walk to George's car. He starts it up but turns off the headlights while we wait. I look toward the finish line and see the moment Reid wins the race and jumps out with his helmet on, no doubt screaming with elation. The Focus comes up behind him when the lights start to flash.

Blue lights illuminate the night, and I watch as a swarm of police cars surround the racers and their fans.

"Time to go," I tell George as I give his arm a squeeze.

I flip down the visor and slide open the mirror, a light above turns on, and I pretend to fix my hair. George puts the car in drive and turns us in the opposite direction of the excitement. From my side-view mirror, I watch as handcuffs are slapped onto Reid's wrists.

50

Sam

My phone rings, and it's the call I've been waiting for. I stopped at a dingy bar south of the Caramel town line and immediately ordered a scotch. Two fingers of booze can go a long way to ease the conscience.

"Come and get him," Jose says when I answer.

"On a scale from one to ten, how angry is he?" I'm not as eager to accept the consequences of my actions as I was when I made the arrangements.

"Fifteen."

The brusque reply and insolent click of the line confirm my suspicion that Reid is so pissed that even Jose, a Marine veteran turned Caramel police officer, doesn't want to deal with him. This favor may have been a bit too much to ask.

George dropped me off at the city impound, and I slipped the clerk the five-hundred dollars promised to keep my car safe and off the record. He was all too happy to accept the cash. When my car was delivered to the front gate, I had never felt so relieved. My beautiful baby survived unscathed, not a single scratch.

Jose was outside the building waiting for me when I arrived at the city lock-up.

"We tossed him in solitary," Jose says.

The news is horrifying. "What the hell? That wasn't part of the plan."

"Jesus, Sam. What did you expect? You gave me less than twelve hours to put this together, and you didn't want him to go to jail. What he was doing, what *you* were doing, was illegal. Hell, what you're driving is illegal." He runs his hand through his chestnut hair with frustration. "There was nothing easy about this, and your boyfriend going bat-shit crazy was not something I planned for."

"You're right. I'm sorry. And, thank you," I tell Jose, batting my eyelashes as I finger comb his mussed hair back into place.

Jose gives me a small smile, and I know I'm forgiven.

"When's he being released?"

He lets out a sigh as if he's just realized this was a no-strings-attached kind of favor. Jose nods to an officer behind a thick, bullet-proof, window. It's a signal which follows with an obnoxious buzz as the door unlocks, and Jose wrenches it open. "We'll be out in a minute."

I sit in a hard, orange chair which reminds me of my second-grade classroom. I wait.

And wait.

I scroll through my social media on my phone in an attempt to kill time. The clock on the wall held securely in place by metal wires tells me I've been waiting almost forty-five minutes.

The officer behind the window has his feet kicked up on the desk, watching a small TV broadcasting *The Andy Griffith Show*. He chows down on a messy sandwich which must be delicious if the barbeque sauce dribbling onto his chin is any indication.

I give a light knock on the window, not wanting to press my luck, but I'm too impatient to wait much longer. "Excuse me." I knock again. "I wanted to check on my friend Officer Mendez. He was helping me with something."

The officer sets his sandwich on the desk and wipes his hands on his pants, dropping his feet to the floor. He doesn't even bother to clean his face with the napkin next to him. "I know about your 'something,'" he sneers. "Mendez had a situation. Someone's back there now helping him out. Have a seat."

"Oh, okay. Thank you." I return to my chair, more nervous now than I was when I first got here. There was no scenario in which I would have expected everything to go this badly. On my end, it worked out exceedingly well given the short time frame to construct everything. Reid was supposed to be angry. Reserving his bed in the crazy house was not something I would have ever considered.

The squeak of the metal door throws me from my thoughts. Reid walks out, his hair matted to his head, his stance a bit too wide for comfort and his boots have disappeared. He's walking the tile floor with bare feet. His arms are still behind his back, and Jose is directly behind him as they walk into the atrium toward me.

"Can you behave yourself now?" Jose asks Reid.

Reid rolls his eyes. "Sure."

Jose unlocks the cuffs, and Reid swings his arms around, stretches his shoulders then rubs his wrists.

"Shoes. Jacket." Reid says without looking at anyone.

"*McCallister,*" Jose calls out. "Gallagher's boots."

The messy officer behind the window stands up and makes quick work of grabbing the items and bringing them around to us.

"Anything else, Officer?" Reid asks, contempt dripping from every syllable.

"We're done here," Jose tells him.

Reid turns his attention from the wall to me and gives me a heart-stopping glare as he walks toward the doors.

Jose frowns as he tugs me by the hips in a slight, but noticeable, sign of affection. "You going to be okay with him?"

I don't know. "Yeah. We'll be fine."

Jose leans in and gives me a slow kiss on the cheek. I hear a loud bang from the door opening, forcing me to turn around. Reid has walked out the door and is now storming the parking lot. I'm not sure where he plans to go.

"Thanks for your help," I tell Jose as I step away from him, using his chest as leverage.

"One of these days you're going to fill me in on why I had to set up and arrest an innocent man."

"One day."

"Be careful," Jose shouts as I thrust open the doors.

Reid is waiting for me in the parking lot, leaning against Spock. His feet are still bare, his boots dangling from his hands. He stares at the ground as I approach.

"I'm sorry."

"Him too?" he asks, his voice low, still staring at the asphalt of the parking lot.

"Who? Jose? I can't speak for him."

He lets out a contemptuous grunt. "I don't care if that cop is sorry. I'm asking if you've fucked him, too."

I unlock the car and walk around to the driver's side and yank open the door. "That's rich," I mutter as I slide into the seat and turn over the ignition.

Reid waits a few more beats, then finally gets in. The ride is silent for most of the way back to our apartment building. We could be in a comic book with the words we aren't speaking. The emotions filling the void are clear, but not expressed. Only conversation balloons above our heads could describe what either one of us is thinking.

When I park Spock in the garage, I kill the engine and lay my head against the headrest. I'm exhausted and disappointed in myself. Despite all that has happened, I just want to curl up in Reid's lap.

"Why'd you do it?"

"How'd you end up in solitary?" I retort.

An exasperated breath is all the answer I get. No

interpretation needed. Reid steps out of the car without saying a word and slams the door behind him.

Space and time are what he needs, and I sit in the car for a few minutes while he heads to his apartment. The one next door to mine. As I wait, I receive a text from George.

George: "How'd it go?"

Me: "As planned, I suppose."

George: "Is he pissed?"

Me: "Beyond my expectations."

George: "Hope it was worth it."

Me too.

51

Reid

Monday was Frank's official retirement. There was a party in the building's cafeteria that afternoon with cake and punch and other shit. People from all over the city stopped in to give Frank their congratulations and to meet the new president of Sterling—me.

Of course, Stella was there, ever the dutiful wife. Moving in next door to Sam was not an ideal situation, especially with the state of our relationship, but I would bunk with Satan if it meant I didn't have to share the same space as Stella.

Sam stopped by for a while and made the rounds. She shook hands and worked the room like a pro with polite conversation. When she tried to start a discussion with me, I stopped her in her tracks. I didn't have it in me to be civil.

I've been working to control my anger, and thus far, avoidance of the people who trip my wire has been the most effective way to achieve positive results. There's a lot of perspective one gains while in solitary. I had my fair share on Saturday. Sometime between Officer Mendez seizing my shoes and belt and the smooth manipulation of the cavity search, I had a revelation. I've harbored too much anger. Anger toward everyone. Toward the world. I need to let it go because there is nothing to be gained.

Frank is sick, and I'm powerless to stop it. There is no decision I can reverse that will change the past. The opportunity to move forward is right in front of me. The fact that Silas Keogh is back in my life isn't forgotten, I just need to finish this fucking deal and then I can leave it behind. I imagine that once Silas sells off Keogh Tower, he'll tuck his tail between his legs and run back to New York.

As angry as I should be at Sam, I'm not. Sure, she had me arrested, but truthfully, I'm more disappointed than angry. I trusted her. God only knows why, but I did. In the end, it all turned out okay, no permanent record or anything, I suppose it's easy enough to forgive.

On Tuesday, I moved into Frank's office. I considered staying where I was, not wanting to step on anyone's toes, but it is imperative to show my employees that I'm the one in charge and taking over Frank's office should do it. It feels good. It's like filling the shoes of my legacy. When I was little, five or six, Frank was my whole world. I wanted to be a carbon copy of my dad when I grew up, but things happened. That little boy is still a part of me, and I need to focus on the good. Frank wasn't a perfect father, but I know he's only wanted the best for me. Unfortunately, sometimes pride gets in the way, and I am no less guilty than him.

It's lunchtime on Thursday, and I decide to walk to Sam's office, and I know Ben will be away from his desk for a late lunch. Sam's picky about appearances and doesn't want anyone to think she's screwing the boss, not that we're doing that anymore. I don't blame her. She may have a reputation as a— whatever the female equivalent for a womanizer would be—but it shouldn't affect people's perception of her. As much as I hate to admit it, she's right. I've been just as judgmental as Delores and everyone else.

When I arrive, Sam's door is shut, and the lights are off. I guess she left for lunch too. I'm a little disheartened. I don't know what I was going to say, but I was hoping to start off with "I love you." I don't want this war to keep raging. I want to hold her in my arms every night. I want to wake up next to her every morning. Sam Valentine is the single best thing to happen to me since Amanda. Something so small, like taking her promotion, won't stop me from getting what I want. What we both want. Not that she knows that yet, but she will, eventually.

I turn to go back to my office, and the phone on Ben's desk rings.

I take the liberty of answering. "Sam Valentine's office, this is Reid."

"Reid," the female voice squeals. "How are you? It's Victoria. Victoria Valentine. Sam's mom? We met on Saturday. You remember, don't you?"

"Of course, I do. How could I forget such a stunning woman?" I think I can hear her blushing through the line.

"You're too kind," she says. "How did it go with you and Sam on Saturday?"

"It was an experience," I tell her, choosing to leave out the part where I was fingerprinted.

"Oh, I don't doubt it. I drove Spock once," she says, referring to Sam's Vulcan. "She had the car transported to a track, a couple of hours south, back when she first bought it. I know it goes fast, but I was so scared to put a dent in it that I couldn't get myself to go over forty," she giggles.

"He handles like a dream."

"He sure does."

"Sam's at lunch right now, is there something I can do for you? Do you want to leave a message? You could call her on her cell phone."

"Oh, I don't want to bother her. I thought if she had a minute, we could talk about the party on Sunday."

"Oh? What kind of party?"

"Victor and I are celebrating our fortieth wedding anniversary. Can you believe that? I've spent more of my life being a Valentine than a Morris."

"That's amazing. Congratulations."

"You should come," she says, sounding more excited if that's even possible.

It's probably a bad idea. No, it *is* a bad idea. "I'd love to. When and where?"

Victoria rambles off the details, and I grab a pen and sticky note from Ben's desk, jotting it down. "I can't wait."

"I'm glad you're coming, Sam will be delighted."

Sam definitely will *not* be delighted. "Oh, and Mrs. Valentine?"

"Please, call me Victoria."

"Okay, Victoria. Maybe we can keep this between the two of us? I want it to be a surprise," I tell her, a plan beginning to take shape.

She laughs. "My lips are sealed."

I grab my suit jacket from Frank's office—correction—my office—and head toward Michigan Avenue.

52

Sam

Lizzie, Grayson, and I walk through the doors of my parent's country club and are greeted by the smell of potpourri and oiled leather. It's a beautiful venue with scenery to inspire painters with its backdrop of Lake Michigan.

I'm surprised Grayson agreed to come with me, but he promised my parents he'd be here, so he didn't have much choice. He didn't speak to me for the entire hour-long car ride.

Lizzie, on the other hand, is ecstatic. This is the first time in over a week that she's left my apartment. She got the results back on the serial blood work she was having done. The growth hormone is rising; therefore the baby is still growing, or something like that. She's on bed rest for the next couple of weeks, and at some point, she'll follow up with her obstetrician, and they'll figure it out from there.

An empty table that sits next to the French doors is calling our name. "Go. Sit," I command. Since Lizzie is still on bed rest, I don't know that she should have come, but she wanted to be here to celebrate with my parents so badly, she cried for three hours straight until I caved. With those crocodile tears sliding down her pouty face, there was no way I could deny her.

"Woof," Lizzie says, smiling as she makes her way to the designated spot.

Grayson and I head toward the open bar.

"I'll take a Cosmo."

"Scotch. Neat," Grayson orders.

When the bartender hands us our drinks, we switch.

Grayson lets out a sigh. "I haven't forgiven you,"

"I know."

"I will though."

"I know that too." I give him a small smile. He returns it and begins to laugh, the forgiveness already underway.

"Grayson," my mom sings as she skitters over to us at the bar. She looks beautiful in a purple fit and flare dress and stunning black heels, her outfit matching the October leaves on the trees. "It's so nice to see this handsome face," she says, grabbing Grayson's chin between her thumb and fingers. "It's been too long."

Grayson gives her a heartwarming smile and leans in to give her a hug. "It has."

When she let's go of Grayson, she turns to me. "Sam, you look radiant." She holds me by the shoulders for a good look. I'm wearing a similar style dress, but white, and it's after Labor Day. I'm such a rebel.

"Hey, kiddo," my dad says, taking his turn to give me a hug. It feels right. His long arms wrap around me and make all my troubles melt away. He's wearing a nice black suit paired with a purple tie that matches my mom's dress. Every time I see him, he looks a little bit older, his hair salt and pepper with a few flecks of auburn.

"Hi, Dad."

"Grayson," my dad says after letting me loose and shakes hands with my friend. "How's Lizzie?"

Me, Grayson, and Lizzie grew up together, all on the same

suburban street. We shared our homes and our parents. We're one big happy family.

Grayson seems stunned by the question, I'm sure he didn't expect my dad to know, but my mom shares everything with my dad. Everything. Hell, he probably knows about Reid too, not that he's said anything to me. He isn't an intrusive kind of man, but he's there if you need an ear. Since I'm not sure what is going on in my life right now, I haven't wanted to broach the subject.

"Victor," my mom chides, swatting him on the shoulder. "Don't ask something so personal. This is a party."

"She's doing well. Still taking it easy. You can ask her yourself, she's right over there," Grayson tells my dad, pointing toward the tables where Lizzie is sitting.

Lizzie is aglow and appears to be enjoying herself while she chats with Grayson's parents. I'm not sure what all they know, or if Grayson has told them they're about to be grandparents.

I sneak off while my mom and dad grill Grayson to grab some finger sandwiches, a flute of champagne, a glass of punch, and make my way over to the table with Lizzie.

"So?" my mom asks, catching up with me.

"So, what?"

"How'd it go last Saturday? With your new neighbor?"

"You mean my boss?"

"Just because he's your boss doesn't mean—"

Here we go, my mother trying to play the matchmaker, convinced the goal of every woman is to marry.

"That's right, he's my boss. Even if he wasn't, I don't think we're compatible."

What I want to say is, "I don't think he'd want me." Not after what I did.

My mother's smile fades, and I hate that I'm the cause of it; it's her fortieth anniversary for crying out loud. "But, maybe one day."

That does the trick, my mom's face brightens with hope

again. "Great. Oh, there's Doctor and Mr. Miller. I'll talk to you in a bit," she says as she glides toward the other guests.

I sit next to Lizzie and hand her the snacks I grabbed.

"Thanks," she says, shoveling her face full of food. "I was starving."

My Aunt Sheila comes up to our table and settles down. Every family has an Aunt Sheila—she's feisty and honest to a fault. "How are you doing, sweetie pie?"

"I'm okay," I sigh, my thoughts drifting toward my new boss. My sexy new boss. The sexy new boss I had arrested.

"I'm not talking to you. I already know your story—top of the world business exec. Boring. Now, Lizzie's life is interesting, isn't it, dear?"

Apparently, Aunt Sheila has no interest in how my life is falling apart at the seams, but this isn't the time or place to discuss it anyway. I'm nibbling on my finger sandwiches when Aunt Sheila turns her attention back to me.

"Are you giving a speech?" she asks.

I choke on my food. "I was supposed to give a speech?"

Uncle Robert, Aunt Sheila's husband, comes up behind her. "You don't have a speech? Well, you should. You're their only child, their testament of love and devotion."

"Living proof of one night of passion shared between a husband and wife," Aunt Sheila chimes in.

"Gross," I mutter.

Aunt Sheila and Uncle Robert are right, I should make a speech. It didn't occur to me since I've been so wrapped up in my own dysfunction. I walk up to the lone microphone at the front of the room. It was probably put there for this exact reason, the mic's presence further shaming me. I give it a tap, and it makes a horrific squeak, grabbing the attention of my audience.

"Hello, I'm Sam, as most of you know, and I'm Victor and Victoria's daughter. I just wanted to say a few words."

The entire room faces the front, and my parents come up to stand next to me. My dad grabs my mom by the waist and tucks her into his side, and she blushes. The reactions of my parent's devotion to each other speak more than words.

"Forty years is a long time," I start.

"Forty to life," my Uncle Robert calls out from the back, and everyone laughs, my parents included. Aunt Sheila swats him on the arm with her purse.

"Forty years of fighting and compromising. Loving and I'm sure a little bit of hatred as well. Eighteen of those years were dedicated to *moi*," I say, with a curtsey, the crowd laughing. "And I'm sure those weren't easy either, but through it all, they stuck together."

The doors to the room open and a man dressed in a black suit slips in. My breath hitches when I realize it's Reid. I have no idea why he would be at my parent's anniversary party, or how he knew to be here, but there he is looking handsome and powerful.

I swallow hard, trying to find my place in this impromptu speech. "A testament that love requires work and dedication, but above all love requires kindness. Every day I watched as my dad treated my mom like a queen, and my mom gave him everything a king could need. Now here we are, forty years later." I raise my champagne glass in the air. "Forty to life."

"Forty to life," everyone repeats with their glasses raised.

My parents clink flutes, kiss each other, and drag me in for a family hug.

"That was so sweet," my mom says, a tear sliding from the corner of her eye.

"Beautiful speech, kiddo," my dad compliments, dropping a kiss on my forehead.

I give them each a peck on the cheek. "Thanks. Now, go mingle with your guests," I tell them, my sight trained on one person.

53

Reid

Sam looks beautiful, practically glowing. It's the first time I've seen her around her family, and she's in her element. It didn't escape my notice the way her breath hitched when I walked through the door. That's a sound I can't wait to hear from her again. In about a half-hour.

"Reid," Grayson says, shaking my hand. "What are you doing here? I had no idea you knew the Valentines."

"Sure. I've met Victoria a few times. She invited me." It might be an exaggeration, but to say it any other way makes me sound like a creeper.

"Sam's going to love this," Grayson laughs as we walk to the bar.

I order a beer. "Oh, she's going to hate it. But, I couldn't say no, it would be rude."

"Come say 'hi' to Lizzie. She's been trapped in Sam's apartment for the past week. She needs all the human interaction she can get."

"I heard. I've had dinner with her a couple of times."

"Really?"

"Sam was working late, and Lizzie wandered over to my apartment." Those dinners were enlightening. Who knows Sam better than her childhood best friend? I learned a lot about her, what makes her tick. Why she's so driven to succeed. "Sam didn't tell you about her new neighbor?"

"Sam and I haven't been on the best terms since Lizzie almost lost the baby. No, no one told me about the new neighbor."

I waggle my eyebrows suggestively.

"No."

I nod with pride.

"Holy fuck. Sam must have lost her shit over that," Grayson laughs.

"That's putting it mildly. She had me arrested."

Grayson's mouth falls open.

"It's a long story."

Grayson glances toward the French doors on the other side of the room. "Sam's grandma is about to corner Lizzie. I should be there to help. Good luck," he says, raising a pink cocktail in salute.

Victor and Victoria are chatting with a couple around their age when I approach to give my congratulations. Victoria is a beautiful woman, and other than her short stature, her daughter is a mirror image. If the myth holds true that a woman's mother provides insight as to how well she will age, I will be an incredibly lucky man.

"Reid," Victoria says, giving me a hug. "I'm so glad you came."

The present I picked out for Sam might as well be burning a hole in my pocket. "Wouldn't miss it for the world. Mr. Valentine," I say, offering my hand to Sam's dad.

I spoke with him on the phone and got his blessing for my plan. He was surprisingly quick to give it to me considering I have known Sam for such a brief time, and the majority of it hasn't been on good terms. Mr. Valentine believes Sam will come around. I have held that same belief.

"Reid, it's nice to meet you in person," Mr. Valentine says, shaking my hand. "So, today's the day, huh?"

I'm nervous as hell, but it's the good kind of nervous. Some men get cold feet. Not me. I haven't had a second thought since the idea first came to me. "It is."

"Reid?" Sam says, walking up to me and her parents. "What are you doing here?" She tries to sound polite, but it comes out irritated.

"Your mom invited me."

Sam's death stare switches focus from me to her mom. Victoria is completely unaffected by the wrath of her daughter and raises her hand in the air, snapping her fingers. Per Mrs. Valentine's signal, the first notes of the song begin to play.

"May I have the honor of this dance?" I grab Sam's hand and drop a kiss on her knuckles. Her mom sighs and her dad smiles—there's no way she's going to tell me 'no.'

Sam chews on her bottom lip nervously. Her eyes harden, and she gives me a resolute nod. She's a smart woman, and she knows there is something up my sleeve.

I lead her onto the dance floor where several others have also begun to dance. Bob Marley's *One Love* plays and I gather her into my arms, her soft body against my hardness warms my heart. A heart that had been like stone until I met her.

"My mom invited you, I can believe that," Sam says as I sweep her across the dance floor. "But what I don't understand is why you would accept."

"I wanted to see you."

She softens at my words. "I'm sorry. I went too far."

"Don't be sorry. I'm not."

She stops moving and gives me a questioning look.

"You did me a favor."

Confusion flits across Sam's face as her brows pinch together. When the song ends, I drop to one knee and offer her a small red box.

Her entire face goes pale. "What are you doing? Get up," she hisses.

Mrs. Valentine brings me a microphone. "From the first moment I saw you, I knew you were special. That you would change my whole world. You can't begin to imagine the ways you've changed my life, how you have changed me. You're kind and caring. Fierce and fun to be around. I was a shell of a man until I met you, sweetheart. You've given my life color and vitality, and I never want to live in a world of gray again. I love you, Samantha Jean Valentine. Will you marry me?"

I open the box with a three-carat, round-brilliant diamond perched in the center. The room is so quiet, I can hear Sam's gasp. There's a long pause as she looks around the room, stunned by my actions and the hopefulness on the faces of everyone watching.

"Say yes," a man begins to chant. The rest of the room joins in, and Sam is backed into a corner. To say 'no' at her parent's anniversary party would be something she would never live down.

Sam holds out her left hand with reluctance. "Of course. How could I say 'no' to that?"

The crowd erupts with cheers and clapping, and I slip the ring onto Sam's finger. I stand and wrap my arms around her, our lips colliding, and slide my tongue into her mouth, needing a taste of my future wife. Sam, on the other hand, nips at my lip so hard it draws blood.

This proposal isn't just another battle in the war between Sam and me. It's going to take a lot to convince her that it's genuine, but I know she'll see things my way. Eventually.

54

Sam

Reid proposed in front of my entire family. What the hell? I had to spend the rest of the afternoon at my parent's anniversary party clinging to Reid like a love-struck dove. My mom was through the roof with happiness, my dad didn't seem to take any issue with a strange man he's never heard about, let alone met, asking for my hand in marriage. What is wrong with everyone?

Reid and I left at the same time but in separate cars. I had to take Grayson and Lizzie home, so at least I had that. When I got to Grayson's, Lizzie hopped out of the car, telling me she was going to stay at Grayson's tonight because a newly engaged couple needs to have alone time. She's right about that. We will certainly need some time alone. A time with no witnesses to the beat-down Reid's about to experience.

After I get home, I toss my stuff on the counter and march the ten feet to his apartment door. I pound non-stop until he answers.

"Hello, fiancée," he greets when he opens the door. He looks deliciously rumpled, still in the black suit from earlier, and his tie loosened at the neck.

"We need to talk."

Reid steps out of my way and follows me to the kitchen. I slip the ring off my finger and set it on the countertop. "I can't accept this." My heart twinges with guilt and disappointment. The ring is beautiful and elegant, but I can't accept the strings attached.

He picks the ring up and seems to inspect it. "You can, and you will." He slides it back on my finger.

I let out a sigh of exasperation, fiddling with the weight on my hand. "This has to stop. It's gone too far. I had you arrested; you proposed in front of my entire family. If we don't stop now, it won't end until one of us is dead."

He laughs, and the sexy sound serves to make me angrier. "This *isn't* a joke."

Swiftly, Reid pins me against the cupboards, the light touch of his thumb grazing my cheek makes me shiver. His lips travel down the column of my throat, his stubble grating against my skin.

"It's not a joke," he says into my neck, continuing to kiss his way to my cleavage.

I'm helpless to stop him. His touch, his kiss is something worth craving. I crave him every damn day.

His hand slips under my dress, and he cups my pussy. "You want me. I can feel it," Reid says, tugging at the thin material and ripping my panties apart.

"Yeah," I admit, grabbing a handful at his zipper. "And you want me."

His fingers slide between my folds, and my entire world tilts.

"Enough to marry you." He dips a finger, then two, inside me.

I grab onto his shoulders, my knees going weak. My mind is muddled from his exacting touch and the words he's saying. There's no way he can be serious about wanting to marry me.

We barely know each other.

He lifts me onto the counter, the cool marble feels divine against the warmth pooling between my legs. I unbutton and unzip his pants, and he shoves them down to his thighs, his cock springing free.

I take a moment to look at him, his shirt untucked, but his jacket still on, his tie loose, and his pants shoved down. It might be the sexiest thing I've ever seen.

"You don't want to marry me," I tell him, a moan escaping my lips as he strums my clit.

He yanks my hips to the edge and lines himself up with my entrance. "More than anything in the world." He juts his hips forward, impaling me with his cock.

I whimper—the feeling part pain, part pleasure. Reid pulls back then pushes in slowly. I'm immersed in feelings. Feelings for this man inside me. I don't know if he loves me, or if this is just another part of the game. If I'm not careful, I could fall head over heels in love with him.

His movements are unhurried and deliberate as he thrusts, hitting my deepest part. A tingle begins to unfurl in my belly, and I'm aching to come around his fat cock. "You don't love me."

"I do love you. More than I ever thought possible," Reid says. "I wake up every morning thinking about you. Every night when I close my eyes, I see you naked beneath me. I want that forever. With you."

"You don't know what you're getting yourself into." I run my fingers down his red silk tie.

"I think I know better than any other man in your life." His pace picks up, warm palms massage my breasts.

The knot of his tie begins to tighten as I pull, staring him in the eyes. My back is digging into a wine rack on the counter, and I could care less, his movements inside me hit just the right spot. I cinch the tie tighter against his throat, and the veins in his neck bulge, I can see the erratic beat of his pulse as he pounds into me.

He roars as he comes, his face turning almost purple, and I quickly loosen the knot around his neck. The thickening and twitching of his cock are too much to resist, and I scream out my pleasure, my body wracked with intensity.

His head collapses onto me, and I hold him against my breasts as we both work to slow down our breathing.

"I mean it, you know."

"I think you think you mean it."

His eyes snap up to mine. "You are the most infuriating woman I have ever met," he says, bruising my lips with a kiss. "Come on," he commands as he helps me down from the counter. "It's been a long day. Let's go to bed."

He grabs me by the hand and we head to his bedroom. It's sparse with a bed and a dresser. I guess that's all he needs.

"I can't stay the night. We have work in the morning."

Reid laughs and yanks back the covers, stripping out of his clothes. "I'll get you up early so you can go home and get ready."

I take off my dress and toss my shredded panties in a nearby trash can. "Very funny."

55

Sam

Reid woke me up early on Monday morning and we made love. At least, I think that's what happened—I've never done that before. The time was filled with gentle caresses and kisses, taking his time to work my body into a frenzy. I've never had an orgasm that intense before, and I can't help but wonder if it isn't because of the man next to me. I'm snuggled into his side, knowing we must leave our little bit of heaven in the next hour to go to work.

"Since we're engaged," I ponder aloud, "does that mean you have to answer any questions I ask? I mean, we should get to know each other on a deeper level before we commit to a life sentence."

I'm not sure I've bought into this whole getting engaged thing quite yet, but last night helped to sway me in that direction. Reid isn't a bad guy. He doesn't objectify and use people for his own gratification, unlike me. I can't imagine a scenario where hitching himself to me would benefit him for anything other than to be with me. I kind of like that idea.

He laughs and tugs me closer to his side. "Marriage isn't prison, sweetheart."

"I know, it's just something my uncle said yesterday. Forty years to life."

"Well then, sign me up for forty years at the Samantha Jean Penitentiary."

"Which brings me to my first question. How do you know my middle name?" It struck me as odd when he used my full name to propose.

"Your resume," he answers directly.

"You looked into me?"

"I wanted to know what made you tick. First in your class at Columbia, a member of the Women's Business Society, and Gosh Yarn It. Got to say, I can't see you sitting in a rocking chair crocheting."

There were a lot of hot guys in that knitting club. Surprising, I know, but the classroom was filled with testosterone-leaded guys who needed a constructive way, besides football or rugby, to deal with their aggressive tendencies. "Yeah, well, my mom was all about teaching me more feminine hobbies. I thought it would be a subtle way to compliment my CV aside from my more career-focused activities. Set me apart a little bit, I guess."

"Speaking of your mom, I also know why you're so hell-bent on proving yourself."

I sit up on my elbow. "Do tell."

"Your mom is a homemaker. She sacrificed her dreams and ambitions for your father's career."

So far, so good.

"But you don't feel like you should have to choose."

Way off. "My mom doesn't want me to choose. She wants me to have it all. It's just that what she values as important—a husband and children—isn't a priority I share."

Reid's face wrinkles with confusion. "Do you see yourself having kids?"

This is why no one should propose to a person in front of

an entire party filled with family—some of the crucial details of a shared life should be discussed. Case in point—children. "Do I see it? Not exactly. I don't hate the idea, but my career is my first priority, my passion. If the other stuff comes along, I'm not going to run the other way."

His eyes light up at my answer, and he rolls on top of me and rains kisses across my face. I think I said something he likes.

I shove at his chest, and he rolls onto his back. "You had your time, now it's my turn."

"Fine, shoot."

"Why are you mad at Frank?"

He scrubs a hand over his face, sighing. "You're going straight for the heavy-hitters, huh?"

"Yup."

"When Frank divorced my mom, he married Stella a couple of months later."

He told me about this before, spinning it as some twisted Pretty Woman retelling.

"I was so angry with him," he continues. "My family disintegrated before my very eyes, and Frank was turning around and marrying someone else. I refused to go to the wedding, and Frank couldn't seem to understand why. He just didn't get it. Anyway, I tried to make my peace with him. My wife, Amanda, insisted on it. She used to tell me if I didn't forgive Frank, and something happened to him, that I'd regret it for the rest of my life. He wasn't as willing to forgive as I had been. It had been three years before I spoke with him again. The only reason I called was to let him know that Amanda died."

Tears well in my eyes as Reid tells the story of the damaged relationship with his father and the lost love of his wife. I want to stop him and smother him with kisses, tell him that everything will be okay, but I selfishly want to hear the rest.

"I don't know what I expected. No, I take that back. I expected he would show up at the funeral. He didn't so much as send flowers. I couldn't forgive him for that, I was a wreck for a long time. Then, when he called me from the hospital, I thought about what Amanda used to tell me, and I didn't want that kind of guilt on my conscience."

Jesus. I don't know what to say to that. Frank was wrong. All the way around, Frank was wrong, and to abandon your son during what had to be the most excruciating pain of his life? That's a new low. I've held Frank in such high regard, and him not telling me about promoting Reid over me seemed out of character with the man I knew and admired. Considering the things Reid is saying, I'm beginning to see Frank in a new light. "Next question."

"Is this one any easier?"

I think about it a moment. I don't want to pry, I don't want Reid to rehash his old hurt, memories that had him fleeing to Barbados, but we can't very well develop a healthy relationship if I don't know the basics. "Harder. What happened to Amanda? How'd she die?"

He doesn't pause and answers me directly. I think he knew the question was coming. "She was in a car accident. We were supposed to go to the Hamptons that weekend, but I had to work late. We decided she would drive there, and I would catch the train the next morning. Needless to say, neither one of us made it."

A tear slides down my cheek, only able to imagine the pain he must have felt. I would give every dime I have if I could go back in time and keep him from feeling that pain. Even if it means losing him forever.

He wipes the tears from my cheek and kisses my nose. "Don't cry, sweetheart. It's not your burden to bear." He rips the covers off us. "Come on, it's time for a shower. We have to get ready for work."

It's on the tip of my tongue to ask him my last question, but I figure I've already put him through the wringer. Instead, I decide to follow him into the shower. There is no way we won't be late for work because I plan to give him a rub down he'll never forget.

56

Sam

It's been two weeks since he proposed. We haven't made the official announcement at work, in part because I'm not ready yet. Nothing about this seems real. I'm not hanging onto the animosity from losing my promotion the way I expected. In fact, that seems even more suspicious. Dare I say it? This is love. I'm still nervous about it. Luckily, Reid seems okay with me dragging my feet, but I can tell he's anxious. He wants to shout our relationship status to the universe.

First, we had to tell his mom. Babs Gallagher is the sweetest woman on the planet. We've talked on the phone several times and have made plans to go to visit her in New York for Thanksgiving. I'm trying to figure out a way to go to The Macy's Thanksgiving Day Parade. That would be the experience of a lifetime. Reid isn't too fond of the idea, complaining that it will be a shoving match with every walk of life. I'm sure that's true, but I still want to go.

Lizzie has moved back into her apartment a few blocks away. She's been given the all-clear as to the pregnancy, but you wouldn't know it by the way Grayson pampers her. He might as well feed her grapes while she directs the girls on stage for rehearsals. Next week, Lizzie is planning to start interviews with potential roommates. She's convinced it will help her save money. Grayson hates the idea, but he doesn't have much say in the matter.

I've spent every night at Reid's since the night he proposed. It's been intimate and domestic. I never thought I would enjoy the company of one person so much. No wedding plans as of yet, I'm not ready to rush into anything, since he proposed while we were at odds, I think we need more time to get to know each other, but we are talking about tearing down the wall that separates our apartments. So that's something.

As we ride the elevator to work, I take a moment to breathe him in, resting my hand on the crook of his elbow. It feels so natural.

"You know what?" I dig into my purse. "I think it's time."

"We've only got twelve more floors to go, I don't think I can be that quick."

"Not that. This." I pluck out the beautiful engagement ring. "Will you do the honors?"

He smiles, his blue eyes filled with love and adoration, and slips the ring on my left ring finger. "Perfect."

The two of us have shared a lot of intimate details about our lives, little by little, but there's one topic I've been purposely avoiding. With this ring on my finger, I can't very well keep hiding. "Listen, I want to tell you, people are going to say a lot of things about me. You know my history with men, and some people aren't as understanding as you. Aside from the jealousy thing, which I hope you've gotten over."

He laughs. "I feel pretty solid about us."

"Good. Just remember, whatever anyone says, I never sleep my way to closing a deal. Never have. I'm going to play the woman card," I warn, "But, because I'm a woman, and various other factors, it's an easy accusation to make. It's not true."

"Understood." The doors to the elevator slide open. "So, do we send out a memo to tell everyone you're going to be my wife?"

I think on it for a few seconds, then grab for his hand. He walks me to the door of my office where Ben is sitting and awaiting my arrival. I give Reid a chaste kiss on the mouth. "That should do it."

Reid smiles, and I love the knowledge that I had the power to give him that happiness. He struts to his office, and I can see him talking to Delores, pointing back to me. Delores's face pinches with disapproval, and I know Reid just told her the news.

I give a small wave. When I turn to Ben, his mouth is hanging open in surprise.

"*No.*"

"It's true. Reid and I are a thing."

Ben looks down at my left hand, the diamond must have caught the light. He rounds his desk and yanks my hand toward him. "Let me see that," he demands, inspecting the ring. "You're engaged?"

"We are."

"I thought we hated him?"

I shrug my shoulders and make my way into my office, tossing my purse on the fainting couch. "I guess sometimes hate turns into love."

"You're joking, right? After everything he did?"

I start up my laptop and slide on my readers. "It takes two to tango. I'm complicit in what happened before, but we're past that now. We're happy—"

"Are you insane? What happened to Sam? Did the aliens get to you? Invasion of the Body Snatchers? Come on. This isn't normal."

I expected some blowback. Ben has been privy to most of my sneaky underhandedness. I can't fault him for being cynical. "People do crazy stuff every day. We're no exception. In fact, we're less crazy because it's going to be a long engagement."

Ben plops down on the chair across from me, resigned and annoyed.

"No more attitude. Be happy for me. Be happy for us. That's an order soldier," I tell him, trying to make light of the situation.

"Aye-aye captain. I want to talk to you about something."

"Sure. What's up?" I give my full attention, the reluctance in his tone gives me the impression that whatever it is, it's serious.

"I've been given an opportunity to go to Peru. To study the Nazca Lines," he says and begins to educate me on the history of the ancient sand drawings of South America.

"That's amazing!" My reaction is over the top, but my excitement is genuine. This is so cool.

"You're not mad?" he asks, sounding surprised.

"Not at all. Follow your dreams, dear Benjamin. I want nothing but the best for you."

Ben and I spend the first two hours of our morning on-line stalking some of the modern-day alien theorists, arguing for or against the proof of alien existence. When lunchtime comes around, I decide it's time to sneak a break with the boss. The guardians, meaning Delores and Ben are out, and I want to check off another item on my naughty-girl list.

I strut into Reid's office, shut the door, and lock it. Reid is on a phone call and looks tense. I know the perfect way to help alleviate that.

"Send over the numbers, and I'll take a look," he says to the person on the other end of the line, keeping his eyes pinned on me as I walk toward him.

I roll his seat back and kneel in front of him, his eyes go wide, and he grins like the Cheshire Cat. My hand cups his crotch, and I'm delighted to find he's already hard.

I unzip his fly, and he helps me by pushing his pants past his hips, still talking to someone on the phone. The beautiful sight of his fat cock makes my mouth water. I run one finger along the shaft and watch as the skin on his thighs pebble from my touch.

A small bubble of precum glints at the slit, and I lick my lips, wanting a taste.

I close my lips over the head, darting my tongue. My fingers glide along the thick veins of his shaft.

"Yeah, um, that would be great," he says to the phone, and I can tell he's having a tough time concentrating.

In a swift move, I sink my mouth around Reid's erection. His hips buck, and I begin to jerk him, working my mouth down farther and farther until I have him nearly to the hilt, swallowing as I go.

Reid pushes his fingers through my hair, and the muscles in his thighs tense. "I'll have to call you back." He hangs up without saying goodbye. "Holy fuck, sweetheart."

I pinch and give a gentle squeeze to his balls, almost making him jump out of his seat. He grabs onto the armrests of the chair, gripping tightly.

His cock is hard as steel on my tongue, and I know he's about to come. I suck him harder, like the fattest straw for the thickest milkshake, until I feel hot spurts of seed sliding down my throat.

When I stand, I look at my work, slouched in a chair with his pants at his knees. I can't help but smile.

He smiles back at me.

"I thought you might want to break-in your new office," I tell him, my voice thick with sex and coated with cum.

He yanks me into his arms and spreads me out on top of his desk. Frank's desk. "Are you sure you want to defile your dad's desk?"

"I've never wanted to defile anything so much in my life," he says, hitching up my skirt.

57

Reid

Every morning, I wake up next to the most beautiful woman in the world. Every morning I'm still shocked as shit that she said 'yes.' The whole idea of proposing was foolhardy, I'll admit that. She could have broken it off the moment we stepped out of her parent's country club, but she didn't. She was angry. Oh man, was she angry, but she still heard me out, and to top that she believed me. I didn't expect it to go quite so smooth, but I guess fate has a way of intervening. The fact that she called to me on the beach that day back in July was fate. Fate intervened when Frank had a heart attack, although I'm sure he would disagree with that sentiment. More than anything else, fate ensured I would take her job, something I wish I could regret. Had I walked away, that diamond ring wouldn't be on her finger right now.

There's a knock on my office door. "You busy?" Sam asks, pushing the door open.

"I always have time for you, sweetheart," I tell her, hoping for a repeat of what happened yesterday. Maybe I should add desk sex to my daily calendar.

"Not for that," Sam says, coming around my desk and sitting in my lap.

I wrap my arms around her, welcoming the feel of her softness. "What's up?"

"A couple of things. First, did you tell Frank about us?"

I can't believe I forgot to tell my dad I was engaged. He isn't my favorite person in the world, but that doesn't exclude him from my life, not anymore at least. I cringe at the thought.

"Oh my God," she says, giving a playful shove to my shoulder. "You *didn't* tell him. The whole office knows. What do you think the chances are that someone hasn't told him?"

Damn, she's cute when she's mad. "Pretty good, since he doesn't work here anymore."

Her eyes go wide as if I have offended her. "You think Delores didn't get on the phone and call Frank the minute you turned your back? You're more delusional than I thought."

I hold up a finger to my lips and press a button on the intercom. "Yes, Mr. Gallagher," Delores answers.

"Quick question. Did you tell Frank about me and Sam?"

"No, sir," she says, and I can imagine the face of disgust she must be making at my mention of Sam. "It's not my place to tell."

"Thank you, Delores." I disconnect the call. "See? He doesn't know."

She folds her arms and pouts out her bottom lip in disappointment.

I run my finger along her lip. "You're adorable when you don't get your way."

She laughs. "You'll be adorable when you realize you have to call him and make arrangements for dinner, with Stella, so we can tell them our good news. The sooner, the better, before he hears it second-hand."

Shit. I loathe the thought of having to dine with Stella. Frank, I can deal with. Stella is going to be a problem. "Fine, but

I want it on our turf."

"Bad idea," Sam says. "Then we lose the upper-hand. They'll stick around as long as they want. If we go to Frank's, we can make plans and be out of there at a reasonable time."

I nod, thinking about the points she's made. "How did you not get this job?"

"Decisions made during near-death experiences are always suspect."

"Fine, I'll call Frank and set up dinner for tonight."

"No can do, I'm afraid. I have a dinner meeting with Silas Keogh tonight. I want to get this deal figured out and behind us."

Silas Keogh has managed to drag out the negotiations with BLH for over three months. Which is ridiculous, considering he's the one who wanted to sell and had a buyer in mind. This contract should have been to the lawyers and back by now. I'm sure he's doing it as a way to torture me. I'm not sure what his end game is yet, but I'll know it when I see it.

"Hello? Anybody home?" Sam asks, waving her hand in front of my face. "Looks like I lost you there for a minute. You okay?"

I scratch my forehead, trying to think how to say what I'm thinking. "Be careful with Keogh. He's capable of more than you think."

"I know all about him. I've been around for a little while. Have some faith."

"You don't know 'all about him,'" I tell her, my defenses rising.

"Is there something you need to tell me?"

I can tell she's suspicious, and for a while too, but she hasn't been able to figure it out. "Silas Keogh was Amanda's father."

Sam's face turns as white as a sheet of paper.

"He's a grade-A prick. He'll use anything and anyone to get what he wants. His own daughter included. Silas tried to arrange a marriage for Amanda with some Middle Eastern businessman, hoping to be able to get into the market in Dubai. When she refused, the result wasn't pretty. A few years later, when she married me, he was irate. Told me I had to work for him because he considered Frank to be the competition. I don't know why. I guess to Silas everyone is the competition. If I didn't, well, let's just say, he made some unsavory threats."

She nods, and I can tell she's trying to absorb the information I've dumped on her. "Okay. I'll be careful. All the more reason to finish this up."

Sam leans in and gives me a sweet, soft kiss on the lips, letting it linger for an extra second. "You know I love you, right?" she asks as she hops off my lap.

"I do. It's just this is the first time you've said it to me."

"No." Her head tilts like she's trying to recall. "That can't be right." She looks up at me, her eyes filled with love. She flashes that gorgeous smile of hers, the one that makes my heart sink with happiness. "I guess you know I mean it then, huh?"

"Yeah, sweetheart, I really do."

58

Sam

The plan is to meet Silas Keogh in the restaurant of Keogh Tower for dinner. This deal between Keogh and BLH has been a monkey on my back, and I will be able to breathe a sigh of relief when it's over. This ends tonight, I don't care what it takes. After learning about Reid's connection to Keogh, it's become imperative to finish this up and leave it in the past where it belongs.

The restaurant is full tonight, and I scan the dining room, looking for Silas, but I can't seem to find him. There is a bartender washing glasses, and I approach him. "Excuse me, I'm looking for Silas Keogh. Have you seen him?"

The bartender sets a glass on a drying rack and wipes his hands. "Are you Sam Valentine?"

I nod.

"Mr. Keogh left a message for you." He grabs an envelope by the register.

He hands it to me, and as I walk toward the lobby, I open it.

Dear Sam,

I've decided it would work best for us to have dinner in my suite.

Please join me in 3110.

Silas

The note puts me on edge. Why would Silas leave me a note? He could have called and made the proper arrangements through the appropriate channels, such as calling Ben, email, or even texting me. The thought looming over my head is—why are we meeting in his suite?

The new location is unseemly, to say the least. As I take the elevator to the thirty-first floor, my stomach roils with apprehension. I shove Silas's note back in the envelope and stick it in my purse. When I step off the car, I walk past a couple of rooms, then give a tentative knock on the suite door of 3110.

Silas answers, wearing jeans and a knit navy-blue sweater. If he didn't give me the creeps, he could be handsome.

"Sam, please come in."

I follow him and let out a breath when I realize the suite is set up like an apartment with a separate living room, kitchen and dining area, and bedroom. We might still be alone, but at least the surroundings feel neutral.

"Sorry about the sudden change in plans," Silas says as he walks to the kitchen. "I needed a quieter place to finish a few things. Would you like a glass of wine?"

"White, if you have it." I take off my coat and set my purse and satchel on the entryway table. I settle onto the leather couch, perching on the edge of the cushion, crossing my feet at the ankles, and keeping my spine straight. My mother would be so proud of my lady-like posture.

"You look divine," he says, walking out to the living room with two glasses of white wine. "I hope I'm not keeping you from anything important."

Divine? I look down at my lap wondering if I have changed my clothes since this morning. Nope, still a pencil skirt and blouse, nothing I haven't worn before during a meeting with him. "Nothing is more important to me than making this deal work, Mr. Keogh," I tell him, trying to shake off the predator vibes.

"Please, call me Silas." He sits next to me, his leg touching mine.

"Oh," I stand up and walk back toward the door. "I need to get the contract." With the most recent negotiations in hand, I sit at the far end of the couch and spread out some papers on the coffee table for him to look over. "You can see for yourself, everything is how we agreed."

Silas leans back and crosses his legs, taking a sip of wine. "Let's not rush, Sam. We have all the time in the world. Why don't you tell me how the transition is going with Frank stepping down."

"It's going well. Reid, Frank's son," I clarify because I'm not sure if Silas knows that I know that he's Amanda's father, "is proving himself. It must be in the gene pool."

Silas let's out a terse laugh. "Good to hear. What's with the ring on your finger? Is there someone special in your life?" he asks, nodding his head toward my left hand.

I instinctively hide my hand under my leg. "Um, yeah. I recently got engaged."

"Congratulations. Anyone I might know?"

I'm not sure how to answer that. The last thing I want to do is tell Silas that it's Reid who I plan to marry. On the other hand, if it comes out before this is over, it'll be nothing but bad news. Because Silas Keogh, himself, is bad news.

"I'm sure you've heard of him. Reid Gallagher?"

Silas doesn't say anything for a beat, and his eyes seem darker than usual, and I realize it's because they're soulless. He's soulless. Reid said he wasn't above sacrificing his own flesh and blood. Who am I, but the means to an end?

"Well, that's wonderful to hear. I'm sure the two of you will be incredibly happy," Silas says, but the sentiment is empty.

Luckily, the knock on the door interrupts wherever this

conversation might be heading. A man dressed in white, wheels in a cart with covered plates, and sets it up at the dining table.

"Shall we discuss over dinner?" Silas asks, pointing at the papers spread out on the coffee table.

As we examine the offer, I'm happy to find that Silas is entirely on board with the new terms of the contract. He doesn't bother to put up a fight when BLH lowered the price they were willing to pay. Why couldn't it have been this easy three months ago? As I swallow the last forkful of poached salmon, Silas rises from the table and positions himself behind me. The hairs on the back of my neck stand on end.

Silas runs his finger down the length of my arm and pushes my hair to the side, exposing my neck. He leans down. "You're a very beautiful woman, Sam," he whispers, the heat of his breath in my ear. "But I'm not going to sign that contract. There's still one more demand that needs to be met."

The salmon turns to stone in my stomach. "What else can we do for you, Mr. Keogh? I'm not sure BLH is willing to bend any further."

"Sometimes, you have to be flexible. You're flexible aren't you, Sam?" he asks, running his tongue along the column of my neck.

"I don't understand." The idea that Silas Keogh expects me to sleep with him seems impossible.

"I think you do." He wraps his fingers around my throat and forces me to look up at him. The look on his face scares the living shit out of me.

59

Sam

I understand what Silas wants. I understand the position I'm in with his hands wrapped around my throat. I'm at his mercy. "I don't know what you've heard." I focus on the painting of a woman and young son hanging on the wall next to me. That could be me one day, holding the hand of the son I share with Reid. Focusing on the gentle brush strokes helps me stay calm. That, and the idea of what the future may hold. "But this isn't how I close a deal."

Silas removes his hands from my neck, and I take a gulping breath. Although his grip was not forceful enough to stop the flow of air, the fright from the threat is enough to keep me from taking a deep breath.

"Of course you don't, Sam," Silas says, walking away, leaving me at the table alone.

Is that it? Are we done? I want to grab my stuff and run out of here as fast as my feet will carry me, but I don't think Silas is finished with whatever it is he's playing at. I'll never know what that is if I leave now. Instead, I choose to sit at the table, waiting patiently, refusing to show fear.

Several minutes later, Silas appears from the bedroom with an orange folder in his hand. He sits in a chair next to me, opens the folder, and with methodical precision lays out each piece of paper side by side. They're photographs. I try not to look, but something catches my eye. Reid. Reid and a beautiful, young brunette holding hands, strolling down the beach.

Silas sits back in his chair, and I can tell he's trying to gauge my reaction, but I refuse to give him one.

"That's my daughter." He points to the picture of Amanda and Reid on the beach. "That's Reid. Did you know he's married to my daughter?" he asks as if his daughter is still alive.

I don't answer.

"I never cared for the man. He was never good enough for her."

Because marrying her off to some Middle Eastern man for a business opportunity was good enough? But I don't say it. I remain mute.

"Do you know how she died?"

"A car accident."

"So, Reid has talked to you about her then, huh? I'm sure some of the more pertinent details were glossed over. Did he tell you why Amanda was driving alone? Why she decided to up and leave her husband behind?"

Again, I don't say anything, not wanting to give him any credence.

He scans the pictures laid out before us and takes his time as he selects the perfect snapshot. He sets a glossy photo in front of me. As much as I don't want to look, I can't help myself. It's a picture of Reid sharing a passionate kiss with a woman. A woman who wasn't his wife. A million thoughts flit through my mind, but I must keep my focus, I can't be distracted by images that could mean nothing. Nothing or everything.

"Do you know who that is?" Silas asks.

The chignon of red is a dead giveaway. I've met Stella

several times, and she's always been cordial, rough around the edges, but cordial none the less. The sight of Reid kissing his stepmother turns my stomach, and I force the bile back down with sheer will.

"This picture was taken a week before Amanda died," Silas tells me. "I knew Reid was a lying cheat the first time I met him, but Amanda wouldn't listen to me. I had him followed, and wouldn't you know, the day his stepmom comes to the city, I get all the proof I need."

I close my eyes, staving off the tears which threaten to fall. I don't know who I'm sadder for, Reid, Amanda, or myself. How long was Reid having an affair with Stella? Is it still going on? Reid did live with Frank and Stella for a couple of months until he got his own place, who's to say they weren't sneaking around behind Frank's back? It would be the perfect way to get back at Frank. Reid harbored so much animosity toward his father. Would he screw Stella to stick it to Frank? I hate that I can't answer with an unequivocal 'no' because how well do I know Reid?

"If he hadn't cheated on Amanda, she never would have been driving on that highway. She'd still be alive," Silas says, his tone sad yet angry.

A small part of me hurts watching this grieving father. Although what he says may be true, I find it strange that he's skewed the situation to absolve himself of any fault. If he hadn't shown Amanda those pictures, she never would have left. She wouldn't have died.

"I've heard enough," I tell Silas, as I stand. I turn on my heel and walk to the entryway; grab my coat, purse, and satchel; and decide to leave the contracts where they lay, on the coffee table.

As I step across the threshold to the hallway, Silas grabs my arm, turning me to face him. I give him a hard stare, but it doesn't deter him. He yanks me toward him and crushes his mouth to mine.

When he releases me, he takes a step back. "Have a good

night, Sam," he says, closing the door.

My brain is a muddled mess of confusion. Absentminded, I walk toward the elevator, press the button, and step into the car. Nothing makes sense. I don't know how to process everything that has happened. What I do know is that I can't go back to Reid's apartment tonight. I don't think I can look him in the face, and with all the emotions flitting through me at the moment, I don't know if I'll fuck him or beat him to a bloody pulp.

I send Reid a text because I don't think I will be able to hold my composure if I hear his voice.

Me: "Hey, going to crash at my place."

As I slide into a cab, I get a reply.

Reid: "Sure. We can sleep there tonight."

It's challenging to ditch your fiancé with any degree of tact when he lives right next door.

Me: "I think I need some time alone."

My phone rings, I knew I was being too hopeful that he would give me some space, no questions asked.

"Is everything okay? Silas didn't give you any trouble, did he?"

The menacing tone in his voice keeps me from telling him anything that happened between Silas and me. I'm not looking to cause problems. I just want this deal done and out of my life. "No. The meeting was fine," I lie. "He seems to be satisfied this time around. We should set up a time to get him and Bennett in the same room and have them sign off on everything. That way if anything else comes up, they can deal with it at that moment."

"Yeah. That's an excellent idea. Listen," Reid says, his voice turning soft. "I don't want you to feel like I'm smothering you. If you want to stay at your place tonight without me, I understand."

My heart fractures. "I don't feel smothered. Not at all. I'm just drained and want to spread out in my own bed."

"That's fine. I'll see you in the morning then?"

"Yeah."

Just before I disconnect the call, I hear him, "Hey?"

"Yeah?"

"I love you."

A tear breaks free because I love him so much, but the weight of those words has never been as clear to me as they are right now. "Yeah, me too."

60

Sam

Reid has been kind and thoughtful all day, sending me a huge bouquet of white roses and never once asking me what happened last night at Keogh Tower. I'm sure he's itching with questions, but he's managed to keep it reined in, and that's precisely the kind of support one should want in a life partner.

It's with that thought in the back of my mind that I toss Reid the keys to Spock.

"Really?" His face lights up with pure joy but morphs into suspicion. "Wait a minute, you're not going to have me arrested, are you?"

I shrug my shoulder. "Maybe," I say as I get into the passenger side.

"Good enough for me." He slides into the driver's seat.

We pull out onto the street and make our way toward Frank's house in the village of Winnetka.

"How'd your talk with Frank go yesterday?" The two men haven't spoken since Frank retired and Reid took over.

"Short, sweet, and to the point," Reid answers as he turns

onto the highway.

We sit there for a few minutes, silent. I fiddle with my phone and he pays attention to the road, the air between us is tense in a way it hasn't been for weeks. Before we got engaged, we knew what had transpired and what we were fighting for, or against, but this is one-sided, and I can tell Reid has picked up on that. I don't think I'm ready to talk about it yet. I'm not sure what to do with the information. Are they all lies? Partial truths conveniently strung together to imply something which doesn't truly exist? I don't know.

"Thanks for letting me drive," Reid says, breaking the silence. "I've been dying to get back behind the wheel of this bad boy."

"Whatever happened to your Ducati?" I ask, thinking back to when we met in Barbados.

He gives a sad smile. "Sold it for a plane ticket to Chicago."

"You didn't have any money?" It's a bit strange that a man with his background would be broke after a few years of not working. With everything he endured, I can understand him running away, starting a new career as a resort bartender. All that makes perfect sense to me. Having not saved any money after working in such a lucrative business as New York real estate—that seems strange.

"No. I did. I'd saved plenty of money when I worked for Keogh. I invested it well and had great returns."

"So, why didn't you use it?"

"I don't know. It just didn't seem right. Felt like blood money."

And my heart fractures a little more for Reid. "How did you afford the apartment next door to me?" Apartments in a building like the Onyx cost millions.

"I thought about it and decided Amanda wouldn't want to see me waste my life pining for her. That I should use the money to find happiness." He reaches over and squeezes my hand. "*You are my happiness.*"

Reid's honesty is the prime reason I have a hard time believing that he cheated on his wife. He's being open and communicative, not holding back the answers to questions. And, let's face it, those questions have been intrusive and brutal.

"I don't mean to pry."

"Don't apologize," he replies. "You need to know these things if you're going to be my wife. I don't want to keep any secrets from you. I want you to read me like a book."

I learned a whole new vocabulary, verbs, onomatopoeias, and other grammar-related terms that were about Reid. About us as a couple. Yesterday morning I knew Reid. I knew he hated when I used his razor, and when he would come out with a dozen tiny pieces of toilet paper dotting his face, he wouldn't complain. He should, but he won't. I also know he ties his shoes like a child, using bunny ears to make and secure the loops. That he can answer the questions on Jeopardy with a disturbingly high percentage of accuracy. The claims Silas Keogh made don't fit the man I love—pure and simple.

"This is it," Reid says as we pull up to Frank's house.

As we walk to the front door, I grab the keys from Reid and tap the button on the keychain, locking up Spock nice and tight. To say I worry that it would be stolen is a massive understatement. Even though Frank and Stella's house is in the most expensive suburb in Cook County, I don't trust anyone. I love my car that much.

Before I can ring the bell, the door of the palatial style home swings open.

"Samantha, darling," Stella exclaims as she bends and gives me an air kiss on both cheeks. "How are you? It's been ages."

Stella Gallagher must have gone to refinement school in the past few years because the last time I ran into her, she was visiting Frank at work, and her greeting of choice was, "Hey, bitch."

"Reid," she says, turning her attention to my fiancé. "Just because you moved out, doesn't mean you have to be a stranger."

She embraces him, the hug anything but innocent.

Did she grab his ass?

Reid pushes his stepmother away gently. "Nice to see you too, Stella," he says with no amount of enthusiasm.

We follow Stella to the kitchen where snacks of caviar and crackers are waiting to be nibbled on. I help myself, spreading on the caviar. It's not the cheap stuff either.

"Dinner will be ready shortly," Stella tells us. "Frank was still getting ready last I checked. Today hasn't been one of his best."

I finish chewing. "What do you mean?"

"He had dialysis today. For some reason, the treatments wear him out for the rest of the day. Sometimes longer."

That sounds awful. I don't know much about dialysis, but I never thought the act of cleaning the toxins out of the blood would be so taxing.

"I feel fine," Frank says, entering the room, straightening his tie as he walks. "She's always worrying," he says, kissing Stella on the cheek.

"I can't help it. I love you and don't want to lose you," Stella responds.

I'm not sure if I want to clasp my heart and say 'awe,' or vomit, thinking back to that picture of Reid and Stella kissing.

Frank releases his wife and draws me into a hug. His body feels cool compared to every other living person in the world, his skin pallid. It's the first time I've realized how close Frank is to death.

61

Sam

The Victorian décor of the dining room doesn't match the impression of what I would have thought to be Stella's taste. I'd expect everything to be swathed in black with accents of gold. There's no particular reason why—it just seems like her style.

"Reid, my boy," Frank says, stabbing at his salad. "How are you adjusting to being president?"

"It's fine. A bit of a learning curve, but I think I'm getting the hang of it," is all Reid says, not giving enough details to satisfy his father's curiosity.

"Sam, how are you getting along?" Frank asks after it becomes clear that he's not going to get much information from his son.

"I'm doing great. Life's good. Ben is planning to take leave for a couple of months." Frank loves office gossip.

"What for?" Frank asks.

"The Nazca Lines in Peru."

"What's that?" Stella chimes in.

I scratch at my forehead, trying to think how best to describe them, and in a way that would make Ben proud. "They're these giant, ancient lines drawn in the dirt of some desert in Peru. Not just lines, like designs, birds and monkeys and stuff. Apparently, they can't be seen to stand next to them, you have to climb a mountain. I guess they can even be seen from space."

"Really?" Frank says. "I wonder what the purpose of drawing pictures in the sand would be if you can't see it?"

This, I know the answer to. "Aliens."

Reid drops his fork, and it clatters as it hits his plate. "What?"

Frank begins to clap his hands. "Of course."

"I don't follow," Reid says.

"What you don't know about the world's best assistant is that he's a conspiracy theorist," I explain.

Reid raises his eyebrow.

"A New World Order existing in an underground city beneath an airport in Denver, a covert American space program that colonized Mars back in the sixties. Stuff like that."

"And do you share these beliefs?" Reid asks, and I can't help but notice his skepticism.

I purse my lips. "Not all of it, but some of it makes sense."

Frank sits back in his chair, folding his hands and smiling, amused by the interaction between the President and Vice President of Sterling.

"Like what?" Reid asks. "And please, be specific."

"Okay." I take a moment to think it through. I need one of Ben's more recent and less crackpot theories. "Area Fifty-One."

Reid rolls his eyes.

"Don't roll your eyes at me. The U.S. government denied the existence of Area Fifty-One since the Roswell incident. They didn't acknowledge the secret military base until twenty-thirteen."

"Oh, come on. Area Fifty-One? Seriously?"

"Absolutely. And do you know why the government decided to fess up? Satellites."

"Satellites?" Reid questions incredulously.

"Yeah, satellites. The images were irrefutable proof that it did exist."

Reid smiles big.

"What?" I ask, not sure what that look is for.

He shakes his head. "I had no idea I was marrying a conspiracy nut," he says, lifting my hand and giving it a kiss.

Stella chokes on her wine and pounds on her chest. "Excuse me?"

"That's what I wanted to talk to you about," Reid says, looking at Frank. "A few weeks ago, I asked Sam to marry me, and she said 'yes,'" he tells them, raising my hand to show the engagement ring.

Frank's smile beams with pure joy. "How did this happen? I didn't know you two were seeing each other. In fact, I thought you were a bit at odds."

I can't help but blush, I'm sitting at the dinner table with my former boss, announcing the fact that I'm sleeping with his son. "We were, but, um, we worked things out."

"It's awfully sudden," Stella says. "You two hardly know one another."

I take a deep breath and remind myself that Stella's a bitch, and I don't care what she thinks.

"Pot, meet Kettle," Reid says with a laughing snark.

"Stop. Please," Frank begs. "This is wonderful news. We should celebrate."

Frank pops a bottle of champagne, and we spend quality time talking about the crazy road that is our love story, and Frank is thrilled with the whole thing.

"Sam, come with me," Frank says, waving for me to follow him to his study. "I think this calls for a nice bourbon."

I look over to Reid, questioning if I should go or stay.

"Go," Reid mouths, giving me an approving smile.

"You sure you should be smoking that?" I ask Frank as he puffs on the end of a cigar.

He laughs. "My doctor would have a coronary if he knew.

But," he takes another puff and exhales, blowing out smoke rings, "life is short."

Frank hands me a cigar, and I work to light it as I sit back in the chair. "Smooth," I say taking a puff. "How have you been feeling?"

"I've been better. It's getting easier though, I guess."

"Really?" He doesn't look too hot.

"No. This dialysis wipes me out. When I'm not hooked up to a machine, I'm sleeping. I ache, everywhere, all the time."

"I'm sorry." I take another puff. "If there's anything I can do, don't hesitate to ask."

"Thanks," Frank says, sighing. "On to happier things. Have you set a date?"

I fill him in on my wish for a long engagement and that no definitive plans have been set yet. "We're still getting to know each other."

"If I know Reid, and I do—better than he would like, I'm sure—he's not going to wait long. He married his first wife the day after they graduated from college. It would have been sooner if she hadn't convinced him they needed to finish school first."

Reid and I discussed this, we're going to wait, there's no need to rush into anything, and although I feel rock-steady in that fact, I don't bother trying to convince Frank otherwise.

I glance at my watch. "It's starting to get late. We should be heading home."

I rise from the chair, and Frank walks me to the study doors.

"Thank you for having dinner with us. You know, I've always thought of you as a daughter, but now it'll be official." He gives a soft kiss to my cheek. "Welcome to the family."

Frank retreats into his office, and I walk to the dining room to collect my fiancé, but he isn't there. So, I check the kitchen, the living room, and the den, but I can't seem to find him. As I approach the front door, thinking he's waiting for me at the car, I hear a crash from the top of the stairs.

The voice in my head screams at me not to go up those steps, that whatever is happening up there will somehow change everything, but I shove the voice to the darkest recesses of my mind, thinking myself ridiculous.

Boy, oh boy, how I wish I would have listened to that voice because as I round the corner at the top of the steps, everything Silas told me, everything I saw in those pictures is in 3-D and ten feet in front of me.

62

Reid

Sam accompanied Frank to his study to talk, about what, I don't know, not that I care. Frank's too worried about getting on my good side to badmouth me, and even if he did, Sam wouldn't buy it. She's learned first-hand what a coward Frank can be. Now, I'm stuck at the table with Stella. Not the most ideal situation, but at least this whole thing will be over soon, and Sam and I can go home where I can spend hours devouring her delicious body.

"You're marrying her?" Stella says. "I'm not sure that's a good idea."

"I don't care what you think." I stare at her, not willing to give her any room for argument.

"After what happened with Amanda? You sure you want to go down that road again?"

I've never in my life thought about hitting a woman, but I'll be damned if I don't have the urge now. "Don't you dare mention her. I never want that name to leave your lips again. Do you understand?"

She swallows and looks down. "I'm sorry, I didn't mean to upset you. I worry that's all. Sam doesn't have a reputation for being exclusive."

"That's rich."

"Listen, I don't want to fight," Stella says as she stands to leave the table. "But I have something I need to show you. Upstairs."

"No way."

"It's not what you think. Please?"

I give in to her plea and my own curiosity and follow Stella upstairs, regardless of every fiber of my being telling me not to. I trail behind her and into one of the guestrooms where she opens the bottom drawer of the dresser and hands me a small stack of black and white eight by ten pictures.

"I thought you should know the truth," she says.

I flip through the pictures, some of them are of Amanda and me in the most intimate moments shared between a husband and wife. Others are of...

"Silas Keogh tried to blackmail me. Said Frank would find the pictures 'enlightening.'"

My heart plummets to my stomach, and I sit on the edge of the bed, my legs losing the ability to hold me up any longer. "Where did he get these?"

"It's from when I visited New York. I stopped by to see you and—"

"And tried to get me to fuck you."

She flinches at my crudeness. "Yes."

I can't believe what I'm seeing. Anyone who looks at these photos will perceive them as two lovers embracing, but that's not what happened. The saying goes that a picture paints a thousand words, but what words does a picture omit? It doesn't say that only seconds later I pushed Stella away and berated her until she cried. Told her that once a whore, always a whore. Words so powerful, I wish I felt sorry for saying them, but I don't.

"When did he try to blackmail you?" I ask, placing the pictures on the bed, face down. I don't want those images in my head a second longer than necessary.

"Last week."

Last week. Huh. "You say he 'tried' to blackmail you. Past tense."

"I persuaded him not to."

I can't imagine Stella has much to offer a man like Keogh. Everything she has is because of Frank. Silas must be aware of that fact.

"How?" I ask, but I'm fairly certain I already know the answer.

Stella's face reddens. "How do you think?" she hisses. "I'm not proud of it, but I would do it all over again in a heartbeat."

"And you're not worried Silas won't try to blackmail you with proof the two of you fucked?"

"I'm sure he will, but I don't care. I know you don't believe this, but I love Frank. These," she says, pointing to the pictures on the bed, "would destroy him."

They would. Images of a man's wife and his son in a passionate kiss could send a man spiraling over the edge. "You're right." The admission is foreign and wrong in this context, with her. "I'm sorry." These words make me want to puke.

Stella sits next to me on the bed. "I know we've had our differences, Reid, but I want us to try to get along. For Frank."

A month ago, her request would have done little to affect me. Now? I don't want to hold onto the resentment. "Yeah, I'll try."

"Yeah?" Stella asks, excited.

"Yeah."

Stella pushes me down so I'm lying flat on my back on the bed, and before I can figure out what's going on, she's straddling me.

"What the fuck are you doing?" I bellow, trying to hurry to the other side of the bed to get out from under her.

"You know you want it. We both do," Stella says, crawling on her hands and knees toward me.

"What happened to 'loving Frank' and all that other shit you were spewing?"

She has me cornered at the edge of the bed, and I swing my arms searching for—I don't know, a 'pause' button maybe—but during my pursuit, I knock a lamp off the nightstand. I'm distracted by the shattering of light. It gives Stella the advantage, and once again she is straddling me.

Stella laughs as she makes quick work of unknotting my tie. "This is going to happen. You and me, we're meant for each other. You can't keep denying it, and in a minute, you'll agree. You'll see how explosive we are together."

She tries to sweep her tongue into my mouth, but I won't part my lips. Three thoughts run through my mind.

One: Is she crazy? That's a definite "hell yes!"

Two: Is she going to...rape me?

Three: Can a man be raped?

That's an affirmative on all counts.

I throw her off with enough force that she rolls twice and falls off the bed and onto the floor with a thud.

"*My arm*," she cries, and I scramble off the other side of the bed.

When I walk around to where she lays, I stare down at her. She's sobbing, cradling her arm close to her body. It's disgusting and unnatural in its position. There is no way that arm isn't broken.

I can't hide my disdain, and I stare down at her as I straighten my tie then walk out of the guest bedroom. When I get down to Frank's office, I run my fingers through my hair, trying to put myself back together. I open the door to find Frank sitting on the leather couch reading a book. Alone. "Where's Sam?"

Frank sets his book down and raises an eyebrow. "She just left. I thought you were with her."

Fuck. She left. What happened? "What did you say?"

"Nothing. We chatted. It was pleasant. She said it was getting late and left. That's all I know," Frank says, raising his hands in defense.

She had to have seen Stella and me. Everything was fine until ten minutes ago. I close my eyes and try to remind myself that, even though Sam and I are in love, we have a relationship built on mistrust and revenge. We've been working on that, but if she walked in on Stella and...This is bad.

"Okay, thanks." I walk toward the door and turn back to Frank. "Your wife's a whore. She slept with Keogh and tried to corner me for a quick fuck. You'll need to figure that out. Have a good night."

Desperate to get away from this madhouse, I take a stroll through the neighborhood and order an Uber. Once I'm in the backseat, I work on a plan to convince Sam that what she saw between Stella and me was completely one-sided.

63

Sam

Home was not the place I wanted to go last night after seeing Reid pinned beneath his stepmom. My mind was a hurricane of fear and heartbreak. After driving around trying to make sense out of total bedlam, I ended up in front of Lizzie's building.

She welcomed me with open arms, and we talked. I let it all spill, what I saw, my own thoughts on whether Reid and I can have a successful marriage with so much going on around us. One thing I know with complete certainty is fate had a hand in us coming together. Reid ended up back in Chicago after being away for years, only months after we first met on an island thousands of miles from home. Now that we've been to hell and back, working through battle after battle—some may have been self-induced—fate wants to tear us apart.

Lizzie is almost four months along, and her ability to see things with reason and objectivity has been questionable. Must be the hormones. In a rare, and inconvenient, moment of clarity, Lizzie asked if I discussed with Reid the photos Silas showed me, or what I saw between Reid and Stella. Of *course,* I didn't. When someone trusts another with their heart, and that trust was fragile from the beginning, further discussing the hurt seems like a terrible idea. Lizzie whole-heartedly disagreed with me, but that's okay because her judgment can't be trusted anyway.

This morning when I walked into the office, I tasked Ben with an errand.

"You owe me," Ben says, walking into my office, bag in hand. He tosses it on my desk.

I peek inside. "You're the best. How many did you get?"

"Four."

"Four?" I have no clue how much I might need, but four seems kind of low.

"It's more than enough. My guy told me only one in a twenty-four-hour period. Any more and he might have to go to the hospital...for relief."

Hmm.

"Don't even think about it, Sam. What you're doing is shitty enough. Don't be that person. You're better than that."

"Since when are you on his side?"

"I'm not. I'm on the side of every man. This is stupid. I don't think you should do it."

"Oh, come on, Ben. It's a harmless prank."

"Tell yourself whatever you want," he says, walking back to his desk.

The meeting between Keogh, Inc., and BLH has been set up for this afternoon. I'll be elated the minute the whole mess of a deal is behind me. I print off the letter I plan to give to Reid and sign it. The initial plan didn't involve my resignation despite not getting the promotion, but here I am. Everything has become so complicated and ugly, and I don't want this to be my life. I want peace, serenity. By the end of the day, Bennett and Keogh will sign off on the contract, and I will have one last payday. It will be a nice chunk of change, so maybe I can take a year off and figure out what I want to do with my life. I sign the paper with a large flowing signature and twirl the ring on my left hand.

I can't do this. I can't marry Reid. He has enough with Frank's illness and taking over as the president of the family company. Oh yeah, and Stella. Can't forget about Stella. A marriage between us would never work. I slide off the ring and slip it into the envelope and seal it closed, leaving it on my desk.

Naturally, I worry about what will happen to Ben. He isn't planning to take his leave until the new year, but if there's one thing I'm sure of, it's that Reid won't toss him out the door when I leave. Reid will find a spot for Ben.

"There's an envelope on my desk. At three o'clock, on the dot, I want you to deliver it to Delores," I tell Ben. I decided not to hand it to him, worried that his nosiness will overpower my instructions and he'll read it. I don't want anything to happen too soon, and I don't want Ben to interrupt negotiations to try to talk me out of it.

"Three o'clock. Got it."

I walk to Reid's office with two cups of coffee in my hand. "You ready for this to be over?" Reid asks as he struts toward me and there's a pang of regret when I see him. His soft blue eyes are filled with warmth, admiration, and confusion. He texted and called me several times last night after I left Frank's, and I didn't respond.

He bends and gives me a kiss on the cheek as he takes the cup I offer him. "We need to talk, sweetheart."

"Later." I make sure to keep my left hand hidden.

Reid nods, and we walk toward the boardroom. When he takes a large sip of his coffee, I know there is no turning back.

Reid makes a sour face. "Does yours taste funny?" he asks, clucking his tongue like he's trying to rid the taste from his mouth.

"Black, remember?" I lift my cup. "Maybe the creamer's bad." I walk around the table and set out the folders containing the contracts, six copies in all.

"Why'd you leave me at Frank's?" Reid asks, following me around, and I can feel the tension rolling off him.

"This isn't the time to talk about it."

"No, it's not. Last night would have been the ideal time to talk about it, but you wouldn't answer your damn phone."

I set down the last folder and turn to look at him. "Later. I promise."

Reid's Adam's apple bobs up and down when he swallows, his eyes heavy with worry. "Are we okay?"

Nothing about us is okay anymore. By the grace of God, Tate Bennett and his lawyer enter the room, and I don't have to answer the question.

"Hey," I greet, walking up to Tate and his lawyer and shake their hands.

As they settle in, Silas and his lawyer file in and take their seats across from BLH. Reid sits at the head of the table, finishes his coffee, and crinkles the cup before tossing it in a trash can in the corner.

"Let's get this over with, shall we? I have some other things that need to be tended too, and these negotiations have wasted enough of our time," Reid says, glaring at Silas Keogh.

64

Sam

The lawyers are tearing the contract apart. I hoped we had more agreeable terms since the two companies have been fighting since day one. I thought we had it finally nailed down. That's why I insisted we have this meeting—put it all out there in the open and come to a compromise both sides can live with. Keogh and Bennett are sitting back, relaxed, letting their lawyers earn their keep.

I steal a glance at Reid, and he almost looks like a puppy tracking a treat. His head is turning side to side as he listens to the lawyers volleying their arguments. With an abrupt stop, Reid looks down at his crotch, his brow furrowed.

"Hey," I whisper, leaning over. "You okay?"

He clears his throat. "Yeah."

It must be working. That was quick. Reid took the last sip of his coffee five minutes ago. I figured it would take at least an hour before it kicked in. Maybe I gave him too much? Ben told me not to give Reid more than one because it could require medical intervention, but I figured that's one of those warnings that happens to one in every ten-thousand during the drug trial. I may have underestimated—

"This is insane," Tate bellows, looking aggravated. "Silas, you asked me to buy Keogh Tower from you. You sought Sam out specifically and asked her to make a deal. Why are you stone-walling?"

Keogh presents his copy of the contract, the one I gave him the other night, and slides it across the table to Tate. "It's signed."

Then why the hell are we here? Why has he let his lawyer make such a fuss over the whole thing if he has already signed the contract?

Reid readjusts himself in his chair, perching on the edge and wincing. "Great. It's settled then."

Silas nods. "It is. Sam here, is one hell of a negotiator."

My lunch begins to slosh in my stomach.

"Sam and I had an interesting dinner the other night," Silas continues, staring at Reid. "Seems your girl here has a special talent for closing the deal." Silas nods to his lawyer, and the lawyer whips out an iPad.

The iPad is set up in the middle of the table, and the lawyer taps the "play" icon.

We all scoot forward to watch, but no one in this room is as eager as I am to see what it will show.

Reid stands lightning-quick and hits the "pause" button. Picking up the conference room phone, he makes his demand to someone on the other side, probably Delores. "Get HR in here." He slams the phone back in the cradle. "I don't want another second to play until Sam has representation."

What is happening? Did I miss something? This has escalated so quickly, one minute Silas has the contract signed and ready, the next I'm under fire for...What? "What's happen—"

"Don't say a word," Reid says, looking around the room at every person, gauging their reactions.

As Reid assesses them, they stare back at him. Except not at his face.

I cover my mouth with my hand to prevent a gasp from escaping. Reid is still standing at the head of the table with a gigantic hard-on fighting to burst through his zipper. His eyes go wide when he looks down to see what everyone is staring at and immediately sits back down.

We wait for twenty minutes, the tension in the room palpable, before the head of HR, Susan, and one of the lawyers, Bill, arrive.

This is bad.

"What's so urgent?" Susan asks, her penciled eyebrows almost touching her hairline.

"Mr. Keogh wants to show us a video," Reid says simply.

"Have you watched it?" Bill asks, the question seems legitimate to everyone in the room except Reid.

"Not yet. I have some concerns about the implications that were made prior. I thought it would be a good idea to have someone here to represent Sam," Reid replies, his jaw ticking.

Bill and Susan both swing their heads toward me and give a look of "it figures."

Silas smiles and gives me a small wink. I want to claw his eyeballs right out of his head, spike them on the tips of my fingernails, and force-feed them to him.

Bill sighs, no doubt thinking about the trouble I've caused over the years. Something tells me that whatever this video shows, it will be the last nail in my coffin. A relief for Bill and Susan, but I didn't plan to get fired before I could resign.

"Can we do this in private?" I ask, believing at the very least, I should be spared some dignity of not being terminated in front of my clients, or anyone else for that matter. Employment termination is a profound and personal experience and shouldn't be a show for some CEOs and their lawyers.

Bill looks to Susan, who looks to Reid. Reid glances down at his crotch and then back up. "Any objections?" Reid asks the room.

The answer is a resounding "no," thank God.

Reid begins to stand but must reconsider because he sits back down. "If you could go down to the cafeteria, grab a coffee and a muffin," Reid says. "I'll send Delores to collect you when we're ready. Shouldn't be too long."

When the room clears, it's just me, Reid, Bill, and Susan.

"Okay, let's see what the fuss is about," Susan says, pressing "play."

When the clip begins, I recognize the hallway of Keogh Tower, Silas's hallway. I can't stifle my gasp when I see myself stepping out of Silas's suite, and I think back to what happened. I look a wreck, my hair's a mess, my clothes disheveled from me grabbing my things to get the hell out of there. To the casual observer, it suggests something far more salacious.

I look to Reid, and he's engrossed in the video, but it's what's coming up which has me worried the most. What will he think? Will he think that what happened was consensual? The tick of Reid's jaw is all I need to see to know that he is witnessing the kiss Silas forced on me. I also don't need to look at Susan and Bill to know what thoughts are creeping through their egg-shaped heads.

"I've seen enough," Reid says, slamming the iPad closed.

I'm supposed to be mad at Reid because he's fucking his stepmom, but why do I feel so deflated at the thought that he might believe what he saw with his own two eyes? Seeing is believing after all. There's no way in hell I'm going to be able to convince anyone that Silas's version of events is a lie.

"Well, shit," Susan mutters. "Bill, what are your thoughts?"

Bill laughs, and I don't find an ounce of humor in the situation. "The same." Bill turns to me. "What's your version of events?"

That's something, Bill's asking for my account instead of assuming I'm guilty. I will hold onto that sliver of hope because, even though I planned to quit, I don't want to be known as the corporate slut who screwed her way to close the deal. It's not what I'm about, and I won't have my hard work made acceptable on those terms. Regardless, no matter which way this goes—for or against me—I still plan to leave.

"It's not what it looks like," I tell Bill, keeping my eyes from straying to Reid's, I don't think I'm strong enough to deal with that fallout. "We had dinner, discussed the updated terms of the contract," Silas put his hands around my throat and showed me suggestive photos, "When he escorted me out, he kissed me. I didn't lead him on, make any kind of promises, he did it without any warning." It's the truth. That being said, it doesn't mean it's believable.

"What are our options?" Reid asks, looking to Susan.

Susan shrugs. "Ask for his statement. See if they match up."

"That's bullshit. You know it won't. Silas is counting on it, or else he wouldn't have put on this little sideshow," Reid says, vehemence dripping from each word.

"That may be, but with Sam's history, it isn't a far stretch," Susan says.

The words hurt. So. Damn. Much.

65

Sam

Angelic is not a word anyone who knows me would choose to describe my personality. I'm far from perfect. I'm loud, I'm boisterous, and I'm sure many refer to me as a bitch. If I were a man, they would call me driven, tenacious, and ruthless. Unfortunately, society has yet to catch up with the evolution of our civilization.

Bill and Susan are no exception.

"What does that have to do with anything?" I ask, now pacing the large boardroom, biting at my nails. I've never been a nail biter, but everything is beginning to spin out of control, and today seems as good a day as any to start.

Susan sighs with annoyance. "Where would you like me to begin? There was the intern three summers ago. The temp in acquisitions. The pastry puff in the lobby," she says, tossing her hands in the air.

"He was nineteen. Completely legal." As if that little fact will somehow help my case.

"Oh, and whatever happened to the assistant you had before

Ben?" Susan asks, picking up where she left off. "I'm surprised Ben hasn't gone running for the hills."

I give Susan a hard glare, but it does nothing to crack her icy demeanor. It's a checkmate of wills. I'm not sure if I hate or admire her.

"Now, there's that young woman from the mailroom," Bill chimes in.

The mailroom.

Girl from the mailroom.

This sounds familiar.

"What girl from the mailroom?" Reid asks, shifting his hips in his seat.

I almost forgot he was here. By the way his face pulls tight, I'm guessing that boner is beginning to get the best of him. I almost feel bad. After all, he's stuck up for me through this whole mess. I'm still confused by the entire Stella thing, but I don't have it in me to worry about it right now.

Bill fills Reid in on the events a couple of months back when I had a run-in with a girl from the mailroom. We'd had an argument about the existence of the term "Hump Day." I'm sure Reid knew about it because I remember him teasing me.

"She cited a 'hostile work environment' during her exit interview," Bill says. "There's a shit storm brewing, Sam. It's about to get messy."

"What are you saying, Bill?" Reid asks, his voice low and defensive.

I feel a migraine coming on, and I pinch the bridge of my nose. I don't have a choice. I know what Bill's going to say. "As of an hour ago, my resignation was delivered to Delores. My hope was that I could close this one last deal, but it's become obvious that my effort has caused more problems than solutions." I stand, straightening my spine and holding my chin high. "Effective now, I am stepping down as Vice President of Sterling Brokerage."

As much as I would like to blame my situation on the sexist

idealisms of the business world, I know such isn't the case. This is a disaster of my own making. Not even a man could come back from this unscathed. He would be forced into the same position I am.

"Sam, don't," Reid says, standing. "Don't do this. We can fix it."

I shake my head and make my way to the door. "I'm going to pack up my office."

The look of relief is written all over Bill and Susan's faces at my announcement.

"I'll call you," I tell Reid as I walk out the door.

As I make my way back to my office, I realize this will be the last time I walk this hall, the last time I will ever sit in that boardroom. When I find Ben at his desk, it's as if he can see right through me. Tears hover in his eyes, a concerned crinkle between his brows. Maybe defeat has a scent, like perfume. I give him a tight smile as I walk past his desk, and I step into the room I have called my office for almost a decade.

I start to pack my things one by one, gingerly placing them in boxes. Not a single tear has fallen, and I'm not sure if it's stoicism or indifference. I planned to resign, and I've somehow managed to beat them to the punch, but it feels different than I expected. I've worked in this building for the past decade. I lived and breathed for Sterling. Now that it's over, shouldn't I be, I don't know, sadder? Because I'm not. I'm not thrilled, but I'm not sad. That's weird, right?

"You don't have to do this." Reid is standing in the doorway, leaning against the jamb with his arms and feet crossed.

A sardonic laugh escapes me. "Yes, I do." I place a miniature Egyptian Sphinx in a box. The limestone replica was a gift from Ben, and the story that complemented the real one's construction was the first clue of my assistant's conspiratorial nature.

"I love you," Reid says as if it's a final plea.

My eyes flick up to him, and I scan his fantastic body, cloaked in a tailored suit. Except for the crotch. Right now that area is so full, I worry the seams will burst. I feel a little bad about what I did, but I won't dwell on it. "I love you too, but it doesn't change anything." I lift the box and walk toward the door, the last of my stuff packed. "It's not good for Sterling, and it's not good for you."

Reid sticks his arm out and blocks my escape. "We'll talk about it tonight over dinner. This doesn't change anything between us."

I'm not sure who he's trying to convince.

I kiss him on the lips. "Tonight."

Saying my goodbyes to Ben was hard, I'll miss him so much. He's been my rock in crazy times and my crazy in rocky times. He's been such a force in my life for five short years, but I know he'll be on to bigger and better things. For the past three years, he's been taking night classes with a focus on history and religion. It will be interesting to see what he grows up to be.

On my way to the elevator, Delores stops me and suffocates me in her bosom for a big brawny hug. She says she's going to miss my attitude, and that I was the best thing to ever happen to Sterling. Are those tears I see welling in her eyes? She tells me she will deny every word if I tell another soul. I think I might miss the old battle-ax. The two of us never got along, but we knew where we stood with each other, and I value that more than anything.

On my way home, I receive a text from Tate Bennett.

Tate: "Everything okay?"

Me: "Yeah."

Tate: "I'm here if you need anything."

Me: "Okay."

Tate: "Gallagher has a boner. It's disturbing."

And for the first time in days, a laugh spills from my lips. It's astounding to realize how my life has changed in the mere course of four months. In July, the idea that I would ever leave Sterling was beyond comprehension. Right now, leaving feels like the most natural thing in the world.

66

Reid

What happened to Sam was disgusting. She was put in a shitty position and forced out, and I hate that there is nothing I can do about it. That's not true, I can do something about it, but she won't let me. What good is being president if you can't save the one you love? She planned to resign when she walked into that boardroom today, and she didn't say a word about it to me.

Then there's the accusation from Keogh. It's a trap, and I'd be a goddamn fool to believe anything else. He set her up. Hell, the whole thing with selling Keogh Tower was probably a ruse. It wouldn't surprise me if he caught wind that I was coming back to Chicago to work for Frank and constructed this entire farce to fuck me over. My misery brings Silas pure joy.

I call Delores and have her deliver Bennett, Keogh, and their lawyers back to the conference room. I pace in front of the windows, trying to command this hard-on into something more manageable, but it just won't quit. What the fuck?

The door opens and the men file in and take their seats. I sit and lean back in my chair. No one speaks, they all look to me, waiting for me to start.

"That was dirty, Silas."

He doesn't respond because he knows I'm right. I'm sure it doesn't bother him at all, and he won't lose a second's sleep over it.

"Someone want to fill me in?" Bennett asks.

"It seems Silas here," I say, pointing toward my former father-in-law, "thought it would be in his best interests to impugn my fiancée's character."

Bennett's face contorts. "Fiancée? You and Sam are engaged?"

"For almost a month now."

Bennett stands and leans across the table and extends his hand for a shake. A real man never sits when shaking hands, one of the few useful things Frank taught me. Because of this fucking erection, I have no choice but to keep my ass planted to my chair.

I grasp his hand.

"Congratulations," Bennett says. "Never saw that one coming."

I laugh. "Thank you. Me neither."

Bennett sits back down. "So, what happened with Sam?"

"We fucked," Silas says, his tone cold and nonchalant, the smug look on his face tells me he's confident he hit the bullseye.

He did hit the bullseye. I leap across the table, the breakneck speed in which I find myself in front of Silas surprising even myself. I yank him from his chair and throw him against the wall, pinning him. "Tell the truth, Silas."

He smiles, a smile of pure evil. "It is the truth."

"The *fuck* it is," I roar.

He laughs at my outburst, and I yank him from the wall and slam him against it again. This time his lawyer decides things may be going too far and runs up beside me, grabbing at my arm.

Silas waves his hand at him. "It's fine, Claude," he tells his lawyer. "It's been a long time coming."

Claude nods and goes back to his seat.

"You're a real bastard, you know that?" I ask, spitting the words in his face.

"No more than you. You think Amanda didn't know about your incestuous relationship with your stepmother?" he asks.

The world around me turns black, my anger so penetrating I'm blind. "You told Amanda I was sleeping with Stella?" I choke the words out, destroyed by the idea that my wife thought I cheated on her. With Stella of all people. Amanda knew how I felt about my stepmother.

"I had proof. She couldn't turn a blind eye any longer. Not with the evidence in black and white right in front of her. If it weren't for you, she never would have gotten in that car. She would never have died. Your Oedipus issues killed my daughter."

I drop my hold from Silas and stumble backward. The idea that the last thought my wife had of me before she died was that I was unfaithful is breaking my heart.

Silas straightens his tie and jacket. "I wasn't about to let Sam go through the same thing as Amanda. She's a good woman, crazy, but a good woman. She deserves better than you."

Sam is a good woman, and if everything Silas has said is true, then she does deserve a better man than me. One with less baggage. One who will fight for her. I don't think I'm that man anymore. This morning, I thought I was, but now, I don't think so.

"Hold on a second," Bennett says. "Did you just say that Sam deserves better than Gallagher after you set her up to make it look like she slept with you?"

Jesus Christ, thank you for the voice of reason. I was so muddled with the idea that Amanda's death was my fault that it hadn't occurred to me that Silas set everything in motion.

"I don't know the whole story here," Bennett continues, "but it sounds to me like what happened with your daughter, and with Sam is in direct relation to your own self-serving interests, Silas." Bennett stands and buttons his suit jacket. His lawyer stands as well. "This farce of a deal has gone on long enough. BLH doesn't do business with people whose primary interests are greed. Have a good day, gentlemen."

Bennett and his lawyer walk out the door, and just like that, months of hard work go right out the fucking window. I don't blame Bennett for backing out. If I were in his shoes, I would do the same. Bennett is a good man, and it's admirable that he would stand by Sam's side.

Now, I'm stuck in this room with Silas, but unlike before with Amanda, I can control the variables. I don't bother to say anything, I just walk out of the room and slam the door behind me.

On my way into my office, Delores hands me an envelope. My name is scrawled across in perfect, feminine cursive. Sam's handwriting.

I scan through the letter. There's nothing heartfelt, just a formal letter of resignation. I crinkle up the paper and throw it in the trash can next to me. As I pick up the envelope, prepared to toss it in the garbage, something falls out. It's Sam's engagement ring.

My entire body goes rigid as I hold the ring in my hand. Blood rushes in my ears. Everything has gone to shit in the course of one day. My balls twinge and my dick aches. What *the fuck* is happening in my pants?

I pick up the phone and dial back my anger before I call Delores. When I'm convinced I can speak in a calm, rational tone, I ask Delores to call Bill and Susan to my office. It's time to set things right.

67

Sam

I don't know if I've ever felt so free in my life. I always thought I would be the one to define my success. There was a core belief that society expected me to marry and have a litter of kids—children, not goats—so I didn't want to conform to the social ideals of a woman's success. Instead, I had let my job define me. I bent over backward, sacrificed nights, weekends, and holidays all in the name of progress. What I didn't realize until today, was that success is based on what makes someone happy. As of late, my job at Sterling has made me miserable. Not just because I lost my promotion. Not just because of the war between Reid and me. Not just because of the nightmare deal between BLH and Keogh. It's all of it. There is more to life than my job.

The knock at the door startles me. I've been lost in my thoughts since the moment I got home. I didn't realize I had taken a shower until I blow-dried my hair, or that I'd mopped the floor until I slipped on the wet tile. I'm now noticing I've been home for almost three hours. When I open the door, I'm greeted by a tall, handsome blond, with a face full of stubble, and the saddest blue eyes in the world. I hate myself for being the one responsible for putting that look on his face.

"Hey," Reid says.

"Hey."

"Can I come in?" he asks, after standing in the doorway a few moments too long.

I jump out of the way. "Oh, yeah. Of course."

He walks past me and sheds his jacket and tie and tosses them on the couch. Not a kiss, not a hug. Just, "We need to talk."

I make a quick scan of his body. Yup, still hard. The clock above my TV tells me we have surpassed the four-hour mark and are making our way toward a second round.

"What's this?" Reid asks, holding the engagement ring I slipped into the envelope.

The taste of blood hits my tongue from biting my lip. Slipping my ring into the envelope with my resignation letter might not have been the most ideal way to break off an engagement. "Looks like a ring."

"Funny," his ocean blue eyes are dark and stormy, "I thought we were getting married, Sam? What the *hell* happened?" he bellows.

Oh, man, it seems Reid has hit his limit. More so than when I set him up to be arrested, and that's saying something.

"You're sleeping with your stepmom," I whisper, ashamed to speak the words. It's like saying it aloud makes it real, and the truth is terrible.

"What did you just say?" Reid asks, his voice dripping with revulsion.

I want to curl up inside of myself and hide, like a potato bug. "I said that I know you're fucking your stepmom." My tone is stronger than my conviction.

Reid closes his eyes as if he's trying to keep himself composed. When he opens them again, he looks into my eyes and shakes his head. "I thought you knew me better than that. Fuck."

"I thought I did too."

"So, what changed? Did Silas get to you? Did he show you some bullshit pictures? Because he did the same thing to Amanda, and—"

I can't let him justify this. To blame it on someone else. Silas Keogh isn't a good guy, but this isn't Silas's fault. It's Reid's. He needs to own it. "Silas showed me some photos—"

"I'm going to kill him," Reid says, making his way toward the door, grabbing his jacket.

"*Stop,*" I yell. "It wasn't him. It was *you*. You did this."

Reid stops, his hand paused on the knob. "What?"

I flop down on the couch, exhausted and wishing like hell I hadn't mentioned anything. I could have lied and told him I needed to try to find myself. That I've made the sudden decision to relocate to Greece. Something, anything. Anything but the truth.

"You have five seconds to explain yourself." He stalks toward me.

"Silas showed me the pictures," I repeat. "But I didn't quite believe it. You looked young. I knew if you had a relationship with Stella, it happened in the past, and I didn't have any right to be angry. It took a couple of days to come to that conclusion."

He sits next to me but keeps a few feet of distance between us.

"But then, when we were at Frank's for dinner, I noticed how infatuated Stella was with you. Still, I remembered you telling me Stella was all over you and that you had to 'beat her off with a stick.'" Recalling the discussion we'd had a couple of months back when we discussed his strained relationship with his dad and stepmom.

"Then what?" Reid asks. His words are clipped, and I can tell he's growing impatient.

"After Frank and I had our little chat in his office, I went to find you, and I found you. With Stella."

"Shit. It's not what you think."

"How can you say that? She was on top of you, and you were

kissing her." A tear slips down my cheek, and I curse myself for being so damn weak.

Reid swipes his finger along my face. "Sweetheart, don't cry. I need you to listen to me."

I want to. I really, really want to. I love this man, and it shatters me to think this is over. I owe it to him, to us, to let him explain.

"What you saw…shit. I don't know how to explain it," Reid says, scrubbing his jaw. "She attacked me."

I raise my eyebrow, not quite believing him.

"It's true." He begins to detail what happened after I left for drinks with Frank. Apparently, Stella lured Reid into a bedroom, wanting to show him the same pictures Silas had shown me. Keogh is enough of a pig that he was blackmailing Stella, and Stella is crazy enough to use this as an advantage to try to have sex with her stepson.

"When I left, I told Frank his wife was fucking Keogh, and you know what? I can prove it." He pulls out his phone and picks someone from his contacts. "Stella called me today, frantic. She was pissed and scared because I told Frank." The call is on speaker, and it begins to ring. "So, I phoned Frank and told him where to find the evidence. I knew she'd be too stupid to destroy it."

"Hello?" Frank answers.

"Hey, it's me," Reid says to Frank. "I only have a minute. Just wanted to see how it went."

Frank sighs. "The pictures were right where you said they would be. I'm sorry, son. I had no idea."

A sigh. That's all the emotion Frank has after the betrayal of his wife? I would have thought he'd be devastated. The perception that his wife and son were having an affair should be enough to destroy a man. Such is not the case for Frank.

"It's okay, Dad. Glad I could help. Talk to you later. Love you. Bye." Reid says and ends the call.

I can't believe what I just witnessed.

"Do you believe me now?" he asks.

"Do you realize what you just said?"

68

Sam

"What?" Reid asks, his head tilted with confusion.

"Did you hear what you said to Frank?" I repeat.

He shakes his head.

"First," I say, holding up my index finger, "You called him 'Dad.'"

"I did?"

"Yeah, you did. And B," I hold up a second finger, "You told him you loved him."

"I did?"

I nod.

"Huh. Weird." Reid shrugs. "I guess I've moved on." He gets up and begins to rifle through my fridge.

I follow him. "Is that all you have to say?"

"This Chinese any good?" Reid opens a white box with a red dragon design on the side and takes a whiff. His face squishes in disgust, and he quickly wrenches it away from his nose. "Nope," he says and tosses it in the trash.

"Chinese? That's what you care about right now? Chinese?"

He pulls out a bag of black grapes. "Mold," and the grapes go the way of the Chinese. "Don't you have anything here that isn't a year past its expiration?"

"Don't try to change the conversation. We need to talk about this. This is *huge*."

"No." He closes the fridge. "We need to talk about what we're going to have for dinner. I'm starving. Pizza?" He walks into the living room and sits on the couch.

"You can't keep deflecting. This is important."

"Ordered," Reid says as he clicks the screen on his phone closed. "You think I'm deflecting?" His voice calm. So calm, it's almost frightening.

I shrink from him, wondering what I've gotten myself into.

"You,"—he points to me—"think I'm,"—he points to himself—"deflecting."

Duh. "Yeah." Has he not been in the room through this whole thing?

He sits back and picks up the remote and turns on the TV. Apparently, we're not speaking. We're not doing anything. We're just inhabiting the same room. Am I in bizarre-o world where the new norm is avoidance of the issues?

When the pizza arrives, the air between us remains unchanged. Our emotions swirl around us like a cyclone, neither one of us will take the leap to be the first to speak. Total communication blackout. That's not true, he does offer me a slice of pepperoni pizza, but that's it. *Die Hard* is on TV and we're eating dinner like nothing has changed. *Everything* has changed.

I toss my crust in the box and wipe the grease on my hands onto my pants and stand. "That's it. You can't ignore what happened. Your indifference is disturbing."

Reid mimics me and tosses his crust in the box and stands. When he was on the couch, I felt confident. On the side of right. Now that he's standing in front of me, his expression hard as he stares me down, I can't help but wonder when the power flipped.

"You think I'm indifferent?"

I give a meek nod.

"I promise you, sweetheart, I'm anything but indifferent. I'm just fighting to keep my sanity. It's hanging on by a thread here."

I don't think we're talking about Frank anymore.

"You quit your job, you don't tell me. You think I'm fucking my stepmom, you don't talk to me about it. You break off our engagement—"

I think that thread is beginning to shred.

"—and I find out from an envelope with your ring in it. You can't give me the courtesy, the respect, to tell me to my face."

Fuck. He's right. My stomach roils with the new-found knowledge of my cowardice.

Reid sits next to me and lets out a sigh. His elbows are perched on his knees, and I'm worried he's given up. I don't know why because I was the one who broke it off with him. This is what I wanted. Isn't it? Now that I know the truth about Stella, I can't help but think I may have overreacted.

"If this is what you want, you have to tell me to my face."

It isn't. It isn't what I want. Right? No. What I want is him. "I...I..." I stammer because the words won't come out.

Reid slaps his knees. "That's all I need to hear."

He gets up and walks toward the door, and for the first time in my life, I feel my heartbreak. It's a sickening, hollow feeling. I thought I knew pain—the sting of a flogger against my ass—but not like this, not with him.

He opens the door, and just as he puts one foot into the hallway, I cry out, "Wait. *Wait*. This isn't what I want. I want you. I've always wanted you. I need you. I love you. I don't want to live a life where you aren't a part of it."

He stops mid-stride and turns to me, his expression soft, and his eyes warm. "This is done, Sam. I won't go through this again."

Oh.

My heart falls to the pit of my stomach, and my lip begins to tremble. It was different when I was the one in control. To hear the words that he's given up? That is a whole different kind of pain.

"No, that's not what I mean. I mean this battle between us, holding back. That's in the past. From here on out, we look to the future. No more games."

I mentally exhale a sigh of relief and the tension in my shoulders dissipates. "I can do that."

"Thank fuck." He charges toward me.

Reid picks me up from the floor, and I wrap my legs around him. Our mouths collide, and we're desperate for each other. He walks me to the couch and lays me down, holding himself above me.

"I love you so damn much," he breathes as his hand slides under my shirt. "You're my days, my nights, my everything."

Our hands are all over each other, both of us desperate with the need to get close. I unbutton Reid's shirt and shove it off his shoulders, running my hands along the magnificent muscles of his chest. At the same time, he unbuttons my jeans, and I wiggle my hips as he slides them down my legs.

Two thick fingers penetrate me, and the sensation is glorious. I feel like I haven't been touched in a hundred years, and I let out a moan.

"Fuck, the sounds you make." He tucks his face into the crook of my neck.

His erection pulsates through his slacks as he grinds into my thigh, and I want nothing more than to help ease that problem. A problem that I have caused. His cock springs free as I unzip his pants. I wrap my fingers around the thick shaft and tenderly stroke it.

"I've been hard for you all day," he says, pumping into my hand.

That's true. "Fuck me," I breathe, "I need to feel you."

Reid rolls over and takes me with him so I straddle him. My

pussy hovers above his hardness, my shirt pushed up past my breasts. With his pupils blown, I know the view must be good.

"Take what you need, sweetheart." He grabs one breast and draws the nipple into his mouth. "I'm all yours."

I take him, and not gently either. I slam down onto his cock, delighting in the vibration as he hits my end. I cry out, the pierce of pain is a pleasure I covet. I'm stretched so full my scalp begins to tingle.

"You're so fucking tight. Shit, Sam," Reid gasps, digging his fingers into my hips. "All day, all I could think about was bending you over my desk. Taking you in my bathroom. Spreading you out on the table in the boardroom."

I continue to ride him, and I can feel his cock grow harder inside me.

"My dick's been hard all damn day, I was afraid I would blow my load in my pants on the cab ride home." He grabs both my breasts and begins to tweak my nipples simultaneously, delight courses down my spine.

"Oh. Oh, God. Reid. Shit." My rhythm falters as I get closer. "Fuck, I'm. I'm. I'm going to—"

"That's it, sweetheart," Reid says as he guides my hips with the pace he wants. "Come for me. I want to watch you fall apart."

Achoo, achoo, achoo, achoo, achoo, achoo, achoo. All the pent-up anxiety and emotions burst from me with each sneeze.

He holds onto my hips tighter, slowing me to a grinding motion. "Fuck, sweetheart. Fuck. Oh, shit." The cords in his neck stretch taut as every muscle in his body goes rigid.

I fall forward onto him, the sweat from our bodies mingling to create a scent unique to us.

He pushes my hair from my face and looks at me. "Tell me again that you're on birth control."

I let out a shaky, satisfied laugh. "I'm on birth control."

"Good," he sighs. "Because that was a big one. So big, if you weren't on the shot, I'm ninety-nine percent positive we would have just made a baby."

He rolls me back onto the couch, in the same position we had started in, except less clothing. He drops a kiss on the tip of my nose. "I'm going to hop in the shower. Want to join me?"

I give him a lazy smile, and that's all. Not because I don't want to talk, because telling him I was on birth control used up all the vocabulary reserve I had available.

After his shower, he comes out and looks down at me on the couch. I haven't moved an inch. I am pliantly sated. He laughs as he repositions me to his liking, my feet dangling over his lap.

His hand slides up my leg followed by a warm washcloth, cleaning up the remnants of our lovemaking. "You know, it's strange. After all that, I'm still hard."

Oh.

"I've taken three cold showers today, and still," Reid says as he lifts his hips, his still-hard cock rubbing against my calf. "It's not like I'm complaining, it's just strange, you know?"

Yeah. I know.

He rubs his hand against his crotch. "It kind of hurts."

I sit up and start to jerk up my jeans. "You should get dressed. We need to go to the hospital."

69

Reid

"It's called priapism," the nurse practitioner in the ER tells me. "Basically, the blood in the soft tissue of the penis gets trapped for some reason or another."

When Sam told me I needed to go to the hospital because of my hard-on, I thought she was crazy. She started citing Cialis commercials and how they say if an erection lasts more than four hours to seek medical attention. She had a good point, and that is how I have come to find myself on a gurney in a backless green gown with my penis on display for the entire medical community to gawk at.

"Any idea how this happened?" the nurse practitioner asks, rolling the stool next to the bed and taking a seat.

I shake my head.

"Any kind of trauma?"

I shake my head again.

"Any history of cancer? Do you take antidepressants?" she prods.

"No, nothing," I answer, growing impatient with this game

of twenty questions.

"Do you take any PDE-5 inhibitors?"

I roll my eyes. "In English?"

"It's a class of medication used to help with Erectile Dysfunction, like Revatio or Viagra," she clarifies.

Viagra? "Getting or maintaining an erection is not a problem for me," I tell her as I wave my hand over my groin. Christ, I'm so hard, it feels like my dick is about to pop off and fly across the room.

"You're sure?" the NP asks incredulously.

"I think I'd know if I needed to take a pill to get hard," I snap.

"Um, about that," Sam pipes up.

I swing my head toward Sam. "Spill it."

Sam begins to fiddle with the hem of her shirt and stares at the ground. "I may have slipped something into your coffee this afternoon."

I knew it. That load of crap Sam fed me about the creamer was bullshit.

The NP takes a deep breath, obviously exasperated. "What did you give him?"

"Viagra, I think," Sam answers sheepishly.

"You're not sure?" the NP asks.

Sam shakes her head.

"Okay, do you know how much you gave him?"

Sam shrugs her shoulders. "I don't know. Three maybe."

The NP scribbles something down on a sheet of paper. "Do you know the dosage? Twenty-five milligrams, a hundred?"

Sam shakes her head once again.

I'm not sure if I want to laugh or cry. Sam dosed me with Viagra of an undetermined amount, and now I have the hard-on of a lifetime. From a distance, it is kind of funny. Up close, it's perturbing that she would do this to me after everything we've been through.

The NP takes another deep breath. "I guess it doesn't matter, what's done is done. Normally, I would suggest we try some ice packs and see if that doesn't help. However, since you've had this erection for over six hours, and we don't know how much Viagra you received," she says, glaring at Sam, "I think we need to be more aggressive."

I straighten up in the gurney, my back as stiff as my cock. Images flit through my mind with medieval torture devices, a porn flick with Ruth Bader Ginsburg as the star, or...*no*. Amputation? I shudder at the thought.

"You *can't* cut it off," I holler, my imagination getting the better of me.

For the first time since I've met her, the NP smiles. "I'm not going to cut off anything. We just need to drain the blood."

My muscles begin to unwind, my fears allayed. Then, "Uh, drain the blood?" I ask, fear striking again. "And how do we 'drain the blood'?" I probe, my voice spiking to a pubescent crack.

The NP waves it off like it's no big deal. "It's a fairly simple procedure with minimal risks. First, we'll numb your penis with some lidocaine, then we'll insert a needle—"

"A *needle*," I scream. "You're *not* putting a needle in my dick. Not happening," I tell her with finality.

"I understand your hesitancy," the NP says, "but, if we don't do something now, you could be looking at permanent damage to your penis."

Permanent damage and penis. These are the only two things I need to hear to convince me that a needle in my dick is reasonable. "Fine," I say, resigned, my head flopping back on a pillow.

The nurse practitioner gives a victorious smile. "I'll get everything ready, and we'll have you out of here in a little bit."

"I can't believe you spiked my coffee," I tell Sam a few minutes after the NP leaves the room.

"I know. Everything was crazy. I thought you were cheating on me with—"

"It's okay," I tell her, interrupting the explanation.

Her face contorts with shock. "It is? You're not mad?"

"Oh, I'm plenty mad," I tell her because I am. "I'm about to have a needle prick my prick. I think that's plenty of reason to be mad. I understand how it happened. I know where your head was at the time. And, I forgive you. Forgiveness and acceptance of each other is part of what being a couple is about, right?"

She hops out of the chair, sits on the gurney next to me, and threads her fingers through mine. "When did you get so wise?"

I stare into her brilliant blue eyes, and I can see myself reflected in them. I want that reflection there for a lifetime. "This afternoon, when I tore up your letter of resignation and fired Bill and Susan."

"You're kidding?" A smile plays at her sensual lips.

"Nope. If they can't figure out how to make it work with your history, and if they won't stand up to defend you, then they aren't doing their jobs. Come back to Sterling, sweetheart. I need you. Sterling needs you."

"I want to say yes, but there's no room for advancement now. I've gone as far as I can with Sterling. I think it's time to find a new passion."

"Come on, Sam. You don't mean that?"

"I do. I think quitting Sterling may have been the best thing I've ever done for myself. I feel free. Like the sky's the limit."

"What are you going to do for money?" I can't help but worry that my fiancée has gone over the deep end. No matter if she has, I'll be there all the way.

"I have some money saved up," she answers. "I think I'll take some time off and try to figure out what it is I want to do. Business, car assembly, panhandling. I can do whatever I want."

"You're amazing, you know that?"

"Yeah," she says, beaming her beautiful smile up at me. "I love you."

"I love you too, sweetheart."

The curtain is yanked back, and the NP and a nurse come

into the room. They set up a tray with gauze, syringes, needles of assorted sizes, a vial of medication, and a bottle of saline. Sam hops off the bed and stands next to me on the opposite side of the procedure area.

"Go ahead and lay back and try to relax," the nurse says. She lifts my gown and begins to spread cream on my penis. "Just some cream to numb the skin, then she'll," referring to the NP, "inject some lidocaine."

My heart begins to whack in my chest, my palms sweating. I want to throw the table next to me and run the fuck out of here. Sam gives my hand a reassuring squeeze.

The NP snaps her gloves, picks up the syringe filled with lidocaine, and squirts some out from the top of the needle. "You ready?" she asks.

I give her a nod, the ability to speak has devolved along with the pulse of the plunger on the syringe. As the NP approaches, and the needle gets nearer, the walls of the room close in on me.

"You're going to feel a little pressure..." is the last thing I remember before the room turns black.

70

Sam

It's Thanksgiving Day, and Reid and I decided to spend it with his mom in New York. Babs is a beautiful and gracious woman. When she greeted us at the airport, she didn't so much as say 'hello' to Reid before she pulled me into her arms and gave me a suffocating mom-hug. I liked her immediately. She's kind and sweet, everything I could ever want in a future mother-in-law. I always found it strange how much Reid doesn't look like Frank, but when he stands next to Babs, the resemblance is uncanny. Frank isn't the most handsome man in the world, and fortunately for Reid, his mother must have powerful chromosomes.

Even though Reid hated the idea of attending *The Macy's Thanksgiving Day Parade,* he's managed to take it up a notch. Not only are we attending, but we'll get to ride on a float. The day is already blustery with snow, nothing I'm not used to. Reid bought me a brand-new white winter coat with a matching hat. It's beautiful with intricate stitching of flowers across the waist, and the hat has a chic veil, very Jackie O. Reid is dressed in a new stark black overcoat, black slacks, and shoes. I hold back a sigh as I drink him in. How is it possible that he becomes more handsome with every day that passes? I'm not sure what I've done to deserve a man as wonderful as Reid, but I'm grateful that he's mine.

"Come on," I tug him toward the door. "I don't want to be late." I'm so excited to see the parade that I keep pinching myself, convinced I'm dreaming.

As we take the elevator to the underground garage, I look at our reflection in the mirrored doors. I laugh inwardly because to look at us, you would almost think we were on our way to get married.

Reid and I hold hands as we take a car to the starting point of the parade. His thumb rubs small circles on the inside of my wrist. If I didn't know better, I'd almost think he was nervous.

"You look beautiful, sweetheart." He raises our intertwined fingers and drops a kiss on my hand.

I feel beautiful. The coat Reid bought must have cost a fortune. I didn't want to accept it since I'm not working right now, but he wouldn't hear of it and told me he wanted to be able to give me the best of everything, including the moon and stars if he could. In a way, he already has, because Reid Gallagher is my entire universe. I couldn't be happier.

He turns me around so I face out the window.

"I have a surprise for you." He reaches into his coat and whips out a silk blindfold the same color as my coat, and covers my eyes.

"Do you have noise-canceling headphones too? Total Sensory Deprivation." I whisper, then begin to laugh.

"Yes, as a matter of fact, I do."

What? "I was joking, Reid, come *on*. I want to get to experience the parade, not be the spectacle on parade."

He laughs. "Don't worry, you'll get to have both." He covers my ears with headphones.

This is not what I expected, and I'm not sure if I'm pissed or excited. What the hell. I guess I'll have to wait and see what he has in store. If he's gone to all this trouble, it must be something pretty great.

Reid helps me out of the car and tucks me into his side so I can navigate the steps up the float. After tripping three times, and Reid hoisting me back up, I settle down on a chair and wait.

Reid

Sam sits on a chair on the float I had specially designed for today. I made the arrangements on short notice and wasn't sure I would be able to pull it off. I lived in New York for several years, and with the business I was in, I made a lot of connections and was able to make the magic happen at the last minute.

"Grayson, Lizzie," I greet Sam's friends as they walk up to the float. "I'm glad you made it."

"And miss this? No way," Lizzie says, shaking her head as she laughs.

I point them to where they need to go and then say hello to the Valentines. "Victor, Victoria," I say, giving Victoria a hug and Victor a firm handshake.

"Hope you know what you're doing," Victor says, raising an eyebrow.

"Me too." The plan is outrageous and spontaneous. It will either be the most amazing experience of Sam's life or the biggest mistake I've ever made.

I lace Victoria's hand in my elbow and walk her up the steps of the float and put Sam's parents in their positions. Victoria giggles the whole way, giddy with excitement.

When my mom and dad arrive, I'm shocked as shit to see they shared a cab. It's been years since I've seen them in the same room, so long that the sight is unnatural. My mom laughs at something my dad tells her, and I can't seem to recall the last time I saw them friendly toward each other.

My mom gives me a hug and kisses my cheek, smudging away any remnants of lipstick. "I'm so happy for you," she whispers, tears in her eyes.

"Son," Frank says as he embraces me and gives me a clap on the back, "let's do this."

&.

Sam

I can tell the moment the float starts moving, and it jars my already nauseous stomach. Not knowing what's happening or going on around me is downright unnerving. I have faith in Reid that he knows what he's doing. I brace myself as the frigid air hits my cheeks.

The motorized float makes a series of turns as we make our way onto the parade route, and here I am, my eyes and ears still covered. It takes every ounce of willpower not to remove the blindfold and headphones. About twenty minutes later, I feel Reid's hand grab mine and give it a squeeze. The feel of his touch instantly soothes my nerves.

A few minutes later, Reid removes my headphones. The roar of the crowd is deafening, and a marching band plays in the distance. The knot at the back of my head becomes loose, and my eyes take in the person in front of me. Except it's not Reid.

"Dad?" I ask, confused by my father's presence on a float in New York City on Thanksgiving. He's dressed in a black suit with a black overcoat and looks so handsome, my heart squeezes.

He smiles at me, his eyes filled with joy. "Who else would give you away on your wedding day?" he asks.

My throat constricts, and my eyes fill with tears. "What?"

I look around. The float I'm riding is designed as a white wedding chapel. My mom, Babs, and Frank are sitting on a pew off to the side. There's a red carpet sprinkled with rose petals making a path to the front doors of the chapel where Lizzie holds a bouquet of white roses. She's dressed in a coat and hat the matches mine, except in a beautiful lavender color, and I can just make out the faintest baby bump.

On the opposite side of the aisle stands Grayson, and he looks handsome, wearing the same suit and jacket as my father. There's the preacher, off to the side of the chapel door. When the door begins to open, my breath hitches.

Reid steps out, and my mouth goes dry, his hair disheveled as the wind blows. He takes a step toward me and extends his hand. As if on cue, the marching band starts to play *The Wedding March*. Reid holds his hand out in invitation, and tears slide down my cheeks.

My father grabs my hand and tucks it into the crook of his arm. "Are you ready?"

More than ever.

Acknowledgments

I would like to thank everyone who helped me to see this book from conception to publication. First, to my good friend Stacey Owens. Had I not been visiting her when she stuck her head out of the car to cat-call constructions workers, this story would have never existed. To my kids for leaving me alone for five minutes at a time so that I can do something important for me. To my mom for giving me life and keeping me alive. To my Aunt Rosie and Aunt Sally for loving me and giving me crap for no good reason. But hey, that's how they show love. To my sister Jill who didn't know I was writing smut. I'd also like to give a huge thanks to my beta readers Rhiyel Ormsby, Rebecca Vanden Top, Beth Yurosko, and Craig Nix. And to my amazing friends at the Fort Wayne Writers Guild who cheered me on the whole way. And I can't forget my publisher, Literary Wanderlust, and my editor Kylee for giving me such a great opportunity.

But, of course, to you dear readers. Thank you so much for taking time out of your lives to read the wacky story of a total stranger.

About the Author

Jacquelyn Marker is a Hoosier through and through. Although she's a bit of a city girl, she's an expert on cooking corn and bacon.

She has two children. The oldest is learning that her mother was right and that the adult world is a cruel place. The youngest is trudging the brackish waters of high school. She has two cats, Atticus and Scout, a mixed breed dog that cries until you pet him, and a crazy corgi pup that never does anything wrong. Ever.

Jacquelyn has had a love for books her entire life, but is in love with reading romance. Since experiencing her first romance novel, she has dreamed of putting pen to paper to bring a new angle to the genre.